Scattered Blossoms

By

John I. Wood

SOUTH MAIN MEDIA
WWW.SOUTHMAINMEDIA.COM
A CREATIVE COMPANY OF
MINDWATERING.COM

Scattered Blossoms

Scattered Blossoms is a work of fiction. Where real people, events, organizations, or locales appear or are implied, they are used fictitiously. All other elements of this novel are drawn from the author's imagination.

To contact the author or publisher:
South Main Media™, a Creative Company of Mindwatering
520 South Main Street, Wake Forest, North Carolina 27587
www.southmainmedia.com, www.mindwatering.com,
contact@southmainmedia.com

Second Edition
International Book Standard Number: 978-0-9909737-8-2
Paperbook and eBook
First Edition Paperbook ISBN: 978-0-9909737-6-8
First Edition eBook ISBN: 978-0-9909737-7-5

Cover design & book layout by South Main Media

Printed in the United States of America

Dedication

To my dearest Randi Leigh
who took me to Nikko
when the blossoms and the snowflakes waltzed
in the gentle springtime breeze.

Reviews

"This dramatic story brings to life the closing days of World War II. John Wood captures the courage, faith, and honor of average citizens - American and Japanese - amidst the chaos and brutality of war."
- Garland Tucker, Author, *The High Tide of American Conservatism*

"John Wood has created a wonderful story which incorporates real history with romantic fiction in such a way to grab the reader immediately. It's a truly beautiful story of World War II, incorporating ethic, racial, and religious themes, while drawing the reader to the main premise of humanity, we are all the same and made in the image of God. John is blessed with a natural storytelling style in which his words roll over the pages carrying the reader to natural curiosity and wonder. It's a magnificent book and I highly encourage the reader to take to heart the underlying promise that love perseveres over everything else. As Paul wrote in First Corinthians, 'So now faith, hope and love abide, these three; but the greatest of these is love.'"
- Colonel Gary I. Gresh, US Army Retired, Author, *Vietnam Soldier*

"Captivating, heart-rending, riveting, spiritual are but a few words to describe this outstanding book - *Scattered Blossoms* ! Through poignant creativity, John Wood built a transformative bridge between fiction and reality. As a boy during WWII, a combat veteran of Vietnam, and a 'born again' Christian, I deeply appreciate this wonderful gift."
- Colonel Richard Toliver, USAF Retired, Author, *Uncaged Eagle*

Author's Foreword

The cherry blossom is the unofficial national flower of Japan. Cherry trees bloom during Hanami, or cherry blossom viewing time, from late March to late May, depending on the location in the archipelago—celebrations of Hanami date back perhaps a thousand years. Symbolic of springtime, to the Japanese, they are a reminder of the transitory nature of life. Small, beautiful, delicate, and ephemeral, the pink and white blossoms last only two weeks, then scatter on the breeze and linger briefly on the ground before fading away. In World War II, Kamikaze and other suicide volunteers were compared to the falling cherry blossoms, pure and radiant, dying for their homeland. The blossoms' beauty inspires awe, poetry, and paintings. Their beauty is a time all too fleeting.

The four-engine Boeing B-29 Superfortress was the largest bomber flown in combat in World War II. Its cigar-shaped fuselage, with its bulbous nose, was 99 feet in length with a wingspan of 141 feet. Fully armed, it weighed 86 tons. It carried a crew of eleven men into combat. It flew as high as 37,000 feet and had a range of 4,260 miles. It cruised at 277 miles per hour but could reach 380 miles per hour. The crew spaces were fully pressurized. On the night of 9 March 1945, 279 B-29s sortied against Tokyo, the capital of the Empire of Japan, scattering 1,665 tons of incendiary bombs targeted at cottage industries and armament factories. The resulting firestorm consumed almost sixteen square miles of the city and killed an estimated 100,000 people. Operating from the islands of Guam, Saipan, and Tinian in the Mariana chain, the XXI Bombardment Command firebombed sixty-seven Japanese cities in 1945. Modified B-29s delivered the atomic bombs against Hiroshima on 6 August and Nagasaki on 9 August 1945. The US Strategic Bombing Survey estimated that as many as 300,000 people died in all the air raids against the home islands. The Emperor and the Cabinet of Japan accepted the Allies' terms on 15 August 1945, averting a catastrophic invasion of Japan and battles of annihilation that probably would have cost millions of lives. The XXI Bombardment Command on Guam controlled three bombardment groups of four bombardment wings each. Each wing was composed of three squadrons, each with approximately 17 B-29 bombers.

The 509th Composite Group flew from, Tinian Island. Its specially designed B-29s delivered the atomic bombs. The city of Nikko lies approximately 73 miles north of Tokyo. It is the site of the Toshugu Shrine, the burial site of Tokugawa Ieyasu, founder of the Tokugawa Shogunate (c. 1600-1867). Tamozawa Imperial Villa was a refuge for the Imperial family during World War II. The city escaped bombing raids. An Anglican Christian Church has been there since the late nineteenth century.

Author's note: While Tokyo time was one hour ahead of the Mariana Islands; for the sake of simplicity, all times in this story conform to Japan's clock. Times and dates will conform to the military standard twenty-four hour clock. For Japanese names, the author uses the Western convention of first name, then last name.

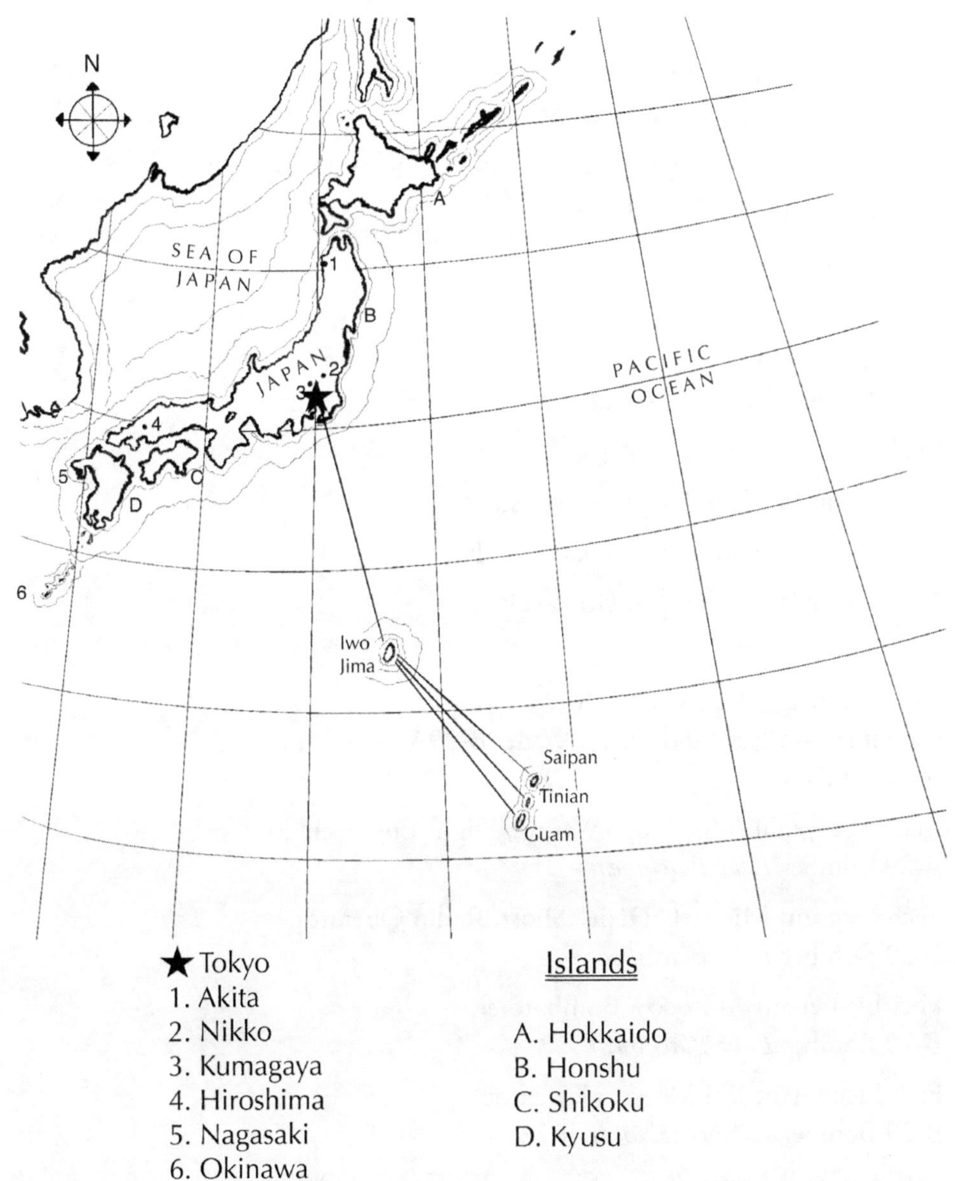

★ Tokyo
1. Akita
2. Nikko
3. Kumagaya
4. Hiroshima
5. Nagasaki
6. Okinawa

Islands

A. Hokkaido
B. Honshu
C. Shikoku
D. Kyusu

B-29 Flight Paths from Mariana Islands to Japan

Cast of Characters

In Nikko, Japan, March 1985

Asaka Okita, a gracious, yet enigmatic host

Riko Sumiko Kurita, his daughter, and her husband Saki

The Rev. Shiro Yamaguchi, a deacon

A visitor from America

In Prewar Nikko, Japan

Dr. Makato Fujita, a physician; his wife Sumiko, a nurse

Yuki, their daughter

Michi Mitsuko, Yuki's younger cousin

An American medical missionary family

Mr. Nakamura, a stranger with a suitcase

In the Mariana Islands, 1945

Captains Sam Reid and Dallas Wade, B-29A pilots and best friends from college days.

Master Sergeant John "Pop" Warner, Flight Engineer,
B-29 Bomber *Lake Blackshear*

Tech Sergeant Michael "Dixie" Short, Radio Operator,
B-29 Bomber *Lake Blackshear*

First Lieutenant Al Rocco, Bombardier,
B-29 Bomber *Lake Blackshear*

First Lieutenant Bill Meeks, Navigator,
B-29 Bomber *Lake Blackshear*

Tech Sergeant Larry Wynns, Central Fire Control Operator,
B-29 Bomber *Lake Blackshear*

Staff Sergeant Tony Costa, Radar Operator,
B-29 Bomber *Lake Blackshear*

Sergeant Steven Lewis, Tail Gunner,
B-29 Bomber *Lake Blackshear*

Flight Officer Leslie Hodges, Co-Pilot,
B-29 Bomber *Lake Blackshear*

Major Maxwell "Max" Adams, assistant operations officer,
Photo Recon Squadron.

First Lieutenant Richard Thomas, Pilot designee,
B-29 Bomber *Pitch Black*

Tokyo Area, 1945
Major Matome Tanaka, an ambitious and ruthless Kempeitai
(Secret Police) officer

Master Sergeant Saito, Tanaka's assistant

First Lieutenant Masao Gunji, medical student,
Imperial Japanese Army Hospital and School

Dr. Kyoji Yahara, a senior doctor at the Imperial Army Hospital

A lost child in a firestorm

The Phantom Tiger, Imperial Japanese Army fighter pilot

Akio, a teenage fighter pilot trainee

Lieutenant Colonel Fujihara Nakamura, a Kempeitai officer and
his wife Ana Oshima

Lieutenant Michio Ida, a Kempeitai officer

Southern Kyushu Military Airfield and Okinawa Area Waters, April 1945
Kenji Ozawa, a teenage Kamikaze pilot trainee

Lieutenant Commander Skipper Orser, US Navy Intelligence Officer

Michi Mitsuko, Imperial Japanese Army Kamikaze pilot instructor

*In these spring days with the tranquil light
encompassing the four directions,
why should the blossoms scatter
with such troubled hearts?*

Ki no Tomonori, Poem #33*

*… they will be like the morning mist,
like the early dew that disappears…*

Hosea 13:3a

*Fujiwara No Teika, *Pictures of the Heart: The Hyakunin Isshu in Wood and Image*. Translation by Joshua S. Mostow. Ann Arbor: University of Michigan, 2015. P 240. Used by the translator's permission.

Prologue

Tokyo
0105 Hours, Early Morning, 10 March 1945

As the firewall advanced, the young woman sensed that she was trapped. The inferno raged before, behind, and to the right of her. A blanket of hot, acrid smoke blocked the other side. Her thick, protective clothing smoldered from the intense heat.

The water she used to soak her turban and outer garments had evaporated. She despaired that her attempts to elude this night of horror had been in vain, as were those of hundreds of terrified victims she had passed on her flight. As the fires continued to spread with a surreal rapidity, fanned by the late wintry winds, new silvery needles of incendiary bombs fell from the darkening and droning heavens.

Running along with the masses of men and women, young and old, with children trying to escape, she had seen people suddenly combust as if soaked in flammable fluid and ignited by a mere spark. Then, staggering, screaming, and falling, they died horribly.

Accepting the futility, she no longer tried helping. Her professional instincts from her medical training and religious convictions were overwhelmed by her urge to survive. There was only the impulse to run, and try to find a safe place, some refuge in a turbulent sea of boiling flames. Hell itself could be no worse – or perhaps even hotter. The pavement seemed to be melting beneath her feet.

Her breathing became more difficult as the heated smoke-clogged air seared her throat and lungs. Her eyes seemed to be melting shut. Her mouth yearned for just a sip of cool water.

She stumbled a few more steps then heard a strange wail above. She looked skyward and beheld the inexplicable image of one of the low-flying silver bombers flying upside-down, illuminated by the bright orange flames. As it passed into the glowing smoke clouds, she offered a prayer for the doomed enemy crew.

Resigned to her fate, she sought forgiveness for her sins and those dying about her. She prayed for the safety of her family and the man she loved, who ironically might be in one of the planes wreaking deadly havoc on the city this horrible night. Then, stopping and breathing slowly, almost serenely, awaiting her immolation, she heard the pitiful cry of a small child.

Above Tokyo Bay
0120 Hours, 10 March 1945

Twice, the night-fighter had flown closely around the American bomber as if daring it to fire its deadly accurate defensive weapons and was now satisfied he had verified the name on the nose of the fuselage; the lone pilot skillfully positioned his plane parallel and a few feet higher than its left wing.

Just out of range, the experienced aviator, known to his colleagues as the Phantom Tiger, knew he could easily dive on her and loose a deadly burst from his cannons into the fuel-laden wing, inflicting a fatal wound that would cause her to plunge to the waters below.

Though climbing, the bomber was ascended slowly at three thousand feet, a low altitude highly conducive to night fighter's maneuverability. Yet the Tiger held back, sensing the conflict, the contradiction between duty and mercy.

Such emotions, he believed, were an unnatural Japanese trait. Duty told him to dive and fire, yet something, perhaps moral intuition, forbade him to kill this particular crew. Suddenly, the voice of his young wingman blared through his headphones,

"Lieutenant, I am going in for a head ram. Please tell my family I died bravely. Banzai!"

Like many young Japanese pilots, short on flying skills, he possessed the desire to die heroically by crashing his plane into an enemy ship and aircraft. The seventeen-year-old flyer now saw such an opportunity. With no prior combat missions and few flying hours in his abbreviated training, the impetuous wingman was willing to pay the supreme sacrifice thus ensuring his soul would be enshrined in Tokyo's Yasukuni national sanctuary commemorating Japan's war dead.

The fool!

The more experienced lieutenant searched the sky ahead, looking for his fellow pilot, and saw him coming, silhouetted against a cloud ahead, diving straight down on a trajectory that likely would result in a tremendous collision of metal and fuel three thousand feet above the surface.

Duty and commitment, skill and conscience, contradictions needing instant resolution, he edged his fighter over, aiming to the front of the B-29's nose. He knew he had but two and a half seconds as he fired a steady burst from his cannons. A brilliant fireball erupted in front of his canopy, momentarily blinding him as he yanked hard on his yoke to pull his fighter up and away.

The forces generated in the maneuver caused him to black out for a few seconds. When he shook his head clear, he was rolling over in an arc. Leveling out, he searched the sky but saw only pieces of flaming debris falling below into the dark sea.

As he headed for his base on the Kando plain, he mentally wrote his report that stated his young wingman sacrificed himself and downed a B-29.

12

One

Nikko, Japan
March 1985

Why I was returning still eluded me. A weekend break from business meetings in Tokyo, my first time on Japanese soil since 1939, provided the opportunity. The invitation to visit appeared sincerely extended. Yet an enticing impulse drove me to take this journey back into the home of my childhood, back to my coming of age.

The train journey gave me time to reflect on the question. After all, the last time I had seen Japan was forty years ago, and then I saw it from about twenty-five thousand feet. Through the carriage window, afar off, I could see the peak of Mount Fuji floating above the clouds, sun-rays basting its snow-covered cone. I recalled the times I observed it from the air on my flight paths of destruction. Had it caused any longing, then? No memories came to mind.

Was this short excursion supposed to answer a hidden longing? Maybe, too much of that time had been buried in my consciousness. Perhaps, I had told myself, it was merely nostalgic curiosity. Maybe, I just wanted to see my old homestead again. Maybe, I just wanted to see how the landscape had changed since my departure. And possibly, I could learn what had happened to the people I had known — and loved — as a child, to see my parents' graves, to be again where I had laughed, played, studied, and wept and developed a sense of self. But that thought seemed so contrived that it held no real chance of answering my deeper thoughts.

More likely, the honest answer would be that I was seeking closure, of haunting memories of a time that seemed surreal or illusory. Was I seeking closure on a time destroyed by time itself, and, of course, obliterated by the war that had been over and done four decades ago?

As I stepped off the train onto the Nikko station platform, a strange longing threatened to overwhelm me. Was it an old familiar odor or the alpine air that triggered the emotion? The scenery had not caused it since I saw nothing I recognized.

Whatever it was, a strange aching cloud of wanting and sadness enveloped me. I almost stepped back on the train. I recalled what the American author Thomas Wolfe had written so many decades ago – something about not trying to go back.

At least not back to the home I knew as a child with all the people and events that were part of my youth. But then, I already knew it would not be the same. It would never be the same. How could it? I finally gathered my senses and walked in the direction of my childhood home.

Despite the obvious late afternoon chill, I carried my parka. My wool sweater blocked the crispness from the penetrating breeze that gently scattered the cherry blossoms, mingling them with a light snow shower – the strange beauty of floating organic pink petals and soft frozen sparkling water crystals waltzing together in the afternoon air.

I knew the house would be there. I had already communicated with the present owner, who graciously invited me to come. As I crossed the Daiya River, I paused to enjoy the view of the water flowing gently beneath the bridge.

Suddenly, mesmerized by the gentle ripple of water flowing over the rapids, the memory of a terrifying day gripped me. Torrential rains had caused the bank to overflow. It was a day, not long before my relocation to the United States, when two teenage boys displayed a serious lack of judgment.

Nikko, Japan
Late April 1939

I asked Michi what would happen if he was called up in the military draft. He answered without hesitation that he would request aviation training.

"Are you concerned about the aggression in China?"

He seemed puzzled momentarily. Then he realized I was speaking of Japan's, not China's, hostility.

"No," he said finally. "They started this. We need to settle it justly."

"What about the atrocities by Japan's Army at Nanking?"

"That's rubbish. Chinese propaganda fueled by Western interests."

"Michi, my father saw pictures of brutal reprisals against innocent women and children. And so did Mama Sumiko and Dr. Sumiko."

Michi said nothing. I could tell he was becoming angry.

"I do not believe those pictures are true."

"But the testimony of so many witnesses – Christian witnesses …"

"No!" he answered emphatically. "They are mistaken. My countrymen would not do such a thing. I just know it."

We were silent as we neared the river's bank. Clearly, Michi did not want to talk on the subject. He was troubled but defiant.

"What about you," he said finally, "when you get back in America?"

"The United States does not have a military draft, at least not now. My parent's home country is isolationist."

"If your country is forced into a war, will you join your army?" He regarded me with knowing eyes.

"I suppose I will have to." After a moment, I added, "I also will seek pilot training." Michi laughed.

"Maybe we will be allies."

I chuckled and said, "Now somehow, I doubt that." The waters surged through the narrow riverbed. We knew there would be no fishing today. We stood on the bank, entranced by the water's relentless flow.

"You really should not listen to Western propaganda," Michi said, staring into the waters.

I am still unsure what happened, but he pivoted toward me to say speak. His foot slipped, and, arms wheeling, he tumbled into the torrent.

Momentarily stunned, I dove toward the bank and grabbed Michi's jacket collar. Panic etched on his face, he turned and thrust his hand toward me. I grabbed and held his slippery wrist. Our grips weakened, and I knew I would soon lose my friend.

The chocolate waters swirled angrily around the lad like a hungry monster trying to devour its prey. Michi's ebony hair clung to his face. His eyes a moment before displayed abject fear, now only resignation.

"Let me go," he gasped. "Save yourself!"

"No!" I shouted above the roar.

Then Michi let go and slipped under the maelstrom of churning water. Horrified, I kicked off my shoes and jumped into the torrent.

Two

Nikko
March 1985

The vision vanished as I heard the word,

"Konnichiwa."

It was the soft voice of a woman. I turned and beheld an elderly, smiling Japanese lady dressed in a traditional kimono. Bowing, I responded politely. She bowed and walked on past me. I watched her briefly, then turned, and continued my journey. As I walked along only a few minutes passed before I recognized the street.

At first, I thought little had changed in the neighborhood, except the trees and bushes had grown taller and wider, and the street must have been paved after the war. The cherry trees still guarded my path, sentinels to a trail into my long-lost past.

I stood before the roofed wooden gate of the scene that was etched into my memory. To the left was a newer gate large enough for an automobile to pass. Taking a deep breath, I opened the gate, into the small yard, I noted the landscaping was still familiar. My father and his host had seen to it that an experienced gardener kept it neat and inviting.

To know that practice had not changed in five decades brought a strange, wistful, yet comforting sentiment. The house, large by Japanese standards, appeared the same as far as I could see.

The roofline displayed the gentle curve I remembered, but the roof itself now consisted of expensive Hinoki bark. Knocking on the front door and then pulling the bell chain, I waited expectantly, my heart beating a little faster. A shuffling sound permeated the wooden portal.

The door cracked and finally opened to reveal a woman, perhaps in her early thirties, dressed in a traditional deep blue kimono adorned with the silhouettes of flying cranes. It was a garment I thought to be appropriate for the season.

Her raven-colored hair rested softly on her shoulders in a Western style that contrasted with her native dress. She bore a lovely soft complexion and was quite pretty. For a moment, I thought I recognized her, but I quickly dismissed the idea.

Her dark eyes gave me a penetrating look, then she smiled, bowed slightly, and opened the door, a clear invitation to enter. Stepping inside, I immediately slipped off my loafers and slid them into the shoe rack to the side of the foyer where I stood.

After I set my overnight bag down and hung my parka on a wall peg, she presented me with soft slippers, then turned, and we stepped up to house level.

Her hand beckoned me into a larger room. It was easily recognizable, though, with the passing decades, certain modifications were evident. It seemed even more spacious than I remembered. She went over to a sliding rice paper screen, pulled it back slightly, and spoke in Japanese.

"He is here."

The young woman then slid the screen wide, stepped back, and gestured for me to enter the spacious, brightly lit room, I noticed the tatami rice mats covering the floor, so I quickly removed my slippers. The man expecting me stood near the opening to the garden at the rear of the house. Like me, he appeared to be in his late sixties and in good physical shape.

His face, marked with light scar tissue, looked severe at first, then turned more cordial as he smiled, appraising and friendly. He wore a light tan kimono, and his thinning silvery hair was pulled back in the traditional short samurai bun. His complexion was deeper than the woman's.

We both bowed, and he spoke first, "Konnichiwa, Reid-san."

"Konnichiwa, Okita-san," I replied.

We knew each other's names from our recent correspondence. His name was Asaka Okita. That much I knew from my Embassy contacts. There was no additional information except he was the current owner of the house of my childhood. Okita gestured toward the sunken table and pillow chairs in the center of the room.

Despite my years, my joints were quite flexible as I sat, dropping to my knees, and sitting on my feet. He gave me an approving look for my latent ability to sit in a polite Japanese style. Then he smiled and said,

"May I suggest we sit comfortably for people our age?"

Nodding, I adjusted my posture so that my legs crossed in front of me. I noticed there were western style chairs and furniture, pottery, a bamboo plant, and rice paper scroll adorning one wall. Smiling tenderly, he spoke to the young woman in Japanese. I recognized he had asked her to bring tea.

As she left the room, he said, "Do not be fooled by my daughter's subservience; she can be quite the modern feminist."

At this he chuckled. I said, "She is as lovely as the cherry blossoms in spring, Okita-san."

He smiled at my feeble metaphor and muttered, "Thank you. She and her husband are quite good to me."

"Do they live with you?"

"No, they have a home near me, but they look in on me daily. Today, however, I think she came to see you. A woman's curiosity, I suppose."

"I appreciate your very kind invitation. It has been a long time since I was here."

"After we enjoy our tea, I will give you a tour of the house. I think you will approve of any modifications you see."

His English was excellent, though slightly accented. I bowed slightly to signal my gratitude.

"May I ask how your business meetings in Tokyo are progressing?" he asked politely.

"Very well. My Japanese counterparts are shrewd negotiators. Yet they are supremely courteous and pleasant to work with on the proposals. It is nice to take this weekend break."

Okita smiled and nodded; then, he stood silent for a few seconds before continuing.

"So, you have come a long way," he continued; gazing out to the garden, he added, "in space and in time."

I noticed a far-away look as he completed the thought. Space and time two necessary conditions of the physical universe – the thought caused me to wonder if I truly was back where my entire childhood had been spent.

"Indeed,"

"You wrote that you had lived here in this house … in the 1930s with Dr. and Mrs. Fujita?"

"Yes, my father and mother were medical missionaries. They met Dr. and Mrs. Fujita at a medical seminar in San Francisco in 1922; the Fujitas invited them to come to Nikko and assist them in their practice. It seems they also shared the same religion. I was not yet three years old when we arrived. Both families shared this house."

"Ah, so desu ka," he nodded.

I sensed that he knew this already.

The screen opened, and the woman entered with a tray bearing a teapot and cups, then, knelt beside our table, and deftly poured a cup, and handed it to me.

"Arigatou gomaimasu,"

I nodded to her, keeping my eyes on her perhaps longer than appropriate. The uncanny sense that I knew her from somewhere returned, but of course, that was impossible. She peered deeply into mine.

Then, she served her father.

"Arigatou," he said with an endearing smile.

Nodding and, smiling lovingly at her father, the woman rose and slipped quietly out of the room. "May I ask your daughter's name?"

"Riko. Riko Sumiko," he replied, eyeing me closely to see my reaction. He must have read something in my face:

"You see, I met the Fujitas during the war; I came to admire their integrity, and so I named my daughter after Mrs. Fujita."

I nodded, "A dear sweet lady."

"Tell me about your time here,"

I paused momentarily, gathering my thoughts.

My story began when we arrived in 1925 by steamer, docking in Yokohama. My parents already spoke Japanese proficiently and were able to find transport for us to Nikko. Dr. and Mrs. Fujita were expecting us. They were native to this area and their extended family was nearby. We lived on one side of the house and they on the other.

"Dr. Fujita was quite well off financially. He maintained an emergency clinic here, but he and my father both worked out of a larger in town."

Okita nodded and told me that the facility still existed. "My son-in-law practices there."

I continued my story of our early years, how my parents adapted to the culture, the deep friendship between them and the Fujitas, and how the Fujitas treated me as a child relative.

"I was coming out of the terrible twos; it seems Mama Sumiko, my name for her, knew how to handle me – and her daughter."

"Ah, yes, little Yuki," he nodded knowingly.

"Yes, we grew up almost as brother and sister, but I must confess I later had a teenage crush on her despite Yuki being almost three years older."

We both smiled, and I continued,

"Yuki helped me learn Japanese – a very patient girl – so I became bilingual in those days. I'm afraid that skill has diminished with time from lack of practice." He laughed but told me my first letter to him, written in Japanese, was entirely correct. He had replied to me in well-written English.

A call from my hotel concierge had arranged my weekend visit.

Our conversation continued as I spoke about how the two doctors developed their practice with their wives balancing nursing duties with child-rearing.

"Did they share their religious faith in their work?"

"I'm not sure. We all attended the Christian church here; the Fujitas were quite active. Of course, the congregation was small. Mama Sumiko taught children's Sunday School."

"Hmm," he grunted. "Yes, that church has existed since the previous century. So, you enjoyed a happy childhood here? Did you make friends easily?"

"Well, yes and no. Mama Sumiko's brother and his family also lived here in Nikko; their son was my age. We became quite close as boys go. It's not that the other boys were unfriendly, but Michi, Yuki's cousin, and I were like best friends. We shared similar interests. He also learned English so we could converse bilingually. Both of us were quite adept in math. We both aspired to be pilots one day."

I decided not to tell of our adventure in the angry river. I paused, steeling myself for the next revelation.

"It was not always a happy time. You see, my mother contracted typhoid and died in 1929. We were all devastated. The two doctors did all they could, but mother went quickly. My father was never the same. Joy seemed to desert him."

I took long sips of my tea showing I wished to move on to another subject.

"Ah, so," Okita whispered. "Understandable. And you?"

He pushed where I had not intended to go. After all, we were strangers, but suddenly, I found myself surrendered to an impelling catharsis, letting go of things buried for decades.

"Yes, me too. Losing your mother at seven is traumatic, and given my father's inability to empathize with me ... well, that did not make it easy."

"Was there no one to help?"

I stared into my cup, and glanced out to the garden.

"Almost immediately, Mama Sumiko adopted me; she was very loving, showering me with affection even my own mother had not given."

Okita looked at me with kindness.

"And little Yuki would come cry with me," I added with a slight smile.

"So, you grew up here," he stated plainly. "You were almost Japanese." Then he added, "But not quite."

He seemed to enjoy this digging into my past. I wondered why. He seemed to have an intimate sense of my life in Nikko. But then I was the one who asked permission to visit his home. "Yes, I learned Japanese well enough to attend the schools.

"However, Mama Sumiko was fluent enough to give me drills in English for my lessons, especially world history. My parents had shipped schoolbooks to Japan, so I learned traditional American as well as Japanese ways. No, my schooling was not a problem.

"When I was old enough I was sent down to Tokyo to the Catholic school the American embassy arranged for me to attend for further development.

"I stayed with an embassy family while schooling there."

"But there were problems," he interjected, "growing up here." His statement, without being accusatory, was an assertion of fact. He knew more about me than one would think.

"Well, my father grew more distant, not that I blamed him." I lied.

"He never got over my mother's death. He remained here after I went back to America to finish school, and I think he died of a broken heart."

"Yes, that seems quite logical. I sense your father was a good man, however."

"I suppose. He was a good doctor, for sure. He seemed to pour his empathy into his patients instead of me." I wondered if my last remark sounded resentful, but Okita continued his line of questioning.

"Did he pray?" he asked, looking steadily at me. *That sounded like a very personal question.* Yet, not wanting to be rude, I answered.

"Yes, but he seemed to have lost his spirit. I never saw him again after I left in 1939. He passed here in Nikko before the war in 1941. Mama Sumiko had the embassy notify me, and then wrote me, but her letter was very late in arriving. He and my mother are buried here."

"What about you? Did you pray in those days?" Now, it was very apparent to me, he asked again about something deeply personal.

It did not seem like a Japanese person would ask this of someone he had just met. Yet I felt a compulsion to reply.

"Mama Sumiko had me say my prayers every night at bedtime," I answered hoping to end the questions.

But he continued, "Did she also school you in the faith?" When he said the faith, I immediately assumed he meant Christianity. But I thought it odd since I also assumed that he would belong to a sect of Buddhism or a practitioner of Shintoism or maybe no religion at all.

"Well, yes, Mama Sumiko was, you might say, a devout Christian. She read Bible stories to Yuki and me and made us recite catechisms, the Ten Commandments, the creeds. We also memorized disciples and saints and all that." After sipping my tea, I added, "But I abandoned such beliefs decades ago."

Okita's eyes opened a bit wider as he stared at me curiously.

"I suppose we should see the house now," he stood up.

I rose and followed him as he led me through the house. First, he showed me the side where my family had lived, and when we came to the room I recognized as my own, I glanced down at the floor.

"You are looking for something?" he asked.

"Hmmm, no," I dissembled, looking away. The house floor plan had not changed dramatically. Of course, there were modern appliances and structural upgrades that one would expect to occur over five decades; still the layout was much as I remembered from my youth, though expanded. The kitchen and bathrooms had notable Western-style upgrades. The clinic room was now a study and home library. The house displayed the wealth of the owner. It made me wonder about Okita's background. Had he done the upgrades, or had a previous owner? I again recalled the Fujitas' apparent wealth before the war. Perhaps they had survived the war and upgraded.

Next, we walked into the garden that separated the houses' two wings, which opened into a larger walled-in area encompassing the rest of the property. It was too early for many flowering plants, but the cherry trees seemed to burst forth with a well-deserved vanity. The air was cool, but neither seemed to mind as we strolled silently along the gravel walks among the various plants. Lingering snow blanketed the flowerbeds.

"Hanami was my favorite season," I said, remembering another faraway time when a beautiful girl and I sat and laughed among the drifting blossoms in this very garden.

"Hmmm," Okita replied, lost in his thoughts.

We stood awkwardly for a minute before I turned to him.

"You have been very gracious to share your time and home with me, but I should be going. I want to see my parents' grave site and check into my hotel."

He quickly turned to me, "You can do that tomorrow; you must stay for dinner. It would be impolite of me not to have you as my guest tonight. And you will stay in your old room. I will call your hotel and tell them your plans have changed."

His manner of speaking left no doubt he would brook no argument, so I bowed slightly and replied, "You are most hospitable."

Breaking the tension, he laughed, "It is very Japanese to be so. Come my friend; you will want to bathe and relax first. Your room has that added

Western feature."

Smiling and, with a slight gesture, he led me back to my old bedroom. Okita advised dinner would be at six-thirty, giving me a good hour to relax, reflect, and prepare for the evening.

I found a robe, slippers, and pajamas neatly folded on my low platform bed, and as advertised, my bathroom was completely Westernized. I undressed and enjoyed a long hot shower using the aromatic soaps and oils. Slipping on the robe after toweling myself, I wandered over to the screen that opened to the garden yard. Evening shadows crept over the walls, muting the colors of the blossoms though not their beauty. Turning back to the room, I noticed paper and pen at the writing desk. A note is written in Japanese, but I am so out of practice I did not try to read it. Instead, I lie on the bed and close my eyes.

Soon, I'm dozing and hear a girl's soft voice, laughing, teasing me with gentle affection. Then, suddenly, I hear the rumble of a bomber's four troubled engines. Images of a dark sea far below me rush up. I'm falling, tumbling, fighting to get control of my body. I hear a crewman perhaps, scream, "We're going down! For God's sake, bail out!"

I thought I recognized the voice. Then I knew. It was mine. I woke with a start. My hand was shaking. Lying still, breathing slowly, I calmed my body.

I quickly rose, dressed, and I stepped into my slippers. There was a gentle tap at my door, and I heard Riko's soft voice say, "Dinner is almost ready, Reid-san."

"Arigatou."

I opened the screen and walked to the dining room. A man dressed in a blue-gray Western-style business suit and tie greeted me, introducing himself as Riko's husband.

"I am Saki, Reid-san, Saki Kurita; it is my great pleasure to meet you."

I learned that Saki was a pediatrician practicing for several years after graduating from medical school in Tokyo. Okita and his daughter joined us, and taking the lead to seat us around a Western-style dining table. Riko served us a delicious Japanese dinner, and we made small talk for a few minutes.

"You are here also to see your parents' graves?" Saki asked politely.

"Yes, they should be in the yard of the English church. If the geography has not changed, I think I remember where my mother's plot is. I assume my father's may be there too."

"Then it should not be a problem. I understand you left Japan right after high school. Was this your decision?" Saki seemed genuinely curious.

"No, it was not my decision. Events leading to the war convinced my father and the Fujitas I had to leave. They seemed scared about what was happening. Even as a teenager, I was aware of international tensions from my embassy friends. The thought of war between the United States and Japan seemed far-fetched to my young mind. I sailed for America in the summer of 1939 to attend college."

"What convinced them they wanted you to leave so soon?" Sumiko asked.

"Well, they saw the militarists asserting themselves more and more. Of course, the United States never recognized Japan's seizure of Manchuria back in 1931."

I recounted the Marco-Polo Bridge incident in July 1937, and when the United States began to discourage trade in 1938, finally terminating the trade agreements in 1939, the year I departed.

"The relations between America and Japan were becoming increasingly tense."

"Shortly before Japan signed the Tripartite agreement with Germany and Italy," Saki interjected, "in September 1940, I believe."

"Yes, I was back in the States by then, a second-year engineering student in college. It was a most disturbing development. I was deeply concerned for Yuki, her family, and my father."

"Is this why you believed your father should leave Japan?" Okita asked.

Everyone watched me. I breathed deeply. Why I decided to tell my hosts, and why they wanted to know intrigued me. Having just met these people who were so hospitable, I was now about to relate part of a history that I had bottled up all my life.

"No, there was something else." I hesitated and watched them lean in to listen to my story. "One day during Hanami, a strange man with Eurasian features visited the Fujita home. He carried a small suitcase. I still remember his name – Mr. Nakamura."

They sat silently, expectantly. My thoughts drifted back to that day in 1939.

Three

Nikko, Japan
2 April 1939

The girl wore a cotton pink kimono contrasting the lad's black sweater and gray slacks. The two teenagers sat in the garden, supposedly studying for exams, but the girl's deep brown eyes occasionally flirted with the boy who kept looking up at her from his calculus textbook. An unexpected tension had developed between them in the last three years. The girl knew what it was; her mother had warned her that things were changing between the two young people who had regarded themselves as sister and brother.

"Your mutual attractions are quite normal," Mama Sumiko had admonished her, "but you must control them. Do not let your passions get the best of you."

For the lad, it was a matter of figuring it out alone. His father was too distracted to notice the changes occurring, and Dr. Fujita did not think it prudent to interfere where the natural father should.

The boy had, not only recognized undergoing a change of his own, physiologically, emotionally, and intellectually, but he also noticed the physical change in Yuki, along with a developing sensuality and sophistication. When he would give her the obligatory goodnight kiss on the cheek, he wanted to embrace her and not say goodnight.

Once, when he had helped her step down from a ladder, his hands, holding onto her slender waist, had pulled her close and held onto her longer than necessary. Yuki looked at him with a teasing, yet endearing smile. In his awkwardness, he had finally dropped his hands and stepped away, his face flushed with puzzling embarrassment. Neither one of them spoke of it after.

Try as he may, he realized the physical and the emotional were dominating his mind. How he looked and thought about Yuki was not how a brother should think of his sister.

But then they really weren't related, were they? Was there a barrier that separated them? He struggled daily with these thoughts, and there was only one person he could talk to about his new urges and feelings.

One day, while they were fishing in a nearby lake, he had broached the matter with Yuki's cousin Michi, who, next to Yuki, was his closest friend. But Michi had only teased him about his infatuation with an older girl.

"And can you imagine a Japanese girl with an American boyfriend?" Michi scoffed. "The neighbors would be scandalized!" Yet both boys knew one of Japan's foremost diplomats had married an American woman.

Late in the day, Yuki again flirted with her adopted American brother, and he had a most difficult time keeping his mind on the boring math problems. He would glance at her sitting on a garden bench across from his own, looking intensely until her eyes would catch his. As typically the case, he blushed and turn back to his book.

"You'd better pay attention to your homework, dear little brother," she said with a coy smile. Yuki spoke in English as they often did, though just as often, they conversed in Japanese.

"Oh, this stuff is easy and boring. How are your studies?" he asked, trying to deflect the moment.

"Quite well; I think I am ready for the boards. Mother thinks so, and she is a nurse and should know. Father is also confident that I am ready."

"What will you do when you pass your boards?"

"I do not know for certain. Perhaps I could work in Father's clinic. There are rumors the Imperial Army is recruiting nurses for the forces in China and Manchukuo."

"Oh, I do hope you will never go over to either of those places!" he sat up suddenly.

"Oh, would you miss me?" Yuki smiled playfully.

"Uh, well … sure. It's just that it would probably be very dangerous for you over there." Both had read only the government's reports of the war in China. Contradicting the reports of victory after victory, it seemed Japan was caught in a quagmire on the Asian mainland – then, there was the wounded son of a neighbor who came home missing a limb.

Trying to ease the tension, she gave a nervous laugh.

"What will you do when you finish high school this spring?" Yuki asked, even though she knew the answer.

"Father says I shall return to America and enroll in college. He wants me to go to theological school, but I am more inclined toward engineering. Anyway, someone in the embassy is trying to arrange enrollment. I'd just as soon stay here."

The girl looked away, "I too want … I wish you would stay."

A different type of tension settled on them, more foreboding than war in China. The idea of their eventual separation weighed heavily on their hearts, though at that moment, there were no words to express their feelings. They knew the day would come, but both had pushed the thought of the pending severance into another dimension of time and reality. Their innocent conversation had opened the door to a future neither wanted to contemplate.

They looked forlornly at one another.

Suddenly, they heard agitated voices in the house.

With their sobering thoughts broken, they gave one another a mischievous look. Placing their books on the bench, they eased to the side of the porch by the partially opened screen and listened attentively.

They heard a shocking conversation.

"What you ask us to do, Mr. Nakamura, is nothing short of treason!" Mama Sumiko said firmly.

"We're not asking anyone to commit espionage," the stranger spoke calmly. "Just signal from time to time when Dr. Fujita sees or hears anything unusual among the military people. Our people will contact you and note what you saw or heard."

"That would be too dangerous for my husband!" Mama Sumiko said even more forcefully. "And why us?"

There was a brief pause. Yuki peered through the crack in the door to see the four adults sitting around the center table. The stranger had unusual features. He was dressed in a dark, business suit. To Yuki, he appeared to be in his late twenties.

"We have a few reasons. It is common knowledge your husband will be in the Hiroshima area for a few weeks advising the Imperial Navy doctors. He would have access to people who may know things of interest. They may let something slip …"

His words startled Yuki. Her father had not mentioned going anywhere. She looked at the boy, but he was also clearly puzzled.

"That's not a good reason," Mama interjected.

"Well, actually, it is," the man replied. "You see," he paused, "We know of your religious values as well as your disdain for the militarism that is sweeping Japan. My contacts want to know where Japan is heading. The smallest bits of information may be quite helpful. It may well help our diplomats to …," he paused deliberately, "well, let's just say it may help avoid war between Japan and the West."

"Don't you have professionals to do this kind of work?"

"Unfortunately, no. The Western authorities have been quite lax in 'reading other gentlemen's mail' as one of the American statesmen put it. They are behind in that area, so some of us Japanese, who fear war is coming, have taken the initiative to contact people we feel would be reliable sources of help."

The man continued, "Again, we are not asking anyone to do anything destructive. Just report anything that seems ominous, shall we say …"

Yuki heard her mother breathe deeply and say, "No! It's too dangerous."

Dr. Fujita had remained silent until now, but he cleared his throat, signaling for Mama Sumiko to be quiet.

"My medical practice here in Nikko is important. The government said my assignment to Kure Naval Base would be just temporary. I am to teach and assist the medical staff with recent innovations in burn treatment and other skills I picked up in the United States a few years back. Surely I will not be in contact with anyone who knows any secrets."

"That's why we think it is safe for you. But the medical staff with whom you will be working may know things that you may overhear from them."

"But I cannot carry that suitcase to Hiroshima. It would be subject to a search, and as you know, all such radios were required to be turned in a long time ago."

"We do not want you to take it with you. It must stay here. No one will think of Nikko as a place for a clandestine radio transmitter. Instead, we will give you a simple code you will include in your letters home, giving no real information at all. Then Mrs. Fujita can send the short contact signal, and one of us will drop by to chat with Dr. Fujita, on his lunch hour or meet him in the post office."

Dr. Fujita looked down at the floor. Shaking his head from side to side, he spoke slowly, "I just don't …"

"It is too dangerous for all of us." Mama Sumiko interjected.

"For heaven's sake, Mr. Nakamura, we have Americans living here. We

– and they – are already subjects of suspicion among the locals because we host the American doctor and his son."

"True. But the fact that the American is a doctor helping the people and his son will soon leave for America will offset those suspicions."

"I cannot accede to your request,"

Yuki heard Mr. Nakamura cough.

"I think you should see these." Yuki watched as he handed Mama a large envelope.

Eyeing Nakamura cautiously, Mama Sumiko opened the envelope, withdrawing what looked like photographs. Her mother flipped through them and gasped. She handed them to her husband, who likewise seemed startled.

"You are holding photos smuggled out of Nanking, China; the victims were innocent civilians. Innocent civilians – women, children, old people. The pictures were taken in December 1937 after the city capitulated. I can assure you they are authentic."

Mr. Nakamura sat quietly.

Mama Sumiko stared at him.

"Surely, our army would do no such thing! His Majesty would be appalled."

"I cannot say what the Emperor knows or would condone," Mr. Nakamura answered. "But I know these pictures speak the truth. Christian missionaries witnessed many of the atrocities and have sworn to their authenticity. It appears to be the world into which Japan's militarists are taking us."

Mama Sumiko sat in stunned silence. Dr. Fujita handed the photographs to his American colleague, who responded with a shocked expression.

"Terrible! Brutal. How could any civilized people do such a thing?"

Dr. Fujita removed his spectacles and rubbed the bridge of his nose.

"What you ask is indeed dangerous. I would happily do as you ask were it not for my colleague who also faces danger."

"Yes," Nakamura admitted quietly. "That is why, we think he should leave Japan quickly."

At this, Yuki squealed, revealing the two youngsters hiding behind the screen.

"Yuki!" Mama Sumiko exclaimed. The two youngsters entered the room and bowed.

"Well, it seems we already have two young spies in this house. What have you heard?"

"Something about a radio and father going to Hiroshima to work with the Imperial Navy," Yuki answered, looking questioningly at her father.

"We were going to tell you soon. Yes, I will leave for Kure Naval Hospital within a few days. The government tells me it is only for a few weeks."

"But your patients here …" Yuki interjected.

"We have adequate staff to handle my patients in Nikko," he answered.

"And what about …" she turned toward her American brother.

Before anyone else could speak, Mr. Nakamura answered, "He will be returning to Atlanta, Georgia in June to finish whatever high school subjects he needs. With his gifts, he will finish easily and enter The Georgia Institute of Technology. If he wishes, his father may return to Emory University to teach in the medical school, and in the theology department. It is all arranged."

A look of dismay fell across Yuki's face as she turned again to her adopted brother.

"But so soon …"

"Even without what I am asking of your parents, it is becoming more problematic for American citizens in Japan. The sooner they leave, the better." Mr. Nakamura spoke with an air of authority and finality.

"I will not leave my work," the American doctor said firmly, "unless the Japanese government expels me."

The room screamed in silence. Everyone looked defeated except Mr. Nakamura.

Dr. Fujita turned to his American colleague. "Will you excuse us while we talk to Mr. Nakamura alone?"

The American doctor nodded and signaled his son to follow. As they left the room, the boy heard the start of the conversation.

"Tell me how this would work," Dr. Fujita said to Mr. Nakamura when they were alone.

Four

Nikko, Japan
March 1985

Mama Sumiko had explained the so-called simple procedure to me, and I still recalled her words as if they had been spoken minutes ago. Dr. Fujita would mention the word 'pleasant' in the opening of any letter he sent home if he had information. Mama would then tap out a code word at a specific frequency three times a day at certain hours. Then a contact would meet Dr. Fujita at the Hiroshima post office at a particular time and day.

The Fujitas would hide the radio under the floor in my bedroom. Mr. Nakamura was probably right; Nikko was an unlikely place to look for a radio transmitter. The time the transmitter was on and transmitting would be a few seconds, not nearly enough time for listeners to triangulate its location.

Dr. Fujita left for Kure Naval Hospital a week later. He came back once before I returned to the States. He never spoke of any discoveries and Mama Sumiko never indicated he needed to convey any information. I don't recall her taking the radio out except to show me how it worked and how to contact her on it if that possibility ever arose.

"You will, of course write to your father, Yuki, and Michi, we do not know how long Japan and America will maintain diplomatic relations and mail exchanges. I fear the world has entered a very dark and evil time. Who knows when we all shall see each other again? If you have access to a short-wave radio, perhaps you can reach me."

I never told Michi about the radio. We said our goodbyes the way boys often do. We went to the river that morning, thinking it would be our last outing. We sat near the riverbank, looking long hard at the turbulent waters.

"You will write to us?" he asked.

"Yes, of course. Perhaps I should send letters to you through Mama

Sumiko. You know, so as not to arouse suspicion."

Michi shook his head in disagreement.

"No! Write to me wherever I am. I can explain our relationship. Our countries are not at war!"

"Okay, but in Japanese."

"Hai." He looked at me and smiled. "I will miss our outings."

"Promise me, promise me you will be careful."

He chuckled and only nodded.

"Michi, where do you want to be assigned if you become a pilot?"

"I doubt I will have a say. My guess is China."

I nodded. "That's where the action is."

"I hear basic training is brutal in the Japanese forces."

"Where did you get this information?"

"Friends at the American Embassy who know. Military attachés' children. I hear they beat their enlistees."

Michi said nothing.

I was to leave the following day. The thought of Michi at war was disquieting.

We sat and watched the muddy waters for a long time. Then he stood, and lost his balance, and slipped into the maelstrom.

The night before I left, I said my final goodbye to Yuki in the garden. I remember holding her tightly; our kiss was not a brother-sister exchange. Yuki wept bitterly. I sobbed uncontrollably. I promised to write.

I did so right up until the time mail exchanges between our two countries ceased. I had to keep my messages simple, as few were without doubt, the mail would be opened by suspicious people on both sides.

The last that I knew, Yuki was a nurse at Kure Naval Base near Hiroshima, where her father had taught in 1939. I learned Dr. Fujita had been called back to serve at the Imperial Japanese Army Medical School and Hospital in Tokyo. He and Mama Sumiko had taken temporary housing in the Honjo ward. Then we lost contact. Michi was in the Imperial Army. I never heard from them again. I feared the worst because of the war. I knew my father died in 1941.

Riko looked at me with sympathetic tears streaming down her face. She looked expectantly at her father. As I followed her gaze, I noticed him shaking his head ever so slightly.

Okita nodded at me. "I will tell you what I know about the Fujitas tomorrow. Tonight, you rest here in your old home."

I arose early in the morning and dressed quickly. I noted that Okita had not locked the door, so I eased out.

Walking in the crisp morning air should have been exhilarating. Yet, a foreboding mood accompanied my journey to the Christian church. I entered the gate leading into the church cemetery; much had changed in the surrounding yard where the grave was located. I was no longer sure I would know where to look.

I strode to the area where the location should have been seared into my memory, but I saw nothing familiar. After wandering for a few minutes, doubt crept in, causing me to think I had been wrong about the spot where my mother had been laid to rest decades ago. So, I turned toward the sanctuary.

Standing in the sanctuary doorway was a middle-aged Japanese man looking at me with a natural curiosity. I approached, and before I could say anything, he asked in perfect English,

"Good morning. I am Reverend Shiro Yamaguchi. I am a pastor here. May I help you?"

Breathing a sigh of relief, I bowed, and told him whose grave I sought without explaining.

He bowed slightly. "Let us check the registry. Of course, the dates you mention are before my time, but perhaps the records can help with this mystery."

We entered a side room where there were several books. He took one down from the 1920s and opened it. Running his fingers down the pages, he finally halted.

"Is this the one you seek?" he asked quietly.

Looking at the place where his finger rested, I read the familiar name.

"Yes," I whispered.

"Hmmm, the plot has been blotted out."

"Why would that be?" I was befuddled.

"It does not say," he answered. "It is possible her remains were moved …" He paused then added, "or perhaps removed. There is no explanation annotated. Is there no one in Nikko who may have known her?"

"No." I sighed. "They are all dead."

"I am so sorry. I wish I could help you. There may be a few of the older members who will recall. I will be happy to ask on Sunday."

For a moment, I almost agreed. Then I changed my mind.

"No, that will not be necessary … at least for now. You have been very helpful, Reverend Yamaguchi."

With this, he bowed courteously.

I half bowed and muttered a quick thank you in Japanese and started to walk away. Then I paused and turned and asked if he could check one other name from 1941. He found no entry at all. Thanking Yamaguchi once again, I left him in the registry, with a feeling of his eyes boring into my back.

As I cleared the gates of the churchyard, another much older Japanese man wearing a clerical collar passed me. He merely nodded. For a moment, I thought I recognized him, but I dismissed the idea.

When I opened the door to the house the aroma of freshly brewed coffee greeted me. Okita, phone to his ear, was standing in the kitchen as I walked in wearing my slippers. He spoke in Japanese, a few words I recognized, "No, let me handle it."

Hanging up the telephone, he turned, bowed briefly, and handed me a cup of coffee. I returned his bow. This morning, Okita wore navy slacks and a gray sweater.

"Sugar or cream?" he asked. I declined with a nod and sipped the hot brew, hoping that it would warm my chilled spirits.

"You were up early. Did you go to the church?" he asked.

"Yes, but I'm afraid I found neither grave. There is no church record of the location of the graves."

"Hmmm, I can ask around if you like."

"Maybe later. I'm not sure I need to see them anyway. I thought that since I was here I would pay my respects, so to speak."

"It is very Japanese to honor one's ancestors," he smiled as he sipped his coffee.

I sat on a kitchen barstool next to a breakfast counter. Okita placed breads, sweet rolls, and rice cakes on the counter.

"Last night you mentioned you knew what happened to the Fujitas," I said, clearly expecting answers. He smiled and sat across from me.

"You are staring at me," Okita ignored my obvious supplication.

Indeed, I was.

"Your scar," I admitted. "It looks like a burn."

He chuckled and nodded.

"It is a war wound, shall we say." He sipped his coffee. Then he continued.

"I imagine you have scars from that war." It was a statement, not a question.

We regarded one another for a long while. The ball was back in my court.

"I served in World War II … in the Pacific war."

He regarded me curiously, tilting his head, clearly expecting me to reveal more.

"I was a B-29 pilot. I bombed Japan."

He nodded.

Continuing, I admitted, "I am not altogether proud of that, but then I am not altogether ashamed either."

"I think I understand," he looked at me intensely with a non-judgmental air.

"I don't think you really do. I don't think anyone can."

He regarded me enigmatically. We then sat silently allowing the tense atmosphere to slowly dissipate.

"Come, let us chat in the garden. It has warmed up a bit. Refresh your coffee." And he walked out, clearly in control of the conversation.

We sat on separate benches facing one another in the chilled air. The soft blanket of snow still clung to edge of the flowerbeds. The sun was peeking through the clouds, and I was comfortable in my sweater. Okita began his story.

"As I know the events, Dr. Fujita was not long at the Kure Naval Hospital. He must have returned within a few weeks of your departure in 1939. I think you said you knew about his assignment to the Imperial Army Medical School in Tokyo." He looked over at me, and held my gaze.

"As far as I know, he never received any intelligence of any importance when working with the Imperial Navy physicians at Kure." He paused, sipped his coffee, and then continued matter-of-factly, "The same was not true for Yuki, however."

I must have looked startled because he nodded his head in confirmation.

"You see, she was sent to Kure in the summer of 1941 to complete her nursing internship. How Yuki became involved with the Navy is another story for another time. Suffice it to say, she worked with military people in the Kure Naval District. It was during this time Yuki became the agent her mother feared she would become."

"Yuki?" I stammered.

"If you lived in their house with her all those years, you know she was strong-headed. Yuki despised the militarists who were leading the country … though she truly loved Japan and her people and held the Emperor in high esteem."

"But her skills …"

"Yuki was not just an excellent medical technician. She had a way of drawing people into confidence without them even knowing. She was also extremely intelligent."

"Yes, we used to test one another. Yuki could easily have been an engineer."

Okita nodded thoughtfully.

"Anyway, she developed relationships during her short time in Kure. Yuki was privy to important developments; and, it almost caused her exposure to the secret police."

I listened to his story with rapt attention.

Five

Kure Naval Hospital, Inland Sea
Ten Miles South of Hiroshima, Japan
Late November 1941

Her patients slept soundly in the dimly lit, cool ward. A few moaned, even under sedation. Yuki made her rounds, checking the status of each patient and ensuring the medications had been dispensed as directed. There was no reason to awaken any of the men.

However, when Yuki came to the young airman named Wasaki at the end of the ward, she paused, taking more time to check his vitals. His cast-covered arms lay across his chest, and his broken right leg hung by pulleys. He arrived earlier in the day in considerable pain. The doctors prescribed heavy dosages of painkillers and sleeping medications. Yuki knew the aircraft carrier pilot had suffered a training accident. Now as she listened to his heart rate, he stirred, mumbling deliriously. She knelt to listen.

At dawn, she handed off her duties and went to her room. Her hastily written letter home began with a notation of the pleasant weather.

Six days later, Yuki sat on a park bench at noon as usual. It was not the first time she had met her contact in this manner. Earlier in her assignment, she had passed on information about fleet movements in southeastern Asian waters. Today, the kimono-clad woman sat near her and appeared to be reading a paper.

"The weather is indeed pleasant," the woman spoke softly, not looking up from her paper.

"But ill winds are blowing from the east," Yuki replied.

"That is most disturbing,"

"A young pilot mentioned the bombing of a place called Pearl Harbor. I looked it up. It is in Hawaii – an American naval base."

"When?"

"I don't know; soon I assume. He was delirious and I could not really question him. They moved him before I could get more details. It is very dangerous. I fear they suspect me. I am not supposed to interact with the patients, only treat them."

"Perhaps it is time for you to leave," the woman rose and walked away.

Yuki did not watch her depart. Pulling a shawl close around her as the chilly wind blew in off the Inland Sea, she strolled back to the hospital. Yuki sensed she was being watched.

The next morning, Yuki received a summons to the hospital commander's office. She knocked, and heard "Enter".

Expecting to see the Imperial Navy captain in charge of the hospital, she was surprised to see a young Imperial Army major standing alone by the window in the office. Yuki recognized the white armband on the left sleeve of his uniform; identifying him as Kempeitai, the secret police. The man sported a thin, dark mustache to compliment his short, dark haircut. A cigarette hung from his lips.

Yuki tried to calm her nerves so as not to lose her composure.

"Excuse me, Sir," she bowed, "I was expecting to find the hospital commander."

The man turned and eyed her with a hardened glare; then he smiled in a most unnerving way. "He was called away, so I could use his office. We need to speak privately.

"I am Major Tanaka. Please sit."

Yuki found a straight chair and sat with an erect and obeisance posture, her head bowed slightly.

"How may I help you, Sir?"

"I will ask the questions, Fujita-san. You are aware of the rules for dealing with military patients?"

"Yes, Sir, of course. Treat them and get them back to their duties as soon as possible."

"Does that include interrogating them?"

"I'm not sure what you mean. Of course, we ask the patient how they are feeling, to see if we can make them more comfortable."

"I mean, do you ask them about their duties – or how they incurred their injuries?"

"No Sir! Of course, the patients often talk on their own. It is difficult not to hear them. Most of it sounds like gibberish to me."

"Do you recall any of this gibberish from a young aviator named Wasaki a few days ago?"

"The young man injured, I presume, in an aircraft accident. He stayed under sedation most of the time. He seemed quite confused."

"Did you ask him about his duties, such as how he was injured?"

"No, Sir! His chart said post-surgical recovery after injuries sustained in an accident. The chart did not specify what kind of accident. But I think we all suspected it was a flight accident; he is an aviator."

"I remind you it is not your business to presume anything about your patients' duties; just treat them!"

"Yes, Sir, of course," Yuki said, keeping her head bowed toward the floor.

Tanaka walked around the desk and stood in front of her. She glanced up and noticed the holstered pistol on his waist belt.

"You sit in a park at noon each day."

Yuki felt her heart quicken. How would he know this? Were they watching all the nurses or just her? Yuki decided to answer truthfully.

"Why, yes Sir. It is most relaxing."

"Is that all you do, relax?" Tanaka asked sarcastically.

"I take a snack with me. But mainly, I rest my feet and legs. We do a lot of standing and walking on the wards. Is there something wrong with this?"

"You meet a woman there. A civilian woman." He accused.

As if confused by the statement, Yuki paused. "Why yes, a woman occasionally comes by and sits there. She is polite but not very talkative. I do not know her name."

That was true. Yuki had never been told who the woman was or where she was from.

"We find it curious she seems to find your bench so available, shall we say?"

"I don't know, Sir. My mind is not on visitors to my bench. I really prefer being left alone."

Tanaka walked around the desk, stubbed his cigarette, and sat down. He shuffled papers, then looked at Yuki for several moments. She could feel his piercing glare on her, even with her head bowed.

"If this woman comes again, we would like you to delay her. We wish to question her."

"Yes Sir, of course."

"You may go."

"Thank you, Sir." Yuki rose and bowed low and turned toward the door.

Why, she turned and asked, she did not know,

"The young airman you spoke of – did he recover? Is he fit for duty?"

Tanaka lit another cigarette and slowly blew out the smoke toward Yuki.

"That is none of your business, Fujita-san," and he quickly took another puff. "But I will tell you anyway. We considered him a risk from, as you say – the sedation. Therefore, we moved him to a hospital ship headed out to the Southern forces. You will not see him again, I am sure."

Yuki bowed and left.

Tanaka sat for smoking his cigarette, then took the file with Yuki's name, and stuffed it in a briefcase and left.

I know there is more than she revealed.

True, her reputation was of a caring person who showed great concern and empathy for her patients. That alone was a reason to question her about her interaction with the pilot Wasaki. Tanaka decided to keep her file active.

That evening Yuki wrote to her mother.

> *"It was not a pleasant day. I do not think I
> should be taking so much time on my breaks in
> the park. The winds feel colder and I must watch
> my health. I also think my superiors want me to
> stay closer to the wards."*

It was a coded message saying, I am being watched; I cannot meet with anyone for the foreseeable future.

For several days Yuki avoided going to the park bench.

A week later, a Kempei non-commissioned officer showed up at her station on the ward.

"I am Master Sergeant Saito, Major Tanaka's assistant." His smile was contrived. Like Tanaka, he wore a thin mustache, but was shorter and heavier.

"We noticed you have not taken your breaks in the park lately."

Yuki composed herself and bowed to avoid his penetrating stare. "I was under the impression I was to avoid the park." She hoped the lie would deflect the sergeant's focus as indeed, it did.

"No, no, we want you to sit there until this woman returns. We think she is attracted to our nurses. We wish to speak with her."

"Very well, I will go today."

The sergeant's smile became a contemptuous sneer, and then he quickly walked away, his cavalry boot heels clicking on the floor.

During her break, Yuki went to the bench, praying the woman would not come. She did not. Yuki went three days in a row, and never saw the woman again. After a week, Yuki asked to transfer to Tokyo to be nearer her family. By now, she had heard of the raid on Pearl Harbor. Japan was at war with the United States.

Mail from America had already ceased. Yuki wondered if the boy, rather the man she loved, had joined the American forces. Her cousin Michi had been inducted into the Japanese Army and assigned to the Air Corps a year before. He had flown missions in China. Michi was a very skilled pilot.

In February 1942, Yuki reported to Yokosuka Naval Hospital near Tokyo Bay. Though she could no longer report and communicate secret information to anyone, there were other closely held secrets learned from patients recuperating there.

Six

"Unbelievable! Yuki knew about Pearl Harbor before the attack?"

"Yes," Okita answered after finishing his coffee. "But, of course, it was too late for the network to get word to the Americans. Before they could contact your embassy, the attack occurred, and then our two countries were at war."

"It's hard for me to accept that Yuki became a spy." My head was spinning from the revelation.

"Maybe you were the reason. But after the war began, there was little Yuki could do. Her network disappeared like the morning mist and never contacted her again during the war. The Fujitas kept the radio hidden here in this house until they moved to Tokyo. Yuki did learn more secrets in her work, however. For instance, she knew about the Japanese naval disaster at Midway in June 1942 even as our government claimed it was a great victory."

"How?" I asked.

"After the Imperial fleet returned to Hiroshima Bay, our wounded sailors and airmen were quarantined on hospital ships in the Inland Sea. Those not wounded were not allowed shore leave and soon sailed in the Southern seas. The officers were transferred to the Yokosuka hospital for recovery, and that is where she overheard them lamenting the loss of four aircraft carriers and many airmen and planes. In June 1942, Yuki already suspected Japan would lose the war."

"Did the war become routine for her?"

"Not really. You see this Major Tanaka Yuki had encountered at Kure later discovered her family connections. Her father and mother were under suspicion because the Fujitas had played host to your American family."

My heart sank. "What happened to them?" I asked anxiously.

He smiled, tilted his head. "Don't you want to know what happened to your father?"

His question caught me off guard. I had always assumed he died of natural causes. Mama Sumiko had written to me only to say he suffered a heart attack. I nodded, ashamed and curious. I thought I knew the circumstances of his death.

"This Major Tanaka was trying to build a case against the entire family. He interrogated your father, as well as the Fujitas. By 1941, it seems your father had moved into a separate living arrangement, but that did not dispel the suspicion. Tanaka and his fellows searched this house and found nothing incriminating. They roughed up the American, accusing him of spying, trying to elicit a confession, trying to make a connection. He denied the accusation of course, and they could prove nothing. But their treatment caused him to suffer a heart attack. He died in the summer of 1941."

"Yes, but I did not know an interrogation caused his death." My anger was evident. "This Tanaka fellow – was he labeled a war criminal?"

"In the sense of the time, he probably was. There was no official record of this event. Your family's name disappeared in government smoke."

He paused, a frown creasing his forehead. "Your father's death caused the Fujitas enormous grief. I do not think they ever recovered. They had been close friends with your father for almost twenty years, lived, and worked as one family. They felt responsible for not encouraging him to leave with you."

"I remember his stubbornness. He would never leave unless he were expelled." I think there was more than a hint of bitterness in my voice as I thought of his refusal to care for me instead of his work.

As we sat, a light flurry of snow mingled with the drifting cherry blossoms. I felt cold, angry, and despondent. Okita noticed my shivering.

"Come, let us go in and refresh our coffee. There is still more to talk about if you wish to continue."

We went inside, but the house's warmth was neither consoling to the body nor my spirit. Knowing my father may have been murdered, in a sense, left my mind in turmoil. I could not explain it to myself. Had I not also slaughtered many innocents? Who was I to judge others?

I sat on the kitchen barstool while Okita poured more coffee. As he returned my cup I noted him looking at me as if seeking to penetrate my inner thoughts.

"Tell me about your war."

I looked away.

"My best friend and I were in college and flight school together. Both of us were bomber pilots and flew out of the Marianas." I paused to collect my wits and memories of the people and events seared in my conscience. I had arrived on Saipan in the autumn of 1944, delivering a new B-29 Superfortress that had been my transportation to the Pacific theater. Because I had been an instructor pilot before deployment, I served only one mission as a co-pilot before becoming an aircraft commander. I knew other pilots with less experience flying high-altitude bombing and reconnaissance runs over the cities of Japan."

I mentioned my transfer to a squadron on Guam, but omitted how I was transferred later to Tinian, the third of the Mariana Islands. Ironically, it was in the Marianas that I ran into my best friend several months after I arrived. Both of us were skilled B-29 pilots. As good a pilot as I was, he was even better. He flew a fateful mission for me. We both had close relationships with Japanese families. He, too, had a Japanese girlfriend. That fact drew us together more than our engineering and flying background. We spent countless hours together in college, and many free weekends visiting and fishing in various lakes and rivers in Georgia and North Carolina. We were closer than brothers.

I told Okita after Michi, a guy named Dallas Wade became my closest friend.

Seven

Above the Western Pacific Ocean
0545 Hours, Wednesday, 7 March 1945

As the giant reconnaissance bomber winged northwesterly toward Japan, First Lieutenant Dallas Wade gazed down on the ocean four and a half miles below. The reflection of the sleepy, half-lit moon shimmered lazily on the waves far below, like shards of glass on a blacktop road. Sunrise would break on their starboard side at about 0600 with clear weather forecast for the Tokyo and Kanto plain area. That would afford the cameras excellent resolution during their reconnaissance run.

There was little to break the monotony of the four droning engines that carried them to a height of more than twenty-five thousand feet. Dallas had ordered the crew to reduce internal radio chatter to a necessary minimum, so the crew had to fight the drowsy tedium within the pressurized cabin.

"Pilot to Navigator," Dallas finally broke the silence. "Bill, I want to run right, over Yokosuka into the Bay, before turning up between the Arakawa and the Sumida Rivers."

Dallas was merely repeating the flight plan worked out before their departure from Guam seven hours before.

"Roger, Skipper." Lieutenant Bill Meeks replied. "I had a good radar fix on the last island. We are still on a good course to hit that peninsula on time." That would put the plane over the target by about 0930. Meeks sat behind Dallas with a semi-open bulkhead separating them. Meeks was adept at using radar to check their position by studying the outline of islands far below. But Dallas knew Meeks had climbed up in the astrodome well before dawn to get a confirming "fix" on the stars with his handy sextant.

"Roger, out," Dallas replied and looked over at his co-pilot, who was studying his instruments as the autopilot held the aircraft in its flight path. There was really nothing more to say for now, so he closed his eyes to contemplate the hours and mission ahead along with more profound thoughts and concerns. A single B-29, or F-13A as this reconnaissance version was designated, probably should not flush a bevy of fighters to harass them, and they would be flying too high for anti-aircraft flak to endanger them.

That was not his main concern. It was the mission itself, even though this was not a bombing run. The films would be used in a few days to help wreak murderous havoc upon the civilian population of a great city, upon people who were not soldiers.

Though Top Secret, Dallas knew what that future mission would be and how deadly for the inhabitants of the city as well as many B-29 crewmen. How he knew this information, he had kept to himself, never wanting to compromise his chatty source in wing operations. That man's lips loosened after two or three beers.

"I tell you Dallas, the old man is nuts!

"He's ordering a low level, fire raid on the capital. And get, this, the planes are to carry no defensive weapons!"

"What? No gunners?"

"Just the tail gunner," was the reply, "just so the brass can add a few more bombs with the weight offset. I'm telling you, it's a suicide mission they're sending those guys out on. Glad I'm not going."

"Yeah, me too," Dallas felt only half relieved that he was an F-13 reconnaissance pilot now. Dallas had already flown a few bombing missions as a co-pilot and a pilot before transferring over to the recon squadron where he had flown several missions. But it was not the lack of gunners that gave him pause. The F-13 was armed with four machine gun turrets and a tail gun like a conventional B-29. The aircraft flew so high that fighters were rarely a concern.

What troubled him was the likely death toll that would exceed anything inflicted before on the civilian population of the enemy capital. Dallas was no pacifist; he had already contributed to the killing on those prior bombing missions. He had personal considerations on his mind that he shared with his best friend, which always made the missions troublesome.

Dallas and Sam Reid had become close friends when they found themselves in the same advanced calculus class at Georgia Tech in Atlanta, Georgia. Both shared similar interests, including fishing and aviation. They resembled each other physically, making it difficult to tell them apart.

After a night of partying, Sam could not rouse himself to take an English literature final exam, not that he had studied much. His good friend Dallas grabbed Sam's identification card, signed in to the auditorium, and took the quiz for Sam, deliberately missing a question. A few days later, the professor congratulated Sam for achieving the highest score in the class. Sam smiled to Dallas, and added he probably would now forget everything he had learned. English literature had little or nothing to do with engineering and aviation.

One of the boys inherited a little money, and they scraped enough together pay for private flying lessons. They enrolled in the Reserve Officers Training Course (ROTC) through Georgia's land grant university system and rose in cadet rank over the three years they attended college.

After the Japanese attack on Pearl Harbor in December 1941, they received early commissions as second lieutenants in the Army Reserves. The young men applied and were accepted for flight training. Their civilian pilot licenses gave them an edge in the various flight programs. By late 1943, they were learning the intricacies of the Boeing B-17 bomber, assuming their first assignment would be to fly missions against Nazi Germany.

Their talents for handling aircraft did not go unnoticed by their superiors.

Later, they both found themselves training as Boeing B-29 bomber pilots. They became so adept at flying the massive machines that they became instructors for new and aspiring pilots.

For a while, it appeared they would spend the war stateside. Then, they received their overseas deployment orders in 1944. They were assigned to different wings on separate islands in the Marianas and temporarily lost contact.

A love of flying was not the only bond between the two young men. What cemented their close relationship was the Japanese girls they loved. One had left his Yuki behind; the other his Mary, now held in a relocation camp with her family in Arizona. It was this sympathy that became their focus and mutual longings.

These old memories stirred in Dallas' mind as they approached the home islands of the Empire of Japan. He wondered where Sam was. There had been little time to try to track him down. He hoped they would meet up and be in the same wing if not the same squadron.

Daybreak interrupted his memories. With a dazzling brilliance, the sun appeared out of the east, turning the inky sky a pale blue. The ocean far below appeared as a slate board with undulating ripples tickling the surface.

A few hours later, Dallas saw Mount Fuji reflecting the sun's rays off its beautiful, rose-colored, snow-covered slopes. He never failed to enjoy the spectacle from a high altitude, especially when the mountain's cone seemed to float on the clouds like a pink parasol. The navigator interrupted his reverie.

"Approaching IP in twelve minutes," indicating the plane's initial turning point that would begin its photography run.

"Okay," Dallas answered. "Bill, why don't you and Dixie come up for a quick view of the mountain? I've seen it several times. I'll move so one of you can grab my seat. Carl, take control for a couple of minutes."

"Great!" came a drawled response from Technical Sergeant Michael 'Dixie' Short, the young radio operator who sat on the right side of the aircraft across from the navigator, who was behind Dallas.

Quickly unbuckling his seat belt, Dallas slid out of his command seat. The other two stood aside as he made his way back to their area. Dixie was quick to take the command seat and stared out the planes left side at the slopes of Mount Fuji.

First Lieutenant Bill Meeks stood between the pilot and co-pilot positions for his view out the rounded plexiglass bubble nose of the aircraft. In the meantime, Dallas sat at the radio operator's station across from Bill's empty navigation position.

Bill was the first to return to his navigation station and Dallas stood and stumbled clumsily as Meeks sat down across the aisle.

"Okay Dixie, get back to work," the co-pilot said as Dallas stood over the young sergeant in his seat. After retaking his position, Dallas reconnected his intercom. "You better check your dials, Dixie; I may have hit one as I stood up."

"Roger, Skipper," he replied. "Yeah, looks like one is off center but no harm."

"Pilot to crew, over IP in two minutes. Let's be sharp, boys; we're now visiting the Empire."

The immense silver bird flew over Yokosuka Imperial Naval base more than four miles below, then flew northwesterly over Tokyo Bay.

The navigator gave Dallas the new heading for the target run and, in a few moments, simply said, "Mark" – the signal to turn toward the city.

"Any sign of fighters?" Dallas asked as he completed his new heading.

His observers reported back in the negative.

"Okay, we're going to chance it at this altitude and make a quick run over the target area to the Kanto plain, bank left and come around over the area bombed yesterday. Bombardier, she's all yours."

That was the signal for the photographer-navigator sitting in the nose of the aircraft to be ready with his cameras. The F-13's six high-resolution cameras rested in the belly of the aft section of the plane.

Dallas watched out his window at the metropolis as they flew over the harbor area. From their high altitude, Tokyo was just a quilt-like pattern of gray patches, neighborhoods undistinguishable one from another. For a moment, he caught site of the Imperial Palace grounds.

The high command forbade bombing this particular piece of real estate, though he doubted most people back home would object to obliterating it.

Anyone on the ground that morning would have noticed, against the deep blue sky, a single silvery silhouette with its white contrail. The Tokyo air raid had sounded briefly, but the city defense masters sounded the all-clear when it was apparent there was only one plane overhead. Rarely did one plane bomb, and when one did, damages were insignificant. Japanese defense officials recognized that a single bomber usually meant a reconnaissance or weather mission.

Of the four million people in the Empire's capital, one particular person ran outside to see the lone bomber span the heavens above.

"Pilot to crew," Dallas banked the F-13 to the port. "We're now going to cross back over the western part of the city to see what happened below the other day."

"Fighters at five o'clock low!" came a cry from the starboard side observer behind the bomb bays. "Looks like three Zeros. They don't seem interested in climbing up here, though."

"Roger," Dallas replied calmly, though his heart rate had increased noticeably. "We stay at this altitude and continue the run. Keep your eyes peeled all around."

"Weapon systems ready," reported the central fire controller sitting in the rear section, his head projecting into the aft observation bubble. As on a regular B-29, the F-13 was armed with two upper and two lower remotely controlled gun turrets housing two .50 caliber machine guns. The tail gunner also operated two .50 caliber guns.

Dallas knew that few Japanese fighters could maneuver at his altitude but more frequently, a lone wolf was willing to sacrifice himself by ramming his plane into a B-29. If such a maneuver occurred on this day, he would risk his powerful but temperamental engines by quickly climbing higher.

However, the photographic run across the western side of the metropolis was uneventful. Eventually, the photographer radioed, "She's all yours, Skipper."

"Roger, I have her," Dallas replied. "Everyone, stay alert up front in case one of those heroes decides he wants to make a headshot."

Over the Bay, Meeks gave Dallas the headings for Guam, and the crew settled in for the long seven-hour flight back to home base.

Eight

"I must see my mother tonight, Aiki; it is urgent. Father is advising the navy doctors at Yokosuka, and is not due to come here until Monday."

"Oh, I am sorry Yuki, but I cannot take your duty tonight. I am on duty myself. Is there no way you can contact them?"

"No. My parents left Nikko to live and do volunteer practice in the Honjo ward. I will have to go there in person. I am afraid it will not be possible until Friday."

"But you do know we will have a full-blown inspection Saturday morning?"

"What!"

"Yes, including all our rooms and belongings in the hostel."

"How do you know this? An inspection is usually unannounced."

"My fiancé works in Army headquarters. He knows someone in the Kempeitai."

"Why would the Kempeitai want to inspect the medical school and our hostel?" Yuki asked incredulously. Her previous encounters with the secret police in Hiroshima had left her unnerved.

"Apparently they are looking into everything now that the war has come so close to home." Aiki paused, and looked around before speaking.

"I sense this war is not going well, and the government is fearful of unrest. They want to make sure those of us in the military remain vigilant."

"Well, we'd better shine the bedpans."

They laughed, relieving the mutual tension that had failed to mask their nervousness.

But Yuki had a graver concern.

Nikko
March 1985

"Okita, Why was Yuki in Tokyo? I thought she was at the Yokosuka Naval Hospital." My question exposed my unease.

"Dr. Fujita had been ordered to teach and practice at the Imperial Army Medical School and Hospital. He used his influence to get Yuki transferred to the Tokyo hospital as a full-time nurse."

"Was the family living together?" I asked.

"No. Yuki lived in a hostel set up by the hospital for the medical staff, Dr. and Mrs. Fujita deliberately took a shanty across the Sumida River. They ministered to residents when not on duty at the Imperial Medical School."

Still concerned, I pressed, "By 1945; when did they all arrive?"

He told me that Dr. Fujita and Sumiko were assigned in January, Yuki arrived in early February. I knew the strategic bombing of Japan had begun in 1944. By February 1945, Tokyo had been bombed several times.

Okita gave me an appraising look. "Are you going to ask me about the raid you Americans called Operation Meetinghouse?"

"First, tell me, were Yuki and her parents in Tokyo when the big fire raid devastated the city?"

Okita eyed me grimly.

I thought back to that night. I had to know right then, so I asked bluntly, "Did they survive?"

Okita face was ever more grim.

"Were you on the Meetinghouse raid?" he asked.

We stared at one another for a moment. The emotional strain started to affect my voice.

I thought back to that night. Could I talk about it at all?

Remembering I was his guest, I confessed, "Yes, I flew that mission and so did my best friend."

Okita cocked his head to the side, waiting for me to continue.

"Neither of us wanted to go, but it was our duty. We were loyal Americans. But we did not like the racial animosity the Asia-Pacific War had uncovered. We expected orders to the European theater. Both of us flew the Meetinghouse mission." I paused, then added, "But neither of us knew where the other was at the time."

Okita remained silent.

I felt compelled to tell the story. It had been a horrible experience for my best friend, though for different reasons.

Nine

North Field, Guam, Marshall Islands
1945 Hours, Wednesday Evening, 7 March 1945

Dallas let his co-pilot taxi the F-13 to its hardstand and cut the engines.

A routine debriefing followed at the squadron operations center. There was little to report other than the milk run over the Empire's capital city and the potential game of tag with a couple of fighters who did not have the heart for the ultimate sacrifice.

The intelligence team took the film from the cameras and disappeared to their studios to develop and analyze the contents. The rest of the crew quickly dismissed to the mess tent and quarters, but Dallas hung around the operations building a bit longer. He wanted to see if he could get any other information on the forthcoming mission to burn a large section of Tokyo.

The squadron's assistant operations officer, Major Maxwell Adams. Pilots and crews called him "The Max," behind his back. Major Maxwell saw Dallas and walked over. The 'Max' was a stickler for pomp and ceremony. He did not brook messiness in airmen's appearance. His own khakis always appeared starched and pressed; his face so cleanly shaven that there was talk he never grew facial hair. Maxwell wore a short crew cut, and strutted around like a squadron commander instead of a second-tier staff officer. His one known vice was chewing tobacco then, spitting it out with an arrogance that belied his competence.

Aside from the obvious differences, he and Dallas shared an intense mutual dislike for one another. Max was fond of spewing racial slurs about the Japanese as well as other ethnic groups. Dallas seethed when forced to hear the terms of degradation. Furthermore, Max seemed to avoid flying missions, even though he was rated a B-29 pilot. No one could point to a single mission he had flown over Japan's home islands.

As Max moved in his direction, Dallas quickly looked down at his flight suit to ensure nothing was amiss. After fifteen hours in the cockpit, he did not feel like any harassment from a prima donna.

"Relax Lieutenant," Max drawled. "Or I guess I should say Captain. Your promotion orders are in the admin shack. Been there almost a week. Guess I forgot to tell you." He chuckled. "Congratulations and all that. So, go get in the right uniform. We don't do promotion ceremonies here."

"Thanks Major. Didn't know my number was up."

"You should pay more attention to your career development, Captain,"

'The Max' started to walk away, stopped, and turned.

"Oh, by the way, there's another set of orders; the 314th Bomb Wing needs a hot-shot pilot for the mission Friday evening. I volunteered you. Take all your stuff; it's a permanent move." He grinned and walked away.

As the obnoxious officer disappeared out the door, Dallas clenched his jaw and fists and muttered an expletive toward the departing prig.

Dallas was designated as a pilot on the suicide raid, a killing mission. With his last reconnaissance mission, Dallas thought he had done enough already. Yet that was not the real issue. The Max had set him up for a mission that was not only suicidal, but also contradicted his deeply held private considerations.

With these troubling thoughts, he returned to his tent to pack up.

The next day, Dallas entered the administration tent of his new squadron of the 314th Bombardment Wing. He was surprised to bump into Master Sergeant "Pop" Warner, the flight engineer on his F-13, along with Dixie Short, Bill Meeks, and Larry Wynns.

"It's sorter like this, Captain," Dixie offered. "We figured you needed old hands like us with you on your new assignment. So, I know someone who knows someone who knows how to cut orders. All legit, Sir." He winked.

Dallas smiled. "Do you guys know what you're getting into?"

"We heard the rumors, Captain." Pop, the non-com curmudgeon, was several years senior in age to any of them. "All the more reason you'll need old hands with you."

A young administration sergeant handed the new squadron members their tent assignments, then told Dallas to see the squadron commander in the Quonset hut next door. After the formalities of reporting in, Dallas requested permission to check out his new aircraft.

"That's fine," Lieutenant Colonel Taylor, the squadron commander said. "I understand your old crew came with you. That's good. Don't know how I got them since I asked only for a pilot, but I'm glad they'll be with you. I'm breaking up the crew that brought the new bomber from the States. The pilot is in the hospital with appendicitis, and his co-pilot is a green flight officer.

"Your bombardier, tail gunner, and radar operator are alright. You'll be taking the one observer. In case you haven't heard the rumors, only the tail gunner is going armed. Your central control gunner will be the observer. So, your co-pilot, bombardier, radar operator, and tail-gunner just flew in with the new ship. They'll need good, experienced mentors for this mission. Your old timers should provide steady hands. It's going to be a tough mission for all of us. I hear its code name is Meetinghouse. A good name for Tokyo, huh?"

Dallas nodded thoughtfully. "Yes, Sir. I suppose it's as good as any."

"Welcome to the squadron, Captain."

Dallas saluted and left to round up his crew. They all caught a ride out to the parking ramps to find the new B-29 in its hardstand. Tech Sergeant Green greeted them, his dirty khakis reflecting his hands-on attention to the temperamental engines. Dallas had learned that Green, a noncommissioned officer, enjoyed a solid reputation for prepping bombers for their missions. The two of them hit it off immediately. Dallas did not throw his rank around. Long ago, he had learned that the plane belonged to the crew chief when on the ground.

"You heard the rumors, I suppose."

"Yes, Sir. I hate like hell sending you guys off without armament."

"Well, you can do me a big favor, Chief. Leave the forward gun turrets loaded, even if you must hoard a few hundred pounds of bombs. I hate head-on attacks."

The chief flashed a quick smile but said nothing.

"I'd better go meet the rest of the crew."

"Most of 'em seem okay, Captain." the crew chief offered. "But keep your eye on your co-pilot, Mr. Hodges. Frankly, I think he's a little …"

He left the sentence hanging, and Dallas merely nodded.

Returning the Chief's sloppy salute with an equally sloppy one, Dallas then rounded up his veterans who were inspecting the new plane. Dixie asked if they could name the aircraft now and order up its nose art. Dallas smiled at the name selected. Nothing tawdry or funny, just a simple geographical name, one that he knew well. Dixie and Dallas claimed Georgia as their home state. It seemed Dixie had fished the same waters. Dallas nodded his okay and signaled for a ride back to the squadron living areas.

After completing his "in-processing" in the new squadron, Dallas checked out the Quonset hut living quarters. The semicircular building housed ten other aircraft commanders and co-pilots, ranging in rank from lieutenant to major. His area consisted of a cot with an air mattress, like the one he had in the recon squadron. He found a crudely constructed plywood desk shared by other inhabitants of the building. He noticed it had a plywood floor as opposed to a cement one. The windows were screened and kept open to allow the tropical breezes to circulate.

The squadron commander had assigned him to read and censor ten or so letters the enlisted men wrote. It took half an hour to review each, to ensure none leaked classified information. After reading the simple love letters to wives, sweethearts, or parents, he tried writing a letter to Mary, but he wasn't in the mood. Crumpling the stillborn missive, he wondered if Mary had heard from Sam. The three of them had vowed to stay in touch.

The afternoon air had turned sultry, so he decided to take a shower at the sprinkler truck. The water, still warm from the tropical sun, was refreshing.

Dallas convened a later meeting with the new crew members in the squadron briefing room. He spent the early evening getting to know them better. His veterans from the recon squadron also sat in but remained quiet after introducing themselves. First impressions lined up with the squadron commanders' and crew chiefs' observations. The bombardier, First Lieutenant Al Rocco, was more than competent. Dallas noted that Rocco had trained as a B-29 pilot before the Army Air Force decided they needed more bombardiers and forced him into that role. He considered the radar operator, Sergeant First Class Tony Costa, and tail gunner, Sergeant Steve Lewis, to be sharp. Unfortunately, his co-pilot left him with a feeling of doubt and unease. The young man did not say much but nervously joked whenever he did.

"I just want you men to know that you have some fine fellow crew members," Dallas told them. "They are veterans of several missions over the Empire. They can fill you in if you have any questions about what to expect. The main thing I need is for you to stay alert when we get near the home islands. If you thought flying across the Pacific from the States was long and boring," he paused, "well, at least you had stops along the way. It's going to be a fifteen-hour roundtrip up to Japan and back, so you may get bored at times. Just be alert as we approach the combat zone."

Dismissing the crew, he stepped out into still humid air, and ran straight into Major Maxwell Adams.

"You!" 'the Max' bellowed, "You stole my crew members!" He pushed

Dallas with his hands.

"I did no such thing, Major; they volunteered to join my new squadron. And don't put your hands on me again!"

"You're a liar, you Jap-loving bastard!" Max sneered revealing his dark stained teeth and a brown stream of tobacco juice running from the corner of his mouth.

"Watch your language, Major. I don't like your tone," Dallas snarled.

"Shove it and the yellow slut you pine for," Max hissed.

It was automatic. One moment he stood face to face with the obnoxious senior officer and the next he was rubbing his fist after slamming it into Max's juice-stained jaw, flooring the man. Dixie and Pop, witnessing the incident, grabbed him, and quickly escorted him away from the scene. Max did not get up; he was out cold.

Ten

Guam, the Marshall Islands
Thursday Morning, 8 March 1945

Dallas was summoned to the squadron commander's office, and reported sharply at 1100. Colonel Taylor waved off his salute and instructed him to sit in a folding chair by the makeshift desk.

Taylor eyed Dallas, taking the measure of his new pilot. Dallas merely returned his gaze, unfazed by the scrutiny.

"I checked your record, Wade. You have the reputation and the credentials of an outstanding Superfortress pilot. That shouldn't surprise anyone, given your trainer status. You seem to know the plane better than those who designed and built her."

Dallas remained stoic. He knew Taylor had not called him in to praise his flying abilities. When he did not reply to the lure, his commander continued,

"So, Wade, you want to tell me about this incident with this Major Maxwell yesterday? I'm not in the mood for a court-martial when we have a big mission on the plate."

Dallas cleared his throat, and thought for a moment. "Not much to tell, Colonel. I got pushed; I pushed back. The witness statements will confirm that."

Taylor gave him a wry smile. "Coldcocking a superior officer isn't exactly pushing back, if you get my drift."

For a few seconds, Dallas looked away, "It wasn't just his unauthorized pushing that sparked my response; it was something he said."

Taylor regarded him with the clear intention for Dallas to continue. When he did not, Taylor asked, "What in the world could he have said to provoke you, laying him out cold?"

Dallas smiled, knowing that Taylor already knew the answer. He answered anyway, "Something nasty… about someone I love dearly – He spoke in the most disrespectful manner."

Now Taylor smiled slightly, confirming he surely knew the answer. "Yes, you know you have a bit of a reputation as a Jap lover."

"Japanese, Sir."

"Well, Captain," Taylor spoke firmly, "from the President on down, the word for our enemy is Japs. So, I suggest you better not get too sensitive to hear the term around here."

"I hear it all the time, Sir. I agree it's natural for our people to degrade the enemy. But when it gets personal as Major Maxwell made it … well let's just say, it's downright rude."

Taylor laughed aloud at Dallas' innocuous understatement. Dallas remained passive, so his new commander continued his lecture.

"Look, Wade, I don't have to tell you that we're in a brutal war out here, and we lose crews and planes almost every mission. With this particular mission, you cannot let your personal feelings get the best of you, and neither do we."

"Sir, I never let my emotions get out of hand …"

"Until Maxwell made a comment you didn't like."

"And shoved me after accusing me of lying!"

Dallas' face now flushed at the memory of the indignation. He caught himself, breathed deeply, and continued, "Look, Sir, I have a very close and dear friend in a concentration camp in Arizona. Mary and her family are loyal Americans. Her brother is fighting for us in Europe. They are as American as apple pie. Yet we disparage them and lock 'em up because of their race. It's just not right."

Taylor leaned back in his chair and sighed.

"I don't see your point. You're a good man as well as an outstanding pilot, Wade. Your former commander vouched for that. I want to make sure you understand you can't jeopardize your crews' chances for a successful mission over an emotional outburst against what words they call their enemy."

"That hasn't been a problem with the guys who came over with me, or with any of my other former crew-mates."

"Good! Because I can tell you I'd hate for you to mess up your career status over an incident like this.

"We have a hell of a mission tomorrow night. I know you've heard the rumors. We're going to Tokyo without gunners, we are going in low, real low. Five to ten thousand feet. And we are going to burn the city to the ground and kill a helluva lot of Japs – Japanese civilians, whether you like it or not. You got that, Captain?"

"Yes Sir," Dallas answered quietly. "I don't like it, but I know my duty – and my oath."

Taylor breathed in deeply and exhaled slowly.

"I want you to assure me you can take this mission. I'm short of good pilots, and need you to be in top shape tomorrow night."

"Sir, I'm taking my crew to Tokyo and bringing 'em back alive. I know how to fly this mission. You won't have to worry about me."

Dallas did not say that he was worried about his green co-pilot.

"Right," Taylor appeared satisfied as Dallas stood and saluted.

"You may want to know, Major Maxwell has a low reputation over at the recon squadron."

Dallas turned and looked at him quizzically.

Taylor continued, "I got that from your former squadron commander. Dismissed."

Eleven

North Field, Guam, The Marianas
Late Friday Afternoon, 9 March 1945

Sitting in a parking stand throughout the tropical day, the giant Superfortress's interior now seemed like a sauna to Dallas and his crew, drenching their simple one-piece flight suits with perspiration. The foreboding tensions eased only a bit when Dallas gave the order to start engines.

His crew had remained reticent after the group briefing. Most crews knew the scuttlebutt already, hoping against hope it was not true.

Yet when the Group commander stood in the half barrel-shaped Quonset hut to brief the crews, noticeable squirming occurred on the back-row benches where the enlisted members sat. No one uttered any words of protest, and all seemed to take the mission order in stride.

However, Dallas knew of the misgivings he silently shared with his crew. Only Pop Warner, the old career soldier and airman, seemed unshaken by the mission, maintaining a business-like manner during the briefing. Even now, as he monitored his instruments, Pop displayed no evident concerns.

The reasons given for the mission were not entirely convincing. The target areas of Tokyo between the Sumida and Arakawa Rivers were factories producing weaponry, surrounded by their many cottage industries that supplied the armament factories. These cottage industries were paper and wooden houses occupied by families who made various war material components, passing these on to the factories. Every Japanese citizen was now considered a military target. The crew was more concerned about their survival than the well-being of the civilian enemy. While the intelligence officer briefed them on the anemic night fighter capability of the Japanese air forces and the supposed ineffectiveness of anti-aircraft flak due to their low altitude attack, few were convinced that they were not going on a suicide mission worthy of their opponents.

The B-29s would be flying singularly rather than in formation. They would drop incendiaries from low altitudes – five to eight thousand feet. As rumored, they were to leave their defensive armament, ammunition, and two gunners behind; only the tail gunner was going with machine guns loaded. The central fire coordinator would fly as an observer.

The real reason for the low-level attack was the high command's frank admission that daylight precision bombing proved to be an expensive failure. At high altitudes, the newly discovered jet stream played havoc, strewing the bombs away from their intended targets by yards, if not miles. Going in low with incendiaries instead of high explosive bombs was the gamble to change the outcome of the strategic bombing campaign. Most of the crews felt it was gambling with their lives.

The briefing officer told them that the lead bombers would mark the target area with a fiery X that would be clearly visible from the flying altitudes. Dallas' crew knew by the time they arrived there should already be a significant firestorm to guide them in. The follow-on bombers would carry the 500-pound M-69 incendiary bombs. Each cluster would contain thirty-six bomblets of napalm. After release, the cluster would break apart, spreading over a wide area. Upon hitting the ground, the bomblets would release 100-foot streams of fiery gel, burning anything in their path.

After the briefings, the crews had wandered back to their quarters, rested, or gone to the mess tents for a quick meal. Men wrote letters, visited the chaplain or whispered prayers. In the late afternoon, the entire crew boarded the trucks for the ride to the airfield and their bombers.

Dallas smiled when he saw the newly painted words on the nose of his bomber. *Lake Blackshear*, named after the reservoir in southern Georgia where he and his best friend Sam had fished for bass, bream, and the inevitable catfish. Dixie had also grown up near there. None of the other crew members seemed to care about the name at all.

The four engines idled gently, shaking the airframe. Dallas checked his gauges and waited for Pop Warner's verdict.

"Everything looks really good, Captain." Pop reported matter-of-factly.

"She's a good ship."

"Okay, Mr. Hodges, close bomb bay doors."

He heard the ka-thunks as the panels of the two bomb bays snapped shut.

Dallas looked at his crew chief. Sergeant Green stood near the front of the B-29 in cut off khaki shorts and sweat-soaked shirt, his cap pulled low over his brow. Dallas smiled at the thought of 'the Max' witnessing the unorthodox uniform alterations. The grizzly sergeant looked up at Dallas raised his arms to his sides, thumbs pointing outward, indicating that the wheel chocks were removed. Dallas smiled and gave the man a thumbs up. He knew the front upper and lower turrets had ammunition, yet the crew chief did not seem to notice Dallas' "Thank you" gesture. He was all about getting the aircraft out of its hardstand and onto the taxi way.

"Close windows." Together, they closed the two open windows by their seats. Now, their plane was sealed and hotter.

The crew chief saluted sharply. Dallas returned the gesture, released his brakes, and began to taxi *Lake Blackshear* out of the hardstand. The crew chief walked them to the taxiway, stood aside, saluted again. Then the bomber was on the taxiway behind another B-29.

The line of bombers slowly made their way down the taxiway, like giant silver beasts, where they would swing around onto the runway. Already, Dallas saw a Superfortress on its takeoff run in the opposite direction parallel to the taxiway. He glanced over to his co-pilot, who seemed focused on the instruments. Dallas had told Mr. Hodges to let him fly the airplane on takeoff. The co-pilot's sole duty would be to call off ground speed.

Dallas turned the giant bomber toward the runway and waited for the B-29 in front of them to begin its run and, following the flagman's direction, pulled the *Lake Blackshear* around onto the long strip of crushed coral. Immediately, he began to rev the engines to full power as he stood hard on the brakes. He looked out to see the Wing chaplain making the sign of the cross at his aircraft.

Dallas smiled cynically. *Might as well rub a rabbit's foot. Consign the cross, silver dollars, lucky charms, and all the other superstitious artifacts to the dustbin of history.* Nothing but skill and courage would bring the crew through this mission. Dallas intended to apply all the skill and courage he had honed over the past several months – or die trying.

The flagman dropped his flag, and Dallas released the brakes, sending his sixty-nine-ton bomber forward with its deadly cargo.

Far down the runway, he could see the B-29 ahead of him lifting into the air. He had just under a minute to get *Lake Blackshear* airborne, or the entire crew and airplane would be smoking wreckage in the Pacific shoals at the end of the island.

Dallas was more than mindful of the four temperamental Wright Cyclone R-3350 engines Pop Warner had to manage with tender care. Their hurried development with limited testing stateside resulted in many unpredictable operational failures, causing the death of entire crews on takeoff. While Dallas relied entirely on Pop's expertise, he knew flaws were beyond the best flight engineer's skills. Yet Dallas' intuitive feel, for the sounds and rhythms, assured him the bomber's four engines were running smoothly.

Mr. Hodges was performing precisely as Dallas had hoped, calling off the ground speed as the heavy Superfortress rolled down the runway at a quickening pace. He glanced at the young co-pilot and saw a tick in his face—nervousness.

Yet, Dallas and the airplane were one; man and machine melded together. He had flown enough in the States and in the Marianas to know the feel of this type of aircraft, and instinctively, Pop was right – *Lake Blackshear* was indeed a good ship. Halfway down the strip, he pulled gently on the half-wheel control yoke to let the nose wheel strut lift slightly but did not try to force the plane off the ground. He would let it fly itself into the air.

As the airflow increased over the wide wings, creating lift, he felt the pressure on the two wing landing gear struts begin to ease, and as the fast-approaching Pacific Ocean filled the front windows; he pulled back ever so lightly, and the plane rose gently into the air without fanfare or drama. The plane flew off the runway and out over the sea.

"Gear up," he ordered to his young co-pilot, and he heard the landing gear folding into the aircraft's inboard nacelles, the outer casings of the plane's engines. They drifted to about a hundred feet over the Pacific waves allowing the four strained engines to cool from the exertions of the takeoff run.

"Okay, Pop, let me know when you want me to climb."

"Roger, Skipper."

Gazing out his windows, Dallas could see the sea turning a deeper shade of gray in the late evening twilight. A few whitecaps were visible, and in minutes the sea darkened almost to a deep charcoal tint.

About fifteen minutes later, Pop Warner radioed Dallas, "Engineer to pilot. Take her to first cruising altitude, Captain."

Checking with Bill Meeks to ensure he was on the correct heading, Dallas brought the B-29 up to four hundred feet, his cruising altitude until they reached the checkpoint near the island of Iwo Jima, where they would ascend to their assigned five-thousand-foot bombing altitude. The first four planes behind him would climb sequentially by two hundred feet to six hundred, then the third to eight hundred until the last reached twelve hundred. Thus, the flight of five bombers would fly in "stacked" staircase formation until it was time to climb to bombing altitude. When Dallas reached his first cruising goal, he set the bomber on autopilot and relaxed as much as an aircraft commander could allow himself. Seven and a half hours of flying lay ahead before bombs away.

Staying awake and alert were the main challenges for the crew en route to the Iwo Jima check point. Dallas ordered the tail gunner to stay alert and watch for trailing B-29s. Just before darkness enclosed them, the gunner reported seeing one aircraft at six hundred feet altitude and less than a half mile behind. That met with expectations, but no one could be sure where all the planes were in their "stacked" formations. None had running lights so in the coming darkness, they would be invisible.

The *Lake Blackshear* had been in one of the last formations to depart Guam. More than three hundred planes had staged from three Mariana Islands – Saipan and Tinian, as well as Guam. Their unit, the 314th Bomb Wing, had started earlier because of its greater distance from Japan. Still, Dallas' squadron was going in on the target later than many of the bombers. The various conditions affecting each flight – aircraft performance, weather, darkness, and navigation errors – played havoc with such spread-out formations comprising three Wings from the three island bases. The mission would be a maximum effort – every mechanically available B-29 with a crew was heading toward the Empire.

After an hour's flying time, Dallas rose from his seat, stretched as best he could in the cockpit, and then made his way to the twenty-six-foot cylindrical "tunnel" next to Dixie's station. He climbed the short ladder and crawled back over the two bomb bays to the aft section of the aircraft. Dallas developed this habit during training. For one thing, it allowed him to use the chemical toilet in the aft section. More importantly, Dallas liked to check on the rear crew members, assuring them that even if they were out of sight in the huge aircraft, they were not just radio voices on the long journey. Everything appeared in order; everyone was alert. The tail-gunner remained in his pressure-sealed compartment but acknowledged Dallas' greetings.

After three and a half hours, they approached Iwo Jima. Dallas could see the storm clouds ahead. Heat lightning lit up the cumulonimbus formations they would be entering shortly. Each flash brought a remarkable beauty, reminding him of the real Lake Blackshear, when the sky's thunderheads suddenly brightened iridescently. Sometimes, bolts would strike out across the heavens, fragmenting into many arteries before fading as quickly as they had appeared. The scene took him back to those summer nights sitting around a campfire in the dark with his college buddy Sam Reid when they had camped at Lake Blackshear almost two years ago.

Twelve

Lake Blackshear, Crisp County, Georgia
Late August 1943

The embers glowed warmly in the campfire. The two young men had cooked their catch of perch earlier in the evening and now lay back against their rolled sleeping bags. Their bodies and clothing reeked of mosquito repellant, making the warm, humid night all the more uncomfortable. Still, they had enjoyed the day fishing and sitting around the fire after sunset.

The distant thunderheads lit up the night sky every few moments with a brilliant display. Despite its pyrotechnic beauty, neither relished the idea of taking a small airplane unnecessarily into such turbulence, having flown together in a storm. From their training, they knew the storm was more than ten miles away, thus dissipating the sound of thunder.

"Thanks for bailing me out on the ole English lit final."

"Well, you owe me one, Shakespeare," Dallas answered, and they both laughed.

They fixated on the still-hot ashes, as another flash of heat lightning lit up their camp.

"You think we'll get our wings?" Dallas asked, stirring the red ashes. He tossed a dry pine stick onto the embers and watched it burst into yellow flames.

"You bet," Sam answered. "Gotta get a commission first as an officer and a gentleman. Here's hoping we get sent to Europe. I hate the thought of fighting in the Pacific."

Dallas grunted. He shared the same emotions and foreboding that Sam harbored.

"Yeah, it must be pretty bad out there. I don't like the idea of fighting those folks. Whatever persuaded them to pick a fight with the United States?"

"You and I are different from the other guys in our class," Sam answered.

"How's that?"

"They hate the Japanese. They and just about everyone else in the country thinks of them as sub-human."

"There have been awful reports coming out of the Philippines and other places." Dallas paused. "The butchery must be awful. Did you ever hear of the Nanking massacre?"

"Yeah, and I hope that's an exception to their national character."

Sam paused, thinking for a moment, then continued, "But you and I know they are just people like us. How else could the two of us feel so strongly about our girls?"

"I got into a fight the other day," Dallas threw another pine stick onto the dying coals.

"Yeah? You didn't tell me." Sam looked over, expecting to hear more.

"You know that know-it-all jerk from New England? The one who thinks he's an expert on everything from women to slide rulers? Well, he made a smart remark about Japanese girls. I tried to let it slide, but then he got vulgar. A classmate told him about the picture on my desk. Called her a filthy name."

"Whoa!"

"You know what he called me?" Sam shook his head.

"A dirty Jap-lover. So, I knocked the hell out of him," Dallas looked over at Sam.

"Guilty as charged," Sam chuckled.

"Yeah, but it is a shame what's going on besides the war and the killing. Both sides have slumped into race-baiting, denigrating the other based on skin pigments and eye shapes."

"I think it's even more than that, Dallas," Sam answered. "It's also the culture. You remember what Mary told us back in June?"

Dallas nodded. The two of them had caught a train out west after spring classes ended to visit Mary Kurahara and her family in the Niesei relocation camp in Poston, Arizona. The Niesei were Japanese-American citizens whose parents were immigrants from Japan. Poor Mary expounded how they were forced to pack immediately and herded into horse stalls at the Santa Anita racetrack near Los Angeles while awaiting relocation. They slept on straw with the smell of horse droppings hanging in the air.

"Concentration camp, if you ask me."

"Who'd believe that the President would sign such an order." He spoke of the presidential executive order that sent West Coast Japanese-American families to centers under the pretense of prevention of sabotage.

"And the irony of it all," Sam continued, "is that her brother is serving in the United States Army." After a moment, he added, "I hate to see this racial hatred from both sides. I bet the Japanese are using our damned Jim Crow laws against us in their propaganda."

"Who could blame them?"

"Well, we are not at war with our minority populations here; at least we let them serve in our military. Did you read about those Tuskegee airmen fellows? I hear they deployed them to North Africa."

"I wonder if we'll let them fight."

"We'd better. I hear the Luftwaffe pilots are real buzzards."

"But so are the Japanese," Sam replied.

They were quiet before Dallas rolled over and mumbled, "I sure hope we don't have to go to the Pacific to fight, Sam."

The next morning, they packed their gear, and headed up US 341 toward Atlanta. Returning to campus in the early afternoon, they found a note from the Professor of Military Science on their dormitory door. The following morning, they both reported to the ROTC headquarters.

A neatly dressed one-armed major, one of their instructors, returned their salutes with his left hand. He had lost his right arm in the Solomon Islands campaign the year before.

"Well, boys, congratulations," he deadpanned, "You've been accelerated for commissioning in December."

They both appeared stunned. The major smiled. "And you both will be attending flight school in Texas, in January. Don't mess up this last semester!"

They looked at each other, then smiled before snapping their dismissal salute. At least part of the dream had come true.

**The Mad Catfish *B-29, North of Iwo Jima.*
*Late Night, 9 March 1945***

As his bomber approached the storm, Captain Sam Reid reflected on the morning events on Saipan. Like most pilots in the 73rd Bomb Group, Sam knew the scuttlebutt about the forthcoming Meetinghouse mission. He hated the idea of taking a crew to Tokyo that night. He had flown missions over the city before – true enough from thirty thousand feet. It was not the impending danger that caused his unease. By now, Sam knew from experience that B-29's accuracy in previous high-altitude bombing attacks was less effective than the plane's designers had hoped.

Sam also knew the effect incendiaries would have from a low altitude.

No, the real problem was that a lot of Japanese civilians would be killed tonight. Sam feared for them. He could not help himself. The painful thought left him moody all morning. When he went to the makeshift barbershop for a haircut that morning, he snapped at the young airman, who served as the squadron barber, trying to make small talk.

"Just cut my hair, Corporal," he had barked out. He later returned to apologize to the young airman, saying he had a headache. The corporal assured him he took no offense, and Sam told him to take care. The "barber" would be a crewman on someone's bomber that evening.

Sam considered feigning illness to sidestep the mission, but he knew that would be a dereliction of duty. He took his oath seriously. True, he swore allegiance to the Constitution and no man, but accepted the commission as an officer with the commitment it deserved. If the crew had to go, Sam had to go with them. He was their leader and mentor. They were a relatively new bunch, having flown three missions over the home islands. He had to take them in and bring them back out.

Several of the crew were devoutly religious, but like his college roommate, Sam no longer ascribed to any faith. He considered himself an agnostic and avoided all the Wing chaplains. Sam never attended Sunday services.

He did have a self-assurance in his flying skills. Yet something in his psyche seemed to nag at him. "Leave me alone!" But, no one was there.

Sam had never been assigned a mission against Kure Naval Base, and he was grateful for that. The last he and Dallas had known, Yuki was there. Both were now thankful that Mary was safe in a relocation camp in Arizona. They did not know where Yuki's parents were now. They surmised the Fujitas may be in a city hospital or, more likely, at a major military base.

Going in low over Tokyo would be dangerous, not only for his crew, but also for his peace of mind. He wondered how Dallas felt and if he were on tonight's raid. Sam knew he was in the Marianas but was not sure where. He learned Dallas was not on Saipan. The squadron personnel office checked to see if they could find him but to no avail. He even wrote to Dallas care of XXI Bomber Command.

He received no reply.

Sam's crew had named their B-29 *Mad Catfish*, a name with a logo that amused him. He and Dallas caught a few of the fish that summer of 1943 at Lake Blackshear. The logo painted on the side depicted an angry catfish riding a bomb.

Later that afternoon, as his forward crew members climbed into the bomber through the nose wheel opening, Sam asked his crew chief the usual questions, seeking reassurance of the mechanics of the plane. The chief assured him the plane was ready.

"But no weapons, Captain," the chief said sadly, "except for your tail gunner. I'm sorry. Orders are orders." The crew chief was a stickler for regulations and orders.

Sam nodded and climbed up into his ship. They took off just before sunset.

As they flew into the tumultuous clouds beyond Iwo Jima, the big bomber bucked and jumped. Without running lights, it would be difficult to see another plane in the darkness. The more religious crew members prayed they would not collide with another B-29. The tempest strained the pilots who tried to keep her on an even keel, and the airframe herself. Sam could hear the engines pitch modulating with his efforts to maintain control.

Checking his altimeter, he knew they had been blown down from their seven thousand feet bombing altitude.

Half an hour later, he received an ominous report.

"Captain, we've got a problem with number four," the flight engineer's voice crackled over Sam's earphones.

"Report!" he answered.

"Don't know what happened. Oil pressure dropping. If I don't shut her down, we may have a runaway prop."

Sam knew the problem well. If the engine valve was burning, it could cause disintegration of the cylinders. If hydraulic fluid was lost, the four-blade prop could fly off or worse, tear the wing off.

"Feather now!" Sam ordered emphatically. The flight engineer complied.

Sam ordered available crew members to check to ensure the prop had stopped turning.

"Prop is still," came the report from the central fire control observer from his dome on top of the fuselage.

The co-pilot concurred from his vantage point.

Everyone relaxed, but Sam radioed his engineer, "Can she still make the mission or should we turn back?"

"Roger, Captain, I see no reason we cannot make the bomb run and go home," The flight engineer replied.

"Keep your eye on it." Sam replied.

An hour later they emerged from the storm lower than the intended bombing altitude. Those in the nose of the B-29 could see the glow of the distant burning capital city. Sam felt sick as they headed for the Chiba Peninsula. But, now, his mind began calculating.

Thirteen

Kempeitai Field Office, Tokyo
1800 Hours, Friday Evening, 9 March 1945

As the late winter sunlight faded, shadows fell across Major Matome Tanaka's desk as he perused his files. There were rumors of a promotion that pleased him immensely. He had been ruthless in his pursuit of enemies of the Empire. The Fujita family held his attention, but he'd never been able to pin anything specific on them. He recalled that an American doctor and his family had lived with them. Dr. Fujita had trained in the United States two decades ago. That meant nothing. Many Japanese had attended schools in America, even marrying American women.

He also recalled the heavy-handed interrogation of the American. Tanaka had seen much worse abuse in Nanking, China. He had remained suspicious of their connection. After Dr. Fujita reported to the Kure Naval Base, Tanaka made another suspicious connection between the doctor and his daughter, Yuki, though no incriminating evidence of conspiracy resulted. After Tanaka made a discreet call and learned that the doctor would be home in the Honjo neighborhood today, he decided to pay them a surprise visit. He wasn't worried, the daughter was being watched.

At 2230, Tanaka summoned Master Sergeant Saito, his assistant. The two Kempei slipped on their heavy overcoats. The wind was picking up, and the early evening promised to turn bitterly cold later in the night. Almost automatically, they carried their padded zukin air raid cowls, the padded hoods meant to protect them from embers and intense heat. The men summoned a military vehicle and rode toward the Sumita River.

Kashiwa Army Airfield, Kando Plain, North of Tokyo
1800 Hours, Friday Evening, 9 March 1945

As they sat eating their modest evening meal, the Phantom Tiger mused on how well the military dined as compared to their civilian counterparts.

He knew obtaining sufficient food for Japan's population was becoming more complex. His caloric intake was barely adequate to sustain an active man of his age, especially one under the daily stress of flying, instructing, and fighting.

He regarded Akio, his young apprentice, and wingman, who ate ravenously, while the Phantom chewed his food more deliberately.

"Eat slowly, my young friend," he told the boy, probably seventeen years old. "You will have better digestion."

"I'm always hungry, Lieutenant," Akio spoke as he chewed. "Why are our rations so few?"

"We have much more than the people in the village. It is getting harder to move all types of supplies – food, medicine, ammunition." The Tiger knew about medicine shortages, having talked with his uncle at the Imperial Army Hospital. "The war situation is … difficult."

"But surely, we are on the verge of victory, Lieutenant!"

"Akio, I dare say Japan is in serious trouble. The B-sans come more frequently to bomb our cities."

"Bah, we will shoot all of them down!"

Akio obviously believed the propaganda. He had never flown in combat.

"Akio, just three years ago, we were told no enemy would ever bomb Japan. Then, the Americans struck six of our cities with medium army bombers flown off an aircraft carrier. Since February, their fleet cruises off our shores, their carrier fighters and bombers struck us. In addition, their heavy bombers flying in from the Marianas are wreaking destruction on our country."

"But surely, they are almost depleted!" Akio believed what he wanted to believe.

"Listen, Akio, you and I are on alert tonight and tomorrow. I don't think there will be any air raids in our sector tomorrow because of the forecast for high winds; we know how it affects their bombs. But we must rest and be ready. If we go up, you stay on my wing and do what I tell you. Understood?"

"Hai, Lieutenant!" But the Tiger knew Akio was reckless and full of patriotic zeal. He was not yet skilled enough to tangle with a B-29.

"The B-29s are heavily armed with very accurate machine guns, Akio. I will show you how to make a pass using speed and deception. So, if it comes to a fight, watch me. But stay out of range until I tell you. Understand?"

"Hai," Akio answered and smiled.

They were silent for a time as they finished their food. Then Akio asked, "Sir, what do you think of the Special Attack Units?"

Without hesitation, the Tiger answered, "I think it is futile, Akio … and I do not believe in suicide."

"Sir, I understand you are a member of the Christian sect. Do you not honor our Japanese gods?"

"Akio, I do not believe the myth about the Emperor, our people descending from the Sun Goddess, or any other gods. Nor do I believe in our racial superiority and virtue. I believe in the one true God who created everything, including all people, in his own divine image.

"And I believe all people are sinful creatures, so no race has a hold on virtue. I also believe that God came to us two thousand years ago as a human and paid for our evil ways by dying for us. Yet I respect your right to believe otherwise."

"Isn't this blasphemy?" Akio asked incredulously.

"If you choose to believe so, go ahead. I'm just telling you what Christians believe."

"But what about the souls of the Special Attack pilots? Don't they become gods to be worshipped at Yasukuni?" The youngster clearly was agitated.

"Akio, it is proper to honor our war dead who fought for our nation. But no, I do not believe they are gods and objects of worship. Worthy of respect, yes; worship no. I worship the one true God."

Akio's face flamed. Was he angry or just filled with zeal?

"So, you would not volunteer for the Special Attack units?" he asked finally.

"Absolutely not!"

"Well, I am considering doing so, Lieutenant."

"I hope you will think about that in a more tranquil moment, Akio. We need pilots, not martyrs."

They finished their meals and headed back to the barracks. The Tiger admonished Akio to get rest. Then the Tiger went to the airfield to check their planes, confirm they were armed, and fueled. He wrote a letter to his parents and then tried his hand at poetry, but his heart was not in it. He kept thinking about Akio's brashness.

At eleven, he turned in for the evening, but he could not sleep. Outside, the winds wailed mournfully as if someone's death was imminent. He stared at the ceiling, thinking how crazy the world had become. He also thought of his old American chum and wondered where he was this ominous night.

As evening skies darkened, a chilling wind racked the narrow streets, causing shoppers to quicken their pace for home. The gusts brought with them the first blaring air raid sirens.

Having completed her shift on her ward at eight that evening, Yuki went to her hostel to change into her monpei pants and a thick fire-resistant jacket. Abruptly as it started, the siren ceased. *But that is supposed to happen tomorrow.*

Yuki turned on her radio and finished dressing. "All clear", blared the announcer, but she decided to take her zukin with her as required. She wanted to wait until dark to carry the suitcase out into the city. Strangely, there had been no talk among the staff about tomorrow's inspection, so Yuki quickly and quietly retrieved the locked suitcase. Yuki checked her appearance to ensure she looked plain in her pants and overcoat, then closed, and locked her door, and walked outside.

Yuki stood at the gate briefly, then stepped through, nearly bumping into Lieutenant Masao Gunji on her way out.

"Yuki, are you leaving?" He asked eyeing her suitcase.

"Oh … no Gunji-san. I am just running over to my parents for the evening and taking them additional rations and clothing that I saved for them. I may spend the night there."

"How thoughtful. I do not go on duty until 2200 this evening. Let me help you. I can carry it."

Gungi was a medical student who worked as an orderly. He was attracted to Yuki and asked her out several times, but she always found an excuse not to accept.

"No, no, thank you. You are so kind. But I can handle it. I hope to catch a taxi."

"I insist, Yuki. I also will hail a car for you."

Tonight, Gungi was not only friendly but also persistent. Seeing that further argument would be fruitless and suspicious, Yuki smiled sweetly and bowed. Lieutenant Gunji found a charcoal-powered taxi, and taking her suitcase, he opened the car door for her. Yuki gave the driver directions, and they were quickly en route to her parent's village in the Honjo neighborhood.

Once across the Sumida River bridge, the driver stopped at the narrow street that would not accommodate his vehicle. Yuki opened her small purse.

"Allow me," Gungi placed his hand mid-air over hers and paid the driver.

They walked quickly down the street for several blocks and reached a narrower path that led to several small dwellings.

"I will take it from here, Gunji-san. Thank you for your help and generosity."

"This suitcase is quite heavy. Are you sure I cannot carry it farther?"

"No, no. I can manage now. Thank you."

"Aren't you going to invite me to greet your parents more formally?"

"Umm, tonight would not be appropriate. I think my mother may be feeling ill. But you will meet with both later in a more personal manner."

Yuki thought his forwardness strange, given he must be attending her father's lectures at the hospital or meeting her mother in one of the hospital wards. Yuki returned his smile to hide her nervousness.

"Very well, see you in the morning." At this, he swung around and marched off into the darkness.

Yuki walked four houses down and knocked on the door of the fifth. There was no answer, nor could she detect any light within. Finding the hidden key in the flower vase, Yuki let herself in. The small three-room house was empty. She set the suitcase down.

Mrs. Kubota, a neighbor across the alleyway, opened her door to Yuki's persistent knocking. "I'm looking for my parents; have you seen them?"

"Oh, they left a while ago for the train station. They left a note for you on the table in the sitting area."

Puzzled, Yuki raced back to her parents' house and found the note:

My Dear Yuki,

We are going to Nikko for a few days; Uncle
Kurita is ill.

Love, Mama

Yuki crumpled the note and sat in a chair by the table. How could she alert her parents about her discovery and what to do with the suitcase's contents? Yuki could not return it to her room. No, she had to hide it, but not in the house. The air raid trench out back! A perfect place where no one will look.

Yuki went outside with the case and removed the bamboo and wood cover from the trench large enough to accommodate two adults. She set the suitcase in the trench, wrapping it with a blanket, then replaced the flimsy cover.

Satisfied she had done all she could to conceal the thing, Yuki returned to the sitting room to write her parents a note in case they returned before she could speak to them. Yuki was relieved they were leaving the city; another raid was coming. She needed to warn her parents and attempt to catch them at the train station. In her haste to leave, Yuki was unaware that the crumpled note from her mother had fallen on the floor.

Yuki swiftly made her way up the narrow street. When Yuki reached the main road, and looked for a taxi, she saw two uniformed Kempei soldiers approaching. Ducking into a dark corner, Yuki waited for them to pass. Peering out, she recognized a familiar face in the dim light and silently covered her mouth with her hand. It was Major Tanaka and his sergeant! She would recognize Tanaka anywhere.

Yuki waited a few seconds and stepped out to see the direction the two walked. Her heart raced as they turned down the alleyway of her parents' house.

She considered following them, but decided that was too risky. She ran to catch Mama and Papa at the train station.

Fourteen

Major Tanaka and Sergeant Saito found the Fujita house and noticed its darkness. They knocked, but no one answered, and no lights came on.

A door opened in the house behind them, and Mrs. Kubota peeked out.

Tanaka immediately walked over. "We are looking for Dr. and Mrs. Fujita."

"They are not in," Mrs. Kubota said, her eyes cast downward in respect. "They went out earlier. They did not say anything to me." The woman was lying, but her obeisant behavior in the semi-darkness fooled Tanaka.

He stuck his head into the front room. "What is your purpose here?" Tanaka demanded.

"My husband makes parts for airplanes," The woman answered quietly. "Then we take them to the factory."

"Very good." Tanaka turned his attention back to the Fujita house. He ordered the sergeant to pry open the door.

"Search the house," he ordered.

Tanaka sat in the chair by the table and waited. In a few minutes, Sergeant Takai reported that he had found nothing incriminating. Tanaka decided to remain in the shelter of the dark house. After ordering Saito to stay awake, he dozed off, resting on a pillow against the wall. When Tanaka's snoring became evident, Saito decided to take a quick nap on the tatami mats. The room's coolness kept him in a semi-conscious state. He awoke with a start. It was 2300, time to wake his superior. He saw no need to stay in a cold house all night.

Tanaka grunted. "Keep searching. Did you look outside?"

Saito hurried out the door, and a few minutes later, he walked in, clutching a suitcase.

"I found this in the air raid trench."

"Open it!"

"It is locked."

"Break it! Now!"

The sergeant flipped opened the lid and both men inhaled audibly.

"A radio, Major!"

Tanaka rubbed his hands together. "Yes," he smiled, "so it is."

He checked his watch: five minutes after eleven.

"Stay here. If the Fujitas return, detain them. I am going to the local koban."

Tanaka left the house and strolled to the main street. The cold wind gusted, blowing trash through the streets. The nearest koban, or police box, was a five-minute walk, and he felt in no hurry. First, he wanted to check with the local officer to see if the Fujitas had requested travel permits.

Tanaka arrived at the station; the attendant was on the phone, and his speech seemed agitated as he listened and took notes. He looked up at Tanaka. Unimpressed with his rank in the Kempeitai, he continued talking.

"Hai!" He ended the call abruptly and turned to Tanaka. "My apologies, Major, but another koban box said they had heard reports of many B-Sans heading toward Japan."

Tanaka cut him off. "The Americans send planes almost daily now, the air raid has not sounded again. We all do our duty and prepare for their futile efforts. We await their invasion so that we can crush them here on sacred soil." And, he quickly changed subjects.

"A Dr. Fujita and his wife live in your area. Have you any reports on them this evening?"

"Hmmm, I know of the Fujitas. He is a doctor at the Imperial Army Hospital School. Let me look at the logs." The officer scanned through his book.

"Hmmm, no; I see nothing about them today."

"You are sure? Very well, you are to call if you hear of them. Here is my number."

The koban box officer, offended by Tanaka's high-handedness, failed to mention that the Fujitas had received approval to travel to Nikko two days before. The Fujitas already departed that evening. *They were good people who helped everyone in the neighborhood.*

Tanaka trekked back to the Fujita house, thinking about the koban box officer's report on the American bombers. If there was a night raid, it could be Tokyo or another city. Their raids were not very effective anyway. He checked his watch; it was now eleven twenty-five. He shrugged confidently and walked on.

Tanaka found Sergeant Saito asleep in a chair.

"You could have missed them if they saw you! You must always be vigilant!" he shouted, striking the man across the face. The sergeant bowed and muttered an apology.

"Take this suitcase back to my office and safeguard it," he ordered. "It will be evidence of their treason. I will remain here and await their return and arrest them. They cannot stay out long in this windy weather. Send the car back to our drop point and tell the driver to wait for me."

Saito bowed, took the radio case, and left immediately. As he walked, Saito changed direction and stopped at one of his favorite hangouts. He was smitten with one of the Geishas. It would only be a few minutes.

In the Fujita shanty, Tanaka pulled the chair to face the door and sat down, pulling his heavy coat tightly around him. Though it was chilly in the room, soon he was snoring. He did not notice the crumpled note Yuki had dropped carelessly on the floor.

Crowds and the lack of taxis had hampered Yuki's efforts to reach the central rail station. She had caught a trolley that brought her near the station, but had to walk the quarter mile. By the time she arrived, the train had pulled away. There was nothing more to do.

The hidden radio and the memory of the Kempeitai duo heading toward her parents' house flooded back to her mind. What if they were going there? Why would they? Were her parents under suspicion? Yuki debated what to do. The best thing would be to retrieve the radio, throw it in the river, and be done with it. She had lived dangerously long enough.

Someone mentioned that the local radio station was warning of B-29s heading for Japan.

Yuki hurried out of the station, and climbed in a waiting taxi. Yuki directed it back to her parents' ward. It was a few minutes after eleven, and the cold wind was blowing more briskly.

The area was quite dark in her parents' neighborhood, around eleven thirty-five. Lights were forbidden in the late hours of the evening, and the Fujita house was no exception. As she approached the door, she noticed it was slightly ajar. So, the Kempeitai were here! What if they found the radio? Her parents would be doomed. Quietly, Yuki peered in and heard steady snoring. Someone was definitely in the house. She backed away and turned to the neighbor's home across the alley. Knocking gently on the door frame, Yuki held her breath, hoping Mrs. Kubota could hear her light rapping. When the door opened, the woman grabbed Yuki and pulled her inside.

"What are you doing here? Do you not know the Kempeitai are here searching for your parents?"

Yuki gasped. "I think one is inside their house!"

"You must leave at once! They have been here tonight asking questions. I told them I had not seen your parents tonight. But I know they left for Nikko this evening."

"I must get to my parents' shelter!" Yuki whispered earnestly, almost pleadingly.

"It is too dangerous!" the neighbor replied, even more determined to end the train of thought.

Yuki sighed, dejected, not knowing what to do next. There were few hours left. The inspection was tomorrow. She needed to think.

"I must act now. Thank you for your help."

Yuki slipped out the front door and crossed to the backside of her parents' house. Moving catlike, she found the shelter cover removed. The suitcase with the radio was gone! Guilt and despair overwhelmed her. Yuki sobbed silently knowing she foolishly had betrayed her parents to the Kempeitai. She crept unsteadily to the neighbor's house, entered, and wept bitterly.

It was too late to make it back to her hostel. Her duty on Saturday would start at noon, but as far as she knew, the inspection was on, and was required to be in her room by mid-morning. Yuki accepted Mrs. Kubota's invitation to sleep on a futon on their floor and leave at dawn.

Yuki closed her eyes and settled herself. The ominous drone of the first wave of bombers sounded at midnight just as Yuki drifted off to sleep. She did not know the 21st Bomber Command's strategy that night was for an early wave of pathfinders to mark out the target area with incendiaries that the following squadrons would key on.

So, you have come after all.

"We must get to our shelter out back," her host said excitedly.

"No, you must run. The Americans are going to burn the city. We must get to Sumida Park, away from our houses. They will burn like the paper and sticks they are!"

"But the neighborhood association requires we stand and try to save our homes!" the woman protested.

"Do that and you will die! Please come with me. We must hurry!"

"No, my husband and I will not leave our home!"

Yuki saw it was futile to plead further, bowed, muttered her thanks, and left.

Then, the air raid siren began its mournful wail.

Yuki looked briefly at her parents' house before turning up the street but did not linger. Following the baleful noises of the B-29s came a sudden red-orange glow seen from afar.

Yuki ran. She ran to the broader road and turned northward toward the park. Yuki looked up and saw the bombs descending like silvery tinsel. Bombs must have hit not more than three blocks away because she felt the heat and watched, terrified, as flames erupted into the sky.

Other people were pouring out of their houses. They futilely tried to decide where to go in their panic and confusion.

"Sumida Park!" Yuki screamed. People heard her and began moving in that direction. Others went back to their homes to get their possessions. Yuki wanted to scream at them to leave them and run.

As bombs fell, the heat increased. More terrifying was the wind fanning the flames. At sixty to seventy miles per hour, the winds whipped the flames into a vortex, spreading them rapidly in all directions. And still, more tinsel bombs were falling. The winds also blew heavy, acrid smoke through the streets, and soon, sparks were falling, igniting people's clothing. Yuki stopped at a rain barrel by one house, filled her turban, and doused her clothes. Yuki kept moving, inhibited by the growing, hysterical crowd.

Major Tanaka awoke to the sound of the air raid sirens. At first, he ignored them and tried to doze again. Then, listening carefully, he heard the staccato rumble of the B-29s overhead. Now alert, Tanaka sprang from the chair and ran to the door. Already visible were the flames not more than a mile away, rising high into the sky. Tanaka knew the Americans had already started using incendiaries, but these seemed to be the only weapons falling. The planes grew louder. Tanaka looked up and saw several crisscrossing the sky above at a very low altitude, releasing silvery canisters.

He hurried to the street and decided to check with the koban officer on the situation. However, as he turned toward the koban, he saw only a wall of flames. The area was engulfed and became a raging inferno. Fear gripped Tanaka, a fear he had never experienced. He could feel the heat and knew this raid would be different. *Where to go,* he wondered. The river! Yes, he must get across the Sumida River at once. Tanaka turned and began to run.

Fifteen

Boso Peninsula, Japan
0055 Hours, Saturday Morning, 10 March 1945

Following his navigator's directions, Dallas turned *Lake Blackshear* northwest to cross Tokyo Bay toward the conflagration over forty miles away. The eerie orange glow already illuminated the cockpit, and try as he may, Dallas could not drive out the maddening thoughts of people already dying, people like the ones he had known and loved. He prided himself on his stoicism and tried to concentrate on his task and his crew, accomplish the odious mission handed to him and get his troops home safely.

The crew maintained a strange silence as if every man's focus was entirely internal, attentive to the task at hand or individual longing or fear.

Suddenly, Larry Wynns, sitting in the rear observation bubble, blurted out over the intercom, "Skipper, B-29 directly above us, bomb bay doors open!"

Dallas glimpsed up as he was already banking *Lake Blackshear* to the starboard. Sure enough, another bomber soared not more than one hundred feet above, flying on the same course. Indeed, her two bomb bay doors were open, signaling an imminent drop of her ordinance. Though his heart raced, belying his outward calmness, Dallas focused on maneuvering away from the other aircraft as quickly as possible. Mere seconds later, the bombs from the other aircraft began falling. Dallas reflected on how close both planes had escaped a sure disaster.

Someone muttered an expletive. Then, the sister ship began to turn away from Tokyo, banking hard to the port side as if to head south and return to base.

"Hey," Wynns shouted, "He's turning chicken! I got his tail number. He's from a Saipan wing. Do you want to report him, Captain?"

"No," Dallas replied. "We don't know; he may have mechanical problems. It happens a lot on these missions."

"Well, he darn near killed all of us."

Dallas smiled. "Good work on your observing, Sergeant. I hope you don't have to display your shooting skills this night."

"You mean those unloaded guns I'm not supposed to have to fire?" Wynns retorted.

Dallas chuckled audibly into his microphone, hoping it would ease the tension among the crew. Then he looked ahead. At two hundred and fifty miles per hour, the bomber was approaching the dock area of Tokyo.

"Pilot to crew, everyone be alert now. It will get bumpy at this altitude with the hot air coming up. Stay strapped in tightly, men."

Dallas' outward coolness contradicted his inner turmoil and a growing sense of trepidation.

When *Lake Blackshear* was a mile from the harbor, the brilliance of the inferno illuminated the cockpit with an eerie aura, reminding Dallas of the hellfire sermons he had heard.

"Open bomb bay doors, Mr. Hodges," he ordered. He looked over at his co-pilot, who stared ahead in frozen shock, obviously traumatized by the spectacle of his first combat mission.

"Mr. Hodges," Dallas spoke louder and more urgently, "Open the bomb bays! Now!"

The young man jolted in his seat and looked over at Dallas, his face wide-eyed in disbelief.

"Mr. Hodges!"

Only then did Hodges move his left hand to the controls and pull the levers.

"Forward bomb bay open," reported Dixie as he peered through the portal window into the forward bay. A moment later, Wynns reported the same for the aft bomb bay.

"Pilot to bombardier, ready to take over, Rocky? Find us a target, and let's get outta here. I'll take control as soon as we release our ordinance." Dallas relinquished control of the aircraft to his bombardier.

"Roger," Rocky replied, "I see a dark spot ahead."

Suddenly, as the plane crossed the harbor into the city, a brilliant light filled the cockpit, blinding Dallas. He heard the familiar whomp of anti-aircraft explosion. The plane was caught in the cross-beams of the city defense searchlights. *Lake Blackshear* had become a lucrative target before one bomb could fall from her belly.

Honjo Ward, Tokyo
0055 Hours, Saturday Morning, 10 March 1945

As Yuki ran, her lungs weighed heavily within her bosom, the heat and smoke taking their toll on her body. Her wet clothes had already steamed dry, and even on this wintry night, the temperature exceeded the hottest summer day. She coughed and ran, trying to focus on reaching Sumida Park's possible haven of safety.

The monstrous firewall advanced rapidly, cruelly aided by new falling incendiaries and the hurricane-force winds. Yuki glanced behind her and saw an older woman stumbling along carrying a sack of her precious possessions, articles she must have deemed more valuable than life itself. Yuki turned and yelled to tell her to drop it and run when a tongue of flame licked out, igniting the poor woman into a human torch. The woman staggered a few steps, then fell. Horrified, Yuki turned and ran faster, whispering a mournful prayer for the woman's soul. The futility of her efforts began to nag at her conscience.

The wind screamed like a thousand banshees and blew ashes about as if a black snowstorm had descended on the streets.

Tanaka and Yuki were mere yards apart. Tanaka had opted to go for the river rather than what seemed a futile effort to reach Sumida Park – the mob pushed around him, each with one thought – survival. Tanaka cared nothing for any of them; his sole objective was to save his skin. He pushed an older woman aside and knocked a mother down, uncaring that she rolled over the infant on her back. The increasing heat swept over him, its intensity goading him to push on more aggressively through the crowds.

As he neared the river, an incendiary had fallen not fifty feet away, bursting to spew hot gelatin flames, igniting many people around him. Their pitiful screams failed to prick his moral sense of duty. But then he noticed his clothes were aflame. Terrified, Tanaka beat at his clothes, burning his hands. The flames leaped up to his head, scalding his face, making him dislodge his zukin cowl.

Screaming, he stumbled the last few yards to the riverbank and propelled himself into the water. The flames seemed to diminish on his body, but the burning sensation remained. He tried to inhale deeply, only to burn his mouth and throat with super-heated air. Tanaka was aware of bodies floating near him, many face-down, obviously beyond help had he wanted to do any humane act. He could see the flames skimming over the water, heating it to near-boiling. Tanaka had to get out, but where? The bank was a solid wall of fire. Then he saw it. A sewer pipe!

Tanaka crawled up the slippery bank and grabbed the lower rim of the pipe with his charred hands. The pipe was just wide enough to house a human body. Suddenly, objects blown by the super-heated wind slammed into his head, knocking him back. Dazed, he climbed back up to the sewer pipe. Reeking at the stench emanating from this orifice, he briefly hesitated. Spurred by the will to survive and the intensifying heat as the firewall advanced, he grabbed the top rim and swung his feet inside. The heat provided more motivation to survive at all costs. Tanaka pushed his body deeper into the fetid pipe, almost gagging from the stench. His face burned, head throbbing, eyes gluing shut. Major Tanaka did not realize the extent of his body's damage. Tanaka felt pity only for his selfish soul, which he was sure was doomed. Now, nearly blind, he laid his head on his singed, filthy sleeve and lost consciousness.

Sixteen

Above Tokyo
0100 Hours, Saturday Morning, 10 March 1945

Dallas squeezed his eyes shut, retaking the controls; he zigged and zagged the aircraft. When he opened them, his night vision, though somewhat diminished, was adequate.

"Rocky, can you see?" he asked urgently of his bombardier.

"Roger, Skipper. Give me the controls." Rocky had a brief warning before the searchlights lit up the cockpit. "Target ahead."

Through the bubble plexiglass nose of the bomber, a dark area appeared ahead among the roaring flames.

A few moments later, Rocky calmly reported, "Bombs away." The big plane lifted noticeably as the heavy payload exited her belly.

Seconds later, Dixie reported, "Bomb bay one empty," indicating he had turned in his seat to check the status of the bomb bay behind him. His report was followed by an affirmative from Sergeant Wynns, who could see the aft bomb bay.

"Close bomb bay doors, Mr. Hodges!" This time, the young co-pilot eagerly pulled the levers, and Dallas heard the thunk of the doors snapping shut. Before Dixie and Wynns could confirm the ship was sealed, a super-heated updraft hit the right wing of the big bomber. Dallas had just taken the controls back from the bombardier yet was surprised at the force that pushed his aircraft over. He looked left out his window and saw hell raging directly below him. He fought to bring equilibrium to the enormous aircraft.

But the bomber continued to roll! Now, he looked "up" through the glass bubble above his head and saw Tokyo ablaze. Stunned, he realized they were inverted, flying upside down. Trash and other loose objects began falling toward the ceiling of the cockpit.

"Ain't supposed to fly this way, Dallas," came a report from Pop, a little more urgently than his normal voice.

"Working it, Pop!" Dallas snapped.

Dallas also felt the thermals pushing his B-29 higher in altitude. Her four engines roared in straining protest. The fuselage shuttered violently. He knew the plane was under tremendous stress and probably would not survive the bucking it was taking from the scorching air.

Still, the same relentless updraft that had pushed them over continued to hit the wing on his side of the ship. Remembering his training in smaller planes, he dropped the nose toward the pyre below. Dallas thought it must have appeared as diving into the pit of Dante's inferno. But the ploy allowed the winds to guide him through a complete rotation. Even as the bucking continued, he deftly flew the big bomber through the sickening maneuver. After what seemed an interminable time, he was flying right side up but heading down at a terrible speed. He pulled back hard on his control yoke. The aircraft shook and shimmied as if the forces of nature would win over the mechanics of mankind and tear the plane apart.

Then, as Dallas struggled with his controls, he gradually brought it to a level position just nine hundred feet above the boiling conflagration. The stench of burning flesh permeated the interior of the fuselage, causing retching among a few airmen in the rear.

"Oh God," came a garbled cry, "What's the smell?"

"Japs burning," came a short reply.

"Knock it off," Dallas ordered. "Navigator, where are we?" he asked urgently.

Bill Meeks replied, "Perpendicular to our original course, Skipper, heading northeast."

"Fine, let's get outta here!" He continued to bank the *Lake Blackshear* to the starboard, heading over a dark, cool area of the city and the Kando plain. "Bill, give me a heading," Dallas barked while continuing his turn. He heard the navigator and radar operator conferring.

"Keep turning until you are one hundred and eighty degrees." Bill Meeks replied calmly. "That will take us back over the Bay. I can get better fixes then."

"Roger," Dallas replied.

The *Lake Blackshear* headed south out over Tokyo Bay, the city, burning off to its starboard side.

Dallas sat back and hoped for a long, boring ride back to Guam.

At midnight, the Phantom Tiger, awakened by the air raid siren, scrambled into his flight suit and jacket and woke Akio. They took off in tandem and headed to the north side of Tokyo Bay. In the distance, he saw the great Tokyo firestorm inferno. He ordered Akio to stay on his port side wing.

As they headed out over the Bay, at six thousand feet, he thought he saw a B-29 below slowly climbing in altitude. He radioed Akio to stay close to his wing. When there was no response, he looked to his left. Akio's plane had disappeared. He tried again to reach him but received no response.

Where is the young fool?

The Phantom Tiger flew down to the level of the bomber, staying out of range of its deadly weapon systems.

In the pale moonlight, he thought he saw a name on the nose and recognized it. He decided to maneuver closer.

Honjo Ward, Tokyo
0104 Hours, Saturday Morning, 10 March 1945

A mere fifty yards from Tanaka's sewer pipe, Yuki looked skyward to see a strange sight – a B-29 flying upside down, pushed higher by the thermal updrafts, then falling toward the blazing earth. She doubted an aircraft could endure the stresses imposed on it by such a phenomenon, and whispered a prayer for the crew and then for her family. Yuki believed she was trapped and prayed for her soul and her beloved man, who probably was the enemy of her country. Awaiting her death, Yuki heard the child's cry.

A little boy stood alone, bewildered by the chaos and confusion around him, no doubt separated from his family. Unexpectedly, a portal in the smoke appeared behind the youngster, and Yuki ran to him, scooping him into her arms, then dashed through the corridor that had miraculously opened. It led to the river's bank, where she stopped. It appeared clogged with logs. Then, to her horror, there were human bodies floating, not giving any sign of life. Yuki turned and saw the bridge shimmering in the heated air. It was filled with people trying to escape to the other side, only to realize the firestorm now raged on both ends.

Yuki had a last desperate idea – to crawl under the bridge abutment where it jutted from the land. The space would provide shelter and a barrier from the heat and flames. Carrying her young burden, she hurried toward the bridge in the stifling air. Yuki stumbled and fell but held onto the frightened child. Oblivious to the screams of pain and terror surrounding her, Yuki slid down the embankment, ducked under the bridge, and crawled up into the eerie red darkness of the abutment. Pushing herself as far as possible, she wedged her body and that of the child into a small cavity that had remained remarkably cool.

The child stopped sobbing and looked at her in awe as if held by an angel. She spoke soft words of comfort and pulled his head to her breast. Then,

Yuki waited for the flames to engulf the bridge and all its surroundings. This space was unlikely to save them, but it was their only hope.

The young boy slept, and then, Yuki, exhausted, lungs aching from the heated smoke, passed out, unconscious. The horrors about her mercifully slipped into darkness and silence.

Above Tokyo Bay
0115 Hours, Saturday Morning, 10 March 1945

Dallas gently flew *Lake Blackshear*, climbing to fifteen hundred feet. He listened intently to the drone of the engines that had been under tremendous strain during the upside-down maneuver. His instruments told him nothing was amiss, but he could not shake the feeling of unease that this mission had taken on him emotionally and physically.

"Pop, how do we look?" he asked his flight engineer. "Can we take her higher now?"

"Roger, Skipper. Go slow, though, got some fluctuations on number one. Also, we are going to have to watch the fuel ratios." Then Pop added, "Looks like I'll be awake all night."

Dallas smiled. "Roger, beginning a slow climb back to five thousand."

As he nudged the great ship toward a bank of clouds above the Bay, he could see the waning crescent moon among myriad stars and was struck by the celestial beauty that contrasted with the destruction behind him. Still climbing slowly, he listened intently to his engine roar, trying to discern any abnormality that may alter his flying.

Suddenly, Larry Wynns screamed over his headset, "Fighter, nine o'clock high!"

Dallas instinctively looked out his window and saw the shadowy image off to his left. He recognized the aircraft as a "Frank," an Imperial Japanese Army fighter. It suddenly banked under his bomber and disappeared.

"Where is he?" Dallas demanded, his voice now expressing the tenseness he usually hid so well.

"Lost him! No, there he is, overhead," Wynns said, equally nervous. "Now he's moving back out to your side, Captain."

Dallas again glanced out his left side window and saw the dark shadow moving away but in a nearly parallel course.

"Larry, are your guns ready?" Dallas asked.

"Roger, Captain. If he comes close again, I'll have him. But he's out of range now."

The tail gunner reported his weapons were armed and ready.

"Okay, everyone, keep alert."

Dallas could now see a cloud ahead as he continued to climb and determined to make for the ephemeral cover. But then Wynns screamed, "Boogie, twelve o'clock high diving on us."

"Shoot, Larry, shoot," Dallas yelled reflexively.

He could see the speck, silhouetted against a dimly lit cloud, streaking toward the nose of the B-29. Dallas knew they had less than a fifty-fifty chance to avoid a ramming. If the enemy plane hit any part of the bomber, the damage would be fatal to the plane and the crew.

As the aircraft loomed larger, he saw tracer streaks and a brilliant, blinding, yellow-orange explosion followed by a meteor-like stream go by his window under the left wing.

As his vision returned from the glare of the explosion, he breathed a sigh of relief and uttered into his throat microphone, "Nice shooting, Sergeant."

A moment passed. Static filled Dallas's earphones.

"Sir," Wynns' tone sounded puzzled.

After a long pause, Dallas asked, "What's the problem, Larry?"

"Sir, I didn't shoot."

There was another pause, "Whadda ya mean you didn't shoot? I saw the buzzard explode right in front of us!"

"Sir," Wynns answered. "My front upper turret jammed. It wouldn't fire. I swear, I didn't get him."

"Well, someone sure as hell did! See any other B-29's around us?"

After a moment's pause, Wynns answered, "No, Sir. I did a 360 scan above and around the top side."

"Okay, anyone else see any aircraft?"

The crew near windows all reported negative sightings. Then they entered the clouds.

"Maybe we just enjoyed a miracle."

A miracle! Now that's a rich idea, Dallas thought. *More likely, an element of chance.*

Then again, he knew he had a few religious members in this crew. Despite his humanism, he would not disparage their beliefs.

For the first time in what felt like hours, Dallas breathed easily. "Pilot to Navigator; okay, Bill, set a course for home."

Dallas again tried to relax, yet every fiber of his body broadcasted his anxiety and shame. Then he looked at Mr. Hodges for the first time in a long while.

"Uh oh," Dallas muttered. Hodges was sitting rigid with a fixed stare straight ahead, his hands gripping his yoke wheel.

"Pilot to Bombardier, Pilot to Radio; we have a problem at my right. Rocky, you and Dixie help Mr. Hodges out of his seat. Rocky, you will have to take over as co-pilot."

The two men made their way to the co-pilot's position. Dixie unbuckled Hodge's seat belt while Rocky gently yet firmly pried his hands off the yoke. The man did not indicate he recognized any attention paid to him. In an awkward but determined manner, the two men lifted him from the seat and stretched him out in the aisle behind the command deck.

"What do we do with him, Skipper?" Dixie asked.

Dallas thought for a moment. It would be too difficult to maneuver a limp body through the tunnel to the rear of the aircraft, where there would be room to lay him out. But the tunnel would still be helpful.

"See if you can get him into the tunnel."

With a bit of difficulty, the two men were able to raise Hodge's body and slide him into the tube head-first, with his lower legs extended.

"That's good enough, let's go home and hope nothing else happens. When we get near the base, radio ahead for an ambulance, Dixie."

When Al Rocco took the co-pilot's seat, Dallas finally relaxed for the first time.

"Captain, we have another problem," Pop radioed calmly, stirring Dallas from a fitful snooze.

By now, *Lake Blackshear* was well beyond the Japanese home Islands. The tail gunner reported he could see the glow from the fires for more than an hour after clearing Tokyo Bay.

"Report," Dallas requested calmly, expecting the bad news.

"Number one is running hot. Also, I think we may have a fuel leak. Maybe that buzzard's debris hit something."

"Should we shut her down? Can we make it to Guam if we do?"

"Roger, recommend we shut number one down. I think I can adjust fuel; we should make it, but it may be close."

"Pilot to Navigator; how far to Iwo?"

"Gimme a second, Skipper," came the easy reply from Bill Meeks. "Forty-five minutes at our current speed."

"I don't want to land on Iwo, Pop. They're still shooting down there. Let's try to make it home. Shut down number one."

The prop whirred to a stop with no noticeable effect on the flight. Dallas felt comfortable placing the aircraft on autopilot and trying to relax.

Dallas' reluctance to land on Iwo Jima was understandable to the crew. Invaded by United States Marines on February 19th, taking the island had proven costly in lives and material. Thousands of Marines were dead, and casualties were mounting daily.

But the captured airfields had paid a dividend for the strategic forces. Earlier in the month, a B-29 with a mechanical problem made an emergency landing on the south airfield despite enemy fire nearby. The bomber was repaired, refueled, and returned to the Marianas. Neither Dallas nor any of his crew wanted to chance a landing on the still-contested island.

Dallas looked out the window to the east. It was still dark, with no hint of a sunrise. They still had more than five hours to go.

Seventeen

Tokyo
Very Late Friday Night, 9 March 1945

After leaving Yuki, Lieutenant Masao Gunji returned to the hospital to prepare for the surprise inspection. He expected to find nothing important now that Yuki had taken the radio to her parents' house in the Honjo district. As a Kempei informant, Gunji had found himself in an uncomfortable position. Quite by accident, he overheard a conversation between his control officer Tanaka and Saito, his assistant. They suspected the woman he loved of disloyalty to the Empire; Gungi knew Yuki could never betray her country. But to be safe, he took it upon himself to search her room at the hostel before the surprise inspection happened. When he found the forbidden radio, he still refused to suspect Yuki of anything wrong. It only increased his desire to know more about the woman he loved and to protect her. Ironically, he had just helped her carry it away to Honjo.

Gunji did not know his control officer, Major Tanaka, had been en route to the Fujitas' dwelling.

Gunji walked to one of the windows facing the city's harbor district. It was dark; the blackout was still in effect. Tomorrow would bring what it would; either a surprise inspection that he knew would not be a surprise at all or a day of rescue operations following an American attack on a different part of the city. He could do little to prepare his teams further for what was coming.

Around midnight, Gungi heard the low hum of the bombers. Returning to the window, the man beheld a sight so unnerving he felt his knees weakened.

First, one, then another orange flame lit up the harbor area like gigantic balls bouncing and glowing along the darker areas where much of the population lived. In a few moments, whole sections burned as the fires spread rapidly. The wind was picking up, whipping the flames from house to house. Still, the bombers came, and then Gungi noticed how low they were flying, dropping their silver needles.

His looked intuitively turned toward the Honjo district where he had left Yuki. "Please, be on the way back here," he whispered.

Gungi watched the flames engulf the area, and his heart sank. The window reflected the eerie rust-colored glow from across the river. He saw his wretched face reflected in the pane. Half of Tokyo was burning. Someone reported that the Americans had spared the Imperial Palace so far. It brought him little comfort. Finally, the noise of the deadly aircraft ended, and the all-clear sounded, a sorrowful action given that the raging flames were still killing people and destroying neighborhoods.

Tokyo
Early Saturday Morning, 10 March 1945

By 0300, Gunji joined the assembly of rescue teams whose duty was to go out and aid the civilian population in the aftermath of an air raid. He would lead one of nine teams with their three vehicles and minimal medical supplies.

After the initial stand-down, the members of the rescue teams gathered in small groups to exchange news from families and friends, trying to avoid complex realities besetting their country.

Around four in the morning, the rescue teams began their onerous task toward the devastation. Their vehicles carried the few supplies the medical school could spare. As his convoy approached the Sumida River, Gunji could see what lay before them. They crossed one of the intact bridges; his mask of hardness melted in despair as he viewed the fateful scene before him.

Driving into the scalding hot wasteland, the drivers carefully picked their way through the wreckage. A burning telephone pole lay across the street, halting their progress. Gunji walked over to a burned-out fire truck to inspect its damage. He discovered the charred remains of the driver and his companion in the cab, carbonized by the intense heat. Absently, he reached out with a baton he carried and touched the black crust of the vehicle. Instantly, the entire structure crumbled. Ashes of the men inside the unplanned crematorium settled around his feet. Gunji thought himself hardened against the realities of war, yet he stepped away, from the shocking scene. It was not the last such horror he would witness this day.

Out of the smoky mist, a few bedraggled figures limped and tottered toward him. Most suffered second-degree burns, for which he could only provide ointments and, for their smoke and ash-infected eyes, washing with a saline solution. The victims continued their futile search for loved ones.

Gunji noticed as he walked that the ashes under his feet crunched; *it was a night of black snow.*

They found Yuki and the boy just after dawn. At first, Gunji thought they were dead from asphyxiation, robbing him of the joy of finding her. But then he detected the soft movement of labored breathing, and his heart throbbed with a new rhythm. Yuki and the child were wedged tightly into the heated bridge abutment. He first moved the boy, who seemed remarkably alert though scared and wide-eyed. Gunji whispered reassuring words and coaxed him to move away from Yuki. He ordered his companions to give the child water; then he turned back to pry Yuki out of the crude shelter.

As he pulled her away and down the embankment, Yuki moaned softly. Gungi saw no injuries other than mild burns on the exposed flesh of her arms and face. When he had moved her from under the bridge, he lifted her upper body and gently touched her blistered face.

"Yuki-san," he whispered and then repeated the supplication with a normal tone. She stared at him, bewildered. He smiled and whispered, "You are safe; we have you."

"The child …" Her voice was raspy.

"He's fine." Yuki offered a faint smile and tried to speak, but he put his finger to her lips.

"We must get you treatment and return to the hospital."

"How?" But her voice failed.

"You found shelter," Gunji answered. "You are a survivor. You and the boy. So many are dead."

He lifted her to unsteady feet and let her lean on him. He called for another rescue worker who came down the bank and helped Gunji walk her up to the top. Around them lay a strange tableau of bodies, some charred, some not burned. Gunji surmised they died of asphyxiation. He carried Yuki to the lead vehicle and gently set her in the back seat.

"Lieutenant, we found another one – alive!"

Gunji turned and saw the man pointing to a sewer pipe.

"Someone is in there, I think. I heard groans, but I didn't want to go in there."

"Get them out!" Gunji ordered.

The men looked at one another, bowed, and slowly walked back to the sewer pipe. When they had extracted the badly burned man from the fetid shelter, they carried him to the lead vehicle. Even through the slimy filth, they saw the partially burned uniform of an Army officer.

"No!" Gunji shouted. "The woman and the boy go there. Put him in the other truck! And you two go with him!"

Gunji sent his team back to the hospital. He sat in the truck with Yuki and the boy, trying to comfort them.

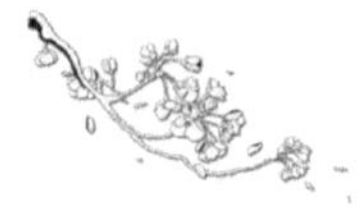

Standing at rigid attention before his squadron commander's desk, the Phantom Tiger stifled a yawn. Still in his flying gear, he had slept little since dawn the previous day. The hours in the air were beginning to wear on his mind and body. Still, he had to be alert to answer his commander's questions.

"Stand at ease, Lieutenant," the older man said, removing his wire-rimmed spectacles. "An interesting report. We commend you for answering last night's alert when so few did. Your initiative reflects highly on your skill and dedication."

"Thank you, Colonel," the weary pilot responded. "I'm surprised we did not have more fighters in the air, especially from the Navy bases." The Phantom and his wingman were the only aircraft from his base to respond to the havoc being rained down on Tokyo a few hours earlier.

"Yes, I agree. You and your young wingman did the right thing." The commander did not mention he had slept through the air raid. "It's too bad we don't have more airmen with the zeal Akio displayed. He surely will be remembered for his sacrifice."

"With all due respect, Sir, it was unnecessary for him to go in for a head ram on that B-san. My cannons were enough to bring her down."

"You must admit it was a noble effort. Akio's action was mathematically efficient. One man takes out – what? Are there not eleven men on a B-san, not to mention the destruction of the flying machine."

"We also lost Akio's aircraft. There are more B-29s. They come in waves now, like the breakers upon a beach. I guess there were hundreds last night."

The senior officer lit a cigarette from the pack on his desk, blowing smoke toward the ceiling. He smiled and offered the pilot the package. The Phantom Tiger declined.

"The B-29 raids are over-hyped by the Americans. They haven't been that effective."

"That's because they have been bombing from 25,000 to 30,000 feet. Their bombs are scattered in the winds and miss their targets. Last night was different."

"In what way, Lieutenant?"

"They came in low, as low as five thousand feet. And they dropped nothing but incendiaries. They burned up a lot of the city last night."

"Couldn't be that bad, surely," the older man said, expressing his doubt about the Tiger's ability to assess damage.

"Sir, I returned after dawn and flew over the city. I assure you the damage is devastating. I can only guess the number of souls that perished last night, but it must be in the thousands."

"Oh, surely not, Lieutenant. Our defenses are more capable than that."

"Colonel, there was a time we were told no one would ever bomb the home islands. But the Americans did in 1942 with medium bombers flown from a carrier. Now they come regularly from just fifteen hundred miles away from land bases."

The commander inhaled a long drag on his cigarette and looked slyly at his subordinate. "You seem to have a rather high estimation of the American capabilities, Lieutenant. Have you not heard of our extraordinary victories, particularly in the Philippine Sea?"

The Tiger shook his head, "Sir, I was there. I flew with our navy forces out of Guam last June. We lost more than 500 airplanes, not to mention the crews."

"Rubbish, Lieutenant! Don't you believe the reports that come from Imperial headquarters?"

"With all due respect, Sir, I believe those reports are inflated."

The commander grunted and puffed on his dwindling cigarette. The man suspected, even believed, the truth behind the Lieutenant's words. When he sat silently for a few moments, the Tiger continued. "Colonel, last June, I fought through the American Navy's combat air patrols, trying to lead our bombers to their fleet. I even took out a few of their planes. When I reached their armada, do you know what I could see from ten thousand feet?"

His commander stared at him, not wanting to hear the rest of the story, but knew the Tiger was an eyewitness; he could only listen.

"I saw hundreds of warships; their vessels stretched to the horizon. If we are sinking so many of their ships, where do they get so many more? We both are aware that now the American Navy is so bold that they sail into the home waters, and their carriers launch strikes on Kyushu and Honshu."

The squadron commander stubbed his cigarette out in an ashtray. He glowered at his pilot.

"You would be advised to watch your tongue, Lieutenant. If the Kempeitai hears your defeatism; you could end up in prison or worse."

"Sir, out of loyalty to you, I felt I owed you my estimate and observations from the air."

"Yes, all well and good. We need more pilots like your late wingman – those so loyal to the throne that they are willing to become cherry blossoms for the Emperor and their homeland."

So, this is where we're heading. No one had pressured him to volunteer for the special attack units before. Now, he guessed that would change with the desperation coming upon the home islands. He had his pre-rehearsed answer.

"With all due respect again, Colonel, my religious faith forbids suicide. If my life is forfeited in this war, it will be in regular combat."

"Aw, yes. You are one of those Christians," he scoffed contemptuously. "Turn the other cheek and that sort of nonsense."

"No one has ever doubted my fighting ability or loyalty to the Emperor or my country." And then he added emphatically, "Sir!"

"What of our national faith and spirit? Are they not important to you?"

The Tiger also had an answer to that obvious question. "We Christians respect others' beliefs. But as far as I know, neither the Emperor nor anyone else in the government compels us to follow the Buddha or worship at any Shinto shrines." He almost added, "Nor could I," but refrained at the last moment.

"Yes, well, you know you follow a Western religion, Lieutenant?"

"Sir, Christianity is a world religion open to all, regardless of ethnicity. It started on the Asian continent. We differ significantly from the Buddhist belief in the permanence of one's soul. We also believe history is going somewhere. But we also would agree with our Buddhist friends that self-indulgence is sinful. Thus, we avoid the flesh-pots." He said this deliberately because he knew his commander's habits of visiting the nearby brothels.

The commander's face deepened in color. He knew the statement was an indirect insult, but he spoke truthfully. He wondered if the brash young officer knew his commanding officer had indeed slept in a brothel last evening.

"I think we have enough information about the raid. That will do for now. You may go, Lieutenant."

After the Tiger had exited the room, the commander lit another cigarette. He was agitated about the young man's moral rectitude and tactical assessments; he wondered if he should keep him. An excellent fighter pilot. Japan needed men like him, even if he would not volunteer for the special attack units. But his tongue could bring disfavor on the squadron and himself. Perhaps the Phantom Tiger should be transferred to a training unit. Let another commander deal with his moral arrogance and defeatism. Let the other commanders answer to the Kempeitai for an insolent young officer. Maybe the

Imperial Navy could use him and convince him to join the special attack forces.

136

Eighteen

Nikko
March 1985

"Yuki did not perish that night?" *What a relief.*

Okita eyed me as if to determine whether I could bear the truth.

"They found her early in the morning, about dawn, unconscious but very much alive. Lieutenant Gunji from the Army Medical School found her."

Quietly, I whispered, "No lasting wounds?"

"She recovered almost immediately after they got her back to the hospital. She had minor skin blisters and a nasty cough. Yuki started working by the end of the day, helping others. The young boy she rescued also came through the ordeal just fine."

"That raid was the worst of the war until the atomic bombs."

"Yes, sixteen square miles of the city burned up in one raid," Okita replied, "and more than one hundred thousand people dead. And another million left homeless."

"The Fujitas' house in Tokyo must have burned."

"Oh, yes, nothing remained."

"Too bad the bombing did not destroy the radio."

"Oh, Tanaka was proactive in sending it back to his headquarters. His sergeant locked it away. It would come back to haunt them."

Okita paused in his story to change the subject.

"What happened to your friend, Captain Wade? Did he survive the war?"

The question startled me. Okita noticed the change in my expression as he regarded me with a sympathetic yet knowing look.

"You understand, we became the closest of friends. It's hard today to recall him without a sense of loss. We both had connections to Japan. We both loved Japanese girls."

Okita waited for me to go on.

"One of us had our Yuki, the other his Mary Kurahara. Even her American first name did not save her from the forced internment."

Yes, the infamous Executive Order number 9066," Okita recited.

Funny, he remembers such details as an American executive order.

"So your friend also flew the fire raid mission that night?"

It took a few moments to answer. "We both were on the mission."

Okita's look bore into me.

"Although we were in the same theater of war, I did not know at the time. He flew from another base in the Marianas."

"What became of your friend, this Captain Wade, I believe you called him?"

Above the Pacific, Aboard B-29A Lake Blackshear
Mid-Morning, Saturday, 10 March 1945

Dallas had ordered all extraneous gear jettisoned to lighten the load. The crew threw flak jackets, helmets, food containers, and unnecessary equipment out of the portholes. He ordered the team to keep the parachutes on.

"Engineer to Pilot," Pop's voice was calm but urgent. "If we've correctly calculated our position, we will land on fumes. I'm cutting number 3. She's running hot."

"Roger, Pop." In case the crew was listening for a hint about his decision, Dallas responded likewise in a reassuring voice. "Shall I begin descending now? We've got to have enough altitude to clear the cliff."

"Roger, Skipper. But make it slow."

The sun now shone brightly in the eastern sky. Dallas thought he saw another B-29 off to the port a couple of miles ahead and a few hundred feet lower. He ordered the crew to keep a watch for other nearby aircraft.

"Navigator to pilot; ten minutes to Guam," Bill Meeks reported.

"Roger. I see the island now. Dixie, radio the tower. We are coming in hot."

The big bomber's slow descent brought the island into focus, and in a few minutes, Dallas saw the runways.

"Shall I drop the landing gear?" Rocky asked.

Ignoring him, Dallas radioed his engineer, "How are we doing, Pop?"

"A good pilot will make it," Pop responded.

"Okay, let's take the right runway, Rocky; it looks clear of any other aircraft. Drop the landing gear on my command."

"Roger, Skipper," Al Rocco answered.

"And be ready to stand on the brakes."

Suddenly, Dallas sat up and leaned forward, staring out the front of the cockpit bubble. Another B-29 had slipped under him and landed on his runway. He cursed, yet he could not blame the pilot of the aircraft whose own B-29 was thirsty for fuel and a haven. He quickly checked the left runway and saw another aircraft landing.

"Al, another B-29 just landed in front of us. Let's hope he clears the end of the runway before we catch him. I cannot stop our approach now, and I don't want to chance ditching."

"Roger, Captain," Al Rocko responded, a bit of tension in his voice.

The runway rose quickly as the giant airplane dropped in altitude. And then another engine sputtered.

"Pop! I need the power to clear the cliff!" Dallas bellowed with a distinct urgency.

"Roger. She's on full rich. Giving you what we have. Bring her home, young man!"

Dallas watched as the cliff, rising menacingly from the sea, loomed higher. He mentally calculated his rate of descent and the distance, knew it would be close. Dallas was thinking of something other than the B-29 on the runway now. He held the yoke wheel tightly, too tightly, and tried to relax. *Let her fly herself down.*

"Drop landing gear!" he ordered. During the forty seconds the wheels needed to extract and lock, Dallas did all the math on the descent, glide path, drag, and touchdown by intuition borne of experience. All the calculus he had learned was of no help now.

Ominously, the cliff approached, starting to fill his view. He felt as if the plane was already level with the runway. At the last moment, he pulled his half-wheel yoke gently back, raising the nose just slightly, and they crossed the threshold of the cliff by mere feet, and then the wheels touched the crushed coral. The big metal beast bounced once, settled down, and sped down the runway.

"Brakes, Rocky!" he ordered sharply, and he and Rocky pushed down hard on the pedals.

Ahead, he could see the B-29 that preceded him slowly turning toward the taxiway, not nearly fast enough. Despite losing weight in fuel, armaments, and extraneous gear, the heavy aircraft defied the braking efforts, and the inertia of weight and speed made everything outside a blur.

"Come on, get off the runway!" He yelled to the obstacle ahead. Then shouted, "Hold on, boys!" Gripping the control yoke, Dallas willed the other aircraft to move, and for a moment, he had a sinking feeling that the two machines would collide. Then the metallic obstruction inched off the runway.

The *Lake Blackshear* roared past the lethargic B-29 now on the taxiway, her right wing-tip barely missing the slower plane's tail. A hundred feet later, *Lake Blackshear* turned onto an exit ramp and stopped, her tires belching smoke from the friction.

"Told you a good pilot could make it," Pop said impassively.

Dallas took a deep breath and radioed, "Dixie, tell the tower we have a casualty." He paused. "And we need a tow."

The peppery old crew chief was happy to see *Lake Blackshear* back in one piece despite his gruff manner about the two engines and the black soot that covered the bottom of the aircraft. He chastised Dallas and Pop briefly and then, rubbing his chin, promised he would have the ship back in shape in a few days.

A crew truck arrived and took Dallas and his team for their debriefing. An ambulance took the traumatized Mr. Hodges away.

The debriefing was routine. Dallas reported the flipping incident and how he brought the bomber through it. Apparently, other crews experienced the phenomenon. His debriefing officer was incredulous when Dallas reported the episode with the two Japanese fighters.

"None of our other crews have reported a fighter. Are you sure?"

Dallas went over the sequence again, describing the two aircraft and how one exploded in front of them, its debris probably damaging number one engine.

"And the other aircraft?"

"He simply disappeared."

"Did you shoot at either of them?"

Dallas smiled, "How could we? The tail gunner was our only armament. They aren't very good for head-ram targets."

His remark brought a reproving look but no comment. Dallas did not tell him the front turrets were armed but failed to fire.

Dismissing the crew, the debriefing officer gave Dallas a knowing look and summoned the next crew's pilot.

Walking out of the debriefing shack, Dixie asked, "Sir, do they think we did okay tonight?"

Dallas was silent for a minute. "Yeah, it went alright tonight. Nice teamwork." He again paused, looking up at the morning sky. "But I think our wing got beat up a bit, though."

"I saw a B-29 going down in flames over the city. Could've been us, huh?"

Dallas nodded grimly. "Yeah, there's always a price." He thought about the eleven men who would have perished. "You did fine, Al, bombing and co-piloting."

"Thanks."

Out of the blue, a young sergeant ran up to Dallas and told him to report to the squadron commander.

The commander's meeting was short. Dallas received orders for a unit on Tinian to preclude any further complications from the incident with Major Maxwell. He left the next day.

Nineteen

Imperial Army Medical School, Tokyo
Saturday Afternoon, 10 March 1945

By early afternoon, Yuki's condition was better than Gunji could have hoped. After treatment for superficial burns and blisters, a change of clothes, and a bowl of watery soup, Yuki seemed refreshed, although her lungs ached whenever she coughed. One of the doctors examined her eyes and pronounced them clear, with no sign of conjunctivitis. Though Gunji wanted her to rest, Yuki insisted on helping with patients.

The triage teams had delivered scores of residents from Sumida Park, including a man pulled from the sewer. He especially needed a thorough cleaning, and Yuki insisted on helping with the horrendous task. Gunji worked with her, both dressed in gowns and gloves. Their surgical masks could not deflect the odious stench emanating from the victim's clothing and skin.

"His eyes are sealed shut," Yuki commented as she gently washed his swollen and burned face and head.

"Yes," Gunji answered. "Here, let's use the saline solution to clean them."

Yuki and Gunji peeled off and discarded the man's scorched, grimy uniform. Continuing their onerous work, they carefully cleaned the filthy and seared body. The man winced from time to time despite their efforts to avoid painful contact. Morphine being a precious asset, Gunji injected a minimal dose. Severe burns covered most of his body, and they could see infection was inevitable where the sewer substances had invaded the wounds and probably seeped into his stomach. A large bump on his head indicated a potential concussion. Examining his mouth, Gunji found the tongue blistered and badly lacerated, obviously from involuntary biting from pain, but his throat seemed relatively clear.

"I hope his trachea is not burned," Gunji muttered. "If so, he is as good as dead."

While they worked, an orderly came in, bowing to Gunji, "Sir, we found these in his pockets."

It was a wallet, identification tags, and a pistol. Gunji nodded and told him to clean them and put them in a bag.

"But, Sir," the orderly insisted. "You should see who he is!"

"I'm busy, can't you see? Just tell me who he is if it's important."

"He's a major. A Major Tanaka," the orderly paused before adding, "He's Kempeitai."

Startled, Gunji looked up at Yuki across the examination table. Had her face expressed fear, revulsion, sadness? Gunji couldn't tell.

"Thank you. Put the items in a bag; make sure you sanitize," Gunji answered and continued to clean Tanaka's body. Gunji observed Yuki's apparent determination to care for the patient, surprising him.

Due to the wounds and swelling, Gunji had difficulty believing it was Matome Tanaka. Once the face was clean, he knew it was indeed Tanaka.

"You know this man, don't you?"

She worked silently for a few minutes before nodding her head.

"He questioned me once," Yuki answered finally, "when I was at the Kure Naval Hospital."

"Questioned you?"

She nodded and wiped her brow with her arm. The room was warm and stuffy.

Gunji walked over and cracked a window. The wintry air blew in. He could smell the acrid smoke even this far from the bombed area. The room cooled. Returning to the patient, he asked, "Better?"

"Yes, Gunji-san. Thank you." There was a tear trickling down her cheek onto her mask. Then, as if she wanted to get the facts right, "He was a young major, as I recall."

Gunji said nothing more.

Finally, Yuki and Gungi finished cleaning Tanaka's body and began to treat his wounds with salves. It was apparent he had suffered second and third-degree burns on his hands, arms, and face. A triage doctor – Dr. Yahara – came by and examined Tanaka. The doctor listened to the man's heart and lungs; then, shaking his head, he opined the man would not survive the night.

"He will not be able to eat. It's better to move him downstairs to the morgue with the others too far gone. We should not waste scarce medicine and time on anyone who will die anyway," the doctor dispassionately intoned.

Gunji nodded to the doctor, who turned and left the room. As Gunji turned to call for orderlies, Yuki spoke softly yet firmly,

"No, Gunji-san. We must try to save him. I believe we can. Please."

Gunji's eyes showed surprise, though his mask hid his mouth.

"Isn't this man a danger to you?" he asked gently.

Yuki did not respond but continued her treatment of his visible wounds. She teared up again. Deciding not to push her at the moment, Gunji continued his treatment of the patient's mouth.

"His face and mouth are burned. He must have inhaled flame. His face will be scarred for life."

"When Father returns, he will treat his burns. He is an expert. He trained in …" she hesitated as Gunji looked at her expectantly. "He trained in America."

Later, orderlies moved Tanaka into a ward. Gunji suggested they go to the dining room for rice cakes and tea. They discarded their gowns and masks and changed into clean nursing clothes.

Yuki sipped her warm tea slowly, grimacing as she swallowed.

"Your throat is sore?" Gunji asked gently.

Yuki nodded. "From the coughing, I think."

They sat silently. Gunji brought Tanaka back into their conversation.

"The man is a threat to you," he stated knowingly. It was not a question.

She finally nodded. Looking around the room to ensure no one could hear their conversation, Yuki spoke quietly. "I made a terrible mistake that endangered my parents."

Gunji remained silent, gazing intently at her.

"I want you to know I am not a traitor, nor are my parents. What I'm about to tell you will seem to contradict that statement. But it's true."

Yuki sipped her tea again, gathering her courage.

"The suitcase you carried for me last night," her voice was as delicate as her face. "It contained a radio transmitter."

She looked straight at Gunji, not in subservience, but with a plainness that attested her honesty. Gunji's face was expressionless, with no emotion, condemnation, or surprise.

"Why were you taking it to your parents' house?"

"A surprise inspection was scheduled for my hostel today. I needed to get it away from here."

"But why did you not simply toss it in the river?"

"I should have. But there is more."

Gunji waited patiently.

"Wednesday, while I was alone in my room, I heard a signal and a simple message. I always listened on Wednesday around noon."

"Message, from whom?"

Yuki breathed deeply. Then she looked at Gunji.

"I must tell you with the deepest respect that I fell in love with an American boy years ago. His parents were Christian medical missionaries who lived with my family in Nikko. We grew up together. He left before the war to study in America. We corresponded until the severance of diplomatic relations and the mails stopped."

"But the radio and the message – surely he could not give you a radio transmitter!"

"No, of course not. A strange man brought that to our home and left it. Mama knew how to use it and hoped the boy would contact us if our countries severed relations."

Gunji wanted to ask what man had brought the radio and why, but he hesitated; he wanted her to continue her story.

"What I heard on Wednesday – I knew Tokyo would suffer a fire raid. However, I thought it would be Friday morning or afternoon."

"What exactly did the message say?" Gunji sat spellbound.

"Simply, 'Mama Sumiko, fire raid Saturday; Get out.' Nothing more. It came through twice and then went dead. Not too long afterward, I heard an air raid siren. I ran out to see a lone B-san pass over the city."

"You think this was your American boy?"

"It could have been. Or a friend of his. I knew he had a friend in college who was engaged to a Japanese-American girl living in California. They shared the information. The other boy knew about the radio transmitter. I know this because of one of the last letters I received."

"Why would his friend send the message from the B-san? Surely he did not know your mother?"

"No, of course not. But he would know the code word 'Mama Sumiko.' I think he would have wanted to warn his friend's loved ones. I hate to think that either one of them participated in the raid. I know they loved our people."

Gunji started to ask why she did not alert the authorities about the raid, then realized that would have betrayed the forbidden radio transmitter.

He reached out and covered her hand with his. She looked deeply into his eyes.

"Gunji-san," her voice choked, "I have sensed your affections. You are a good and decent man. I must tell you of my affection for a man who is your hated enemy. You must understand I can hate no one. I am a Christian and have been taught since my earliest moments to love my enemies."

"Are you blind to what our enemies did to our city? The reports coming in suggest tens of thousands of innocent people died in the fires."

"Were not the Chinese people – women and children in Nanking innocent?"

Gunji cleared his throat. He had been a private soldier in Nanking during the massacres, though he had not participated.

"I know we should not compare brutalities," Yuki continued. "War is an awful tragedy. Now we are all reaping a whirlwind."

"I cannot understand how you can love your enemies when they burn us out of our homes and kill innocent women and children. I confess I had no love for the Chinese in Nanking, but I did not murder them."

"It is not easy to love someone who reviles and persecutes you, Gunji-san. My Master, the Lord Jesus, the Christian God, forgave his enemies from a cross where they nailed him after brutalizing his body. He did not hate the sinners, just their sins."

Gunji dismissed this line of talk. "You did not tell me exactly how your family came to have this radio and why they kept it after the government ordered all such devices be turned in. You only mentioned a stranger brought it to your home."

"Yes, in 1939. He asked my father to report if any indications of war were brewing when he was sent to Kure Naval Hospital to teach burn treatment. Father never did. Mama and Papa kept the radio, hoping to stay in contact with our American friend, not to spy. I guess that's a weak defense."

"Very weak, Yuki-san," Gunji responded in a more serious, almost hostile voice.

Yuki bowed her head.

Gunji sensed her shame. "Where is the radio now?"

"I fear Major Tanaka found it. I hid it in the air raid trench behind my family's house. When I looked later last night, it was gone. Tanaka was in their house waiting. I ran when the air raid sounded."

Gunji's facial expression displayed alarm. "You should have thrown it in the river."

"I intended to do so. I wanted to relay the message and warn Mama to leave the city. I did not realize they had already left to see to a sick relative in Nikko."

"Tell me about the man who brought the radio."

"I remember his name – Mr. Nakamura – He spoke excellent English as well as Japanese. I never saw him after the day he left the radio."

Yuki decided not to talk about the woman who came to the park in Kure.

Gunji was silent for a moment.

"I, too, have a confession." Squirming in his seat, he continued, "I know Major Tanaka. I report to him."

Yuki's face betrayed her surprise. "Are you part of the Kempeitai too? A kempei?"

"No! No! I am an orderly and medical student hoping to become a doctor. My job as an informant is suppressing defeatism, especially among the staff. If I were to find any overt activity, I am – was to report it to Major Tanaka."

"And have you?"

"No, but today's inspection was a stepped-up effort to discourage such thoughts."

He paused, "I found your radio case one day while you were on duty in the wards."

Startled, Yuki gasped, "You were in my room?" Invasion of privacy was something she loathed.

"Yes," Gunji answered, "and I had the authority to be there if necessary. However, I went for another reason. I found out Major Tanaka was suspicious of your activities. I searched your room before the inspection to be sure nothing would raise suspicion."

"But if you found the radio, why did you not turn me in?"

"I planned to search your room myself."

Gunji looked deeply into her eyes and squeezed her hand gently.

"Is it not obvious?"

Yuki looked down, embarrassed by this confession. A tear ran down her cheek, and her lips trembled. Finally, she put her other hand over his.

"Oh, dear Gunji-san, you are so kind to me. But you now know my true affections. How can I share any part of me when my heart is with another?"

"Someone you see as a hated enemy? Do you think this affection you hold can survive this war?" he asked. "Soon, they are expected to land on our shores. Probably this year. It will be a terrible battle. The Empire will call upon us to fight as well as heal."

"I cannot fight, Gunji-san. My faith forbids me to kill another human being. I wish we could settle this conflict peacefully. I wish our leaders would see the futility of this struggle."

Gunji's tone turned bitter, "The Americans have demanded unconditional surrender. They will destroy our way of life, dethrone the Emperor, probably emasculate our population, and abuse our women."

"This may be true, but I do not believe the Americans would abuse us. Not the ones I have known."

Gunji looked away angrily but did not respond. He had never met an American.

Yuki continued, "You know we suffered a terrible defeat in 1942 at a place called Midway?"

Gunji looked up in surprise. "Did your radio tell you this?"

Yuki smiled involuntarily. "Oh no; I overheard it from our Naval officers at the Yokosuka Naval Hospital. Did you know we lost four aircraft carriers and many pilots in that battle?"

"That cannot be true!"

"Gunji-san, it is now no secret that the Americans are advancing closer to our home islands. Why are they so close if we had won all those battles?"

Gunji did not respond but looked down. He knew he had no answer. Yuki had heard classified information, information the military government did not want to be publicized.

"Will your religion save you when they come?" he asked contemptuously.

She squeezed his hand, "I am already saved, Gunji-san, maybe not from death in this world. Last night, I thought I was going to die. I was sure of it. I had resigned myself to a fiery death."

"But you did survive, and I found you!"

"We must consider that a miracle then. Think about this. I had given up when I heard and saw that little child. Behind him, I saw an opening, a way through the horror. I found a place of refuge. But I still should have died. You saw all the bodies near where you found me. Those who did not burn to death died for want of clean air. Why was clean air provided to me in my hiding place? It should not have been. I praise my God for sparing me. But I do not know how – or why – He did this for me. I know I am here alive."

Gunji stayed silent.

Yuki continued, "You found me; that was a miracle to me. And you found Major Tanaka. He is still alive. That, too, is a miracle."

"If he does not die, he will come for you and your parents." Gunji sounded resigned and resentful.

"I must try to save him. It is more than my professional duty as a nurse. It is my duty to my God. I now believe he spared me to help Major Tanaka."

"You have a strange God," Gunji said derisively. "He saves you and so you can save your enemy, who will probably have you shot – if indeed he does survive!"

"That is beyond my control. I must trust in my Lord's purposes."

They sat in silence for a while.

"You must rest," Gunji sighed. "We have a long day tomorrow."

Yuki nodded, "I want to check on Major Tanaka before I go to my room."

He nodded, got up, and left her.

Yuki returned to the ward and found Tanaka's bed. She knelt beside him, placed her hand over his bandages, and prayed silently for his body and soul. Yuki also offered a prayer for Gunji. Then Yuki went to her room.

The next afternoon, her father returned and began treating Tanaka.

Twenty

"Wait, you're telling me Dr. Fujita and Yuki were involved in saving a man who was seeking to kill them?"

Okita smiled at me. "Oh, the whole family would ultimately be Tanaka's caregiver. But that's another story."

He proceeded to relate how Dr. Fujita went about Tanaka's restoration. "The man lay in a coma for several weeks, wrapped in bandages, mummy-like. Conjunctivitis left him temporarily blind; the damage to his throat precluded speaking, and his hands were bound in heavy bandages."

Okita also related how the doctor, who had triaged Tanaka and wanted to consign him to the morgue, had clashed with Dr. Fujita. "Dr. Fujita was all in for saving Tanaka, but his colleague, Dr. Yahara, insisted it was a waste of precious resources. Fujita finally played the Kempeitai card, saying he would not be responsible for the needless death of an officer of the secret police. Yahara relented grudgingly and became a foil in a later plot to save the Fujitas." Okita chuckled.

"So, you see," Okita smiled, "Tanaka was quite harmless, but only for a while. When he regained consciousness, he could not see who cared for him. His hearing was not acute enough to discern whose voices were speaking to him."

"Surely, he remembered he had found the radio?"

"Yes, you can be sure he did. But there was nothing he could do at the time. Unable to ambulate, talk, or write, his ability to communicate was quite limited. Again, it was weeks before he could even walk to the toilet alone."

"How long did he remain in this semi-vegetative state?" I asked.

"Several weeks. Not until the spring. Early on in 1945, Dr. Fujita restored Tanaka's burn-scarred features with a few skin grafts. Dr. Fujita was an expert and taught his colleagues. That is until Dr. Fujita was transferred. He turned the grafting over to the medical staff. Yuki continued treating Tanaka; her voice must have been a pleasant distraction over time as his hearing returned. He still experienced severe discomfort."

"Did he ever know who cared for him?"

Okita laughed. "Once Tanaka's vision improved well enough for him to see her. I am sure he could only gape in shock – and probably humiliation and fear. Yuki began his physical therapy as soon as he could stand."

"How did he respond?"

"Tanaka was in no shape to do anything. Therefore, he snarled at Yuki, but she spoke kindly. As a matter of fact, he had a severe concussion and was often sedated."

"How do you know all of this wartime intrigue?"

At this, Okita did not smile, but looked away with an enigmatic expression that seemed to take him back in time and space.

"I'll be honest with you, Reid-san, I had close encounters with the people of whom I speak. I frequented the Imperial Army Hospital often and spoke with the medical staff. I got to know Tanaka's situation quite intimately. It was not difficult to piece together what happened."

"Were you on the medical staff?"

Okita laughed. "Far from it. But let us say I became closely acquainted with these people and Tanaka." He paused, still looking beyond me. "Yes, I got to know the man better than he knew himself. And my knowledge of the Fujita family was from close encounters. Very close."

"Did you know my Japanese family before the war?"

"No, it was not until 1945 that I really became acquainted with them."

"How?"

I knew my question sounded impulsive the moment it escaped my lips. Yet, throughout my encounter with Asaka Okita, I had the impression that he knew far more about the Fujitas – and me – than he had revealed.

The two of us were playing a game. We were trading one confidence for another confidence, slowly revealing a history, not only about people we knew but about ourselves. His elaborate narrative belied the earlier admission that he was merely acquainted with the Fujita family. I wondered what he was hiding and why. But then, I also was holding my cards close. There were confidences I kept to myself, not just now, with this stranger, but from many others and for a long time.

Okita's face disclosed nothing. He turned away from me, and I heard him exhale.

Finally, he answered, "At the Imperial Army Hospital. You see, I witnessed these events firsthand. Other people told me about the Fujitas and their adventures."

That seemed plausible, and I let the thought go. I was suddenly curious about the damning evidence Tanaka found.

"But what about the radio? Didn't you say he told his sergeant to secure it?"

Okita smiled. "Now, that is quite a story."

Kempeitai Field Office, Tokyo
Late Morning, Wednesday, 14 March 1945

Lieutenant Masao Gunji's first inclination was to lure Master Sergeant Saito out of his headquarters, take him somewhere, and shoot him with Tanaka's pistol. The more he thought about it, the more he knew he could not kill the man in cold blood. Furthermore, he had to know what evidence Tanaka had accumulated on the Fujitas. So, he developed another ruse and asked Yuki to help him. Although feeling reluctant, Yuki finally agreed.

Saito was at his desk when Gunji arrived. Having met several times previously in Tanaka's presence, they exchanged cordial greetings. Gunji noticed several blisters on Saito's face and hands, and he appeared to suffer discomfort.

"Were you injured in the raid?" Gunji asked.

"Insignificantly," Saito answered bravely. He did not think the young officer needed to know of his narrow escape from his unauthorized escapade when he should have returned straight to the office with the suitcase. "Stray sparks hit me, ruined my heavy coat and a uniform, though. I was lucky." Saito was fortunate to get back across the river. He assumed the car and driver perished. *Where was Major Tanaka?*

Gunji thought otherwise about Saito's condition; the man was in more pain than he would admit, but Gunji was sympathetic and didn't mention the wounds on his face. Instead, he asked, "Were you with Major Tanaka during the raid?"

"Yes, we had been in the Honjo district on a case. I left just before the bombing. Frankly, I am worried about the major. It's been almost four days, and he has not reported to headquarters. I fear he may not have survived."

"Oh, then you did not know. I bring you good news!" Gunji exclaimed. "We have him at the hospital. He is severely injured, but he will recover. I have helped in his treatment!"

Saito eked out a smile. "That is indeed good news."

Gungi continued to observe the man. *His good disposition seemed contrived. Perhaps Saito did not care for his overbearing boss as much as he pretended.*

Saito sat back and lit a cigarette.

"Well, it will take time," Gunji rubbed his chin, "Major Tanaka was very fortunate that we found him when we did."

Sensing he had an advantage, Gunji paused, while Saito smoked.

"Did you report him missing?"

Saito looked up defensively.

"Yes, of course."

Gunji knew that was a lie. Dr. Yahara had reported the news to his source at Kempeitai headquarters a day after the raid. That was the first information that the secret police had on their officer.

"Tell me, Lieutenant," Saito said as he blew smoke in the air. "Did the Major say anything about what we were doing that night?"

"He has not been able to speak very much. It's funny, though. He did say he learned that Dr. Fujita is being framed," Gunji paused and added, "if that makes sense."

Saito's squinted, and then he looked at Gunji. "Framed?"

"Indeed. I was quite shocked. It's also ironic that Dr. Fujita is treating him. Saved his life."

Gunji was taking his time, letting the conversation develop. He wanted to see how Saito was taking in his story. Let Saito do the fishing for information.

"Strange indeed," Saito grunted. "As you know, we have been watching this family closely, including the daughter."

"Oh yes," Gunji nodded. "He assigned me to keep watch on her. I have tried to play the interested lover. Not doing very well on that score, I'm afraid." Gungi shrugged.

"Any leads there on possible treason?"

"None that I can detect. Both the father and mother appear loyal, and they all revere the Emperor. Yuki also was instrumental in saving the major's life. One of the doctors wanted to triage him to the hopeless ward and let him die. Yuki Fujita intervened on Tanaka's behalf."

Saito drew on his cigarette. *Too bad the girl had been so dedicated to her work.*

"Tell me, did he say why he thinks Dr. Fujita is being framed?"

Gunji sensed Saito was not buying his story. At least he was doubtful, and indeed fishing.

"No, not specifically. That's what Tanaka mumbled during one of his lucid moments. Something about a witness seeing someone at the Fujita house with a bundle: of course, he goes in and out of consciousness. He was badly burned."

Gunji decided not to mention the head injury that was causing the coma, "I have not been around all the time. Once, he insisted that you come and bring your reports and evidence."

Saito up straighter. Now, he was suspicious.

Realizing Saito had dismissed the idea of visiting Tanaka, Gunji explained, "Frankly, I'm not so sure we should let him do any work right now. The medical staff says he needs rest and time to recover. Perhaps I should tell him you are too busy if that would be appropriate? If he regains any conscious state, that is. However, we must inform his superiors he survived the bombing raid."

Gunji nodded but remained silent. Saito seemed talkative on his own.

Saito lit another cigarette as they rode slowly through the streets toward he hospital. "You know, I find it interesting that a witness saw someone at the ujita house with a bundle, as you say. We questioned one of the neighbors, hey had seen no activity or were unaware of much activity at the Fujitas that vening. Only that they had gone out earlier."

Gunji saw an opening. "That's not surprising. The Fujitas were in Nikko that evening. They had received permission from your headquarters."

Saito turned to Gunji, obviously surprised by this information. "Really? I wonder why Tanaka did not know."

Gunji remained silent. Saito had posed an interesting question. Since the Kempeitai had to approve travel permits, an officer in headquarters or the field office must have signed off.

As they were approaching the hospital, Gunji let the thought drop. The next phase of his plan was imminent. He hoped his ruse would work. If not, he would be taking more decisive action.

When they arrived, Saito marched imperiously into the ward where Tanaka lay unconscious. He summoned an orderly, demanding to see a doctor. A tall man in a white lab coat strolled in, a stethoscope draped around his neck.

"I am Dr. Yahara. You wish to see me?"

"You are treating Major Tanaka? I wish to know his condition."

"And who are you?" Dr. Yahara appeared unimpressed with Saito's attitude.

"I am Kempei Master Sergeant Saito, his assistant. I need to know his condition and if he has spoken."

"His condition is quite serious, but we think he will pull through with

Saito finished his cigarette in one extended inhalation, slowly blowing out the smoke. He seemed to be thinking about his options.

"Our superiors will be delighted to know he is alive. And you are there to watch over him – and the suspects. But it is more appropriate that I should be the one to inform them, Lieutenant."

He lit another cigarette. He offered one to Gunji, who declined politely.

"Yes, you are probably right, Sergeant."

"They need to know one of their senior officers is safe but under treatment."

"You know this is so strange," Saito continued to smoke his cigarette. "We found very incriminating evidence at the Fujita house. I am surprised the major would now say someone is framing them."

Gunji blinked in a puzzled manner. "Evidence?" he asked innocently.

"Yes, Lieutenant. I have it locked up here. If Tana – if the major did not report today, I was going to his superiors with it."

Gunji wanted to tell the sergeant he should talk to Tanaka first but decided he should not push. He feared he would appear anxious. Better to let Saito figure it out.

Saito continued to smoke, thinking, oblivious that the commissioned officer Gungi was in his presence. The senior sergeant could not have been less impressed with junior officers.

Finally, he opened his desk drawer and removed a key. Then he walked over to a closet and, using the key, unlocked the door and pulled a suitcase from the interior. Gunji recognized it at once as the one he had carried for Yuki that awful night.

"This, Lieutenant, is the evidence I spoke of."

Gunji tried to look puzzled. Saito, a cigarette hanging crookedly from his mouth, brought the case and set it on his desk. Opening it, he smiled.

"I'm surprised; that's a radio transmitter!"

"Yes, Lieutenant, a forbidden radio transmitter I found at the Fujita house the night of the raid in their air raid trench. The major felt it was evidence of treason and told me to safeguard it. He planned to arrest Dr. and Mrs. Fujita that very night."

Gunji remained calm, displaying a false curiosity. He was, after all, a lowly medical student. Yet he needed a way to seize the case and make it disappear. Then the idea came to him.

"I will let Major Tanaka know you are safeguarding it. I am sure the hospital commander will notify Kempeitai headquarters that the major survived and is recovering from the raid."

Saito looked up sharply, calculating he did not want his superiors learning of Tanaka's safety from any other source. Saito was not one to lose face or lessen his importance. He sat silently for a minute, then exhaled more smoke, "Perhaps I should go with you now and check on the major personally before reporting to our superiors. Maybe you could persuade the medical staff to let me speak with him."

"Possibly, especially if you insist. But you must not give away my cover." Gunji desperately tried to play a convincing role as a secret informant while remaining calm and assured.

"Yes, I will come with you to see the good Major Tanaka. But we will safeguard the evidence here." With that, Saito returned the suitcase to the closet. After locking it, Gunji saw him place the key in his right jacket pocket. Gunji wondered where the file on the Fujita family was.

"Shall we go, Lieutenant?"

On the ride to the hospital, Gunji remained silent. Finally, Sergeant

Saito broke the silence.

"Did you know I met the Fujita girl once at the Kure Naval

"Really? I knew she had served there and at Yokosuka."

"Yes, Tanaka was suspicious because it seemed Yuki met woman on a park bench during her breaks. Then the woman disappea sloppy. I should have immediately apprehended this woman when I her. The girl denied knowing her and having any meaningful conversa

Gunji sat quietly for a moment. Then he asked, "Why would y been curious about her sitting with this woman?"

"No obvious reason." Saito paused. "Except the girl worked on where highly classified information could leak. It was just before we att the American base in Hawaii. There was a young navy pilot who was in training for the mission. He had a reputation for being talkative."

"And you suspected she talked to him about this training?"

"Or that he talked in his sleep. We were covering all possibilities. had the Imperial Navy transfer him to a hospital ship sailing to the south fleet."

"But surely that alone is not enough to suspect the Fujita family treason!"

"Oh no, Lieutenant, not at all. However, we also knew they had close relationship with an American family before the war. Tanaka interrogat one of the Americans but got no useful information. Still, they stood out. addition, the Fujitas are Christians." Gunji noticed the disdain in Saito's voic

"I understand there are many loyal Christians in Japan."

"Maybe. It is a Western religion, you know, white man's religion."

time. He has spoken very little since he came in. His voice box is quite sore. We do not want him trying to talk right now."

"What did he say when he spoke?"

"Nothing much. Only gibberish about one of our doctors."

"What gibberish?" Saito demanded.

Dr. Yahara appeared put off by Saito, but answered.

"He said something to me about Dr. Fujita being set up. I asked what he meant. He told me a neighbor saw a stranger in the Fujitas' house in Honjo."

"Is that all?"

"That's the gist of it. Major Tanaka was delirious at the time."

"Can you wake him?"

"No! Absolutely not!"

Saito glared at the doctor, who looked curiously at Saito's blistered face.

"Were you in the firestorm, Sergeant?" Dr. Yahara asked.

"Yes, but I escaped before the worst. Why do you ask?"

"Did any sparks hit your body other than your face?"

"A few burned through my heavy coat."

Dr. Yahara asked Saito if he had been treated.

"No; I rubbed salves on my face and body."

"Come with me, Sergeant," the doctor said with authority. In his private office, Dr. Yahara ordered Saito to remove his jacket.

"Why?" Saito asked suspiciously.

"We have found these burns caused by the incendiary gels are toxic. We need to know how badly you've been burned. Your face and hands are a mess."

"First, I wish to speak with Dr. Fujita. I really must insist, Dr. Yahara." Saito glared at the physician.

"Very well. Lieutenant Gunji, will you summon Dr. Fujita to my office?"

Shortly, displaying a curious demeanor, Dr. Fujita entered the room.

"I apologize for interrupting your valuable work, Doctor, but Sergeant Saito of the Kempeitai wishes to ask you a few questions about Major Tanaka."

Fujita turned to Saito and, tilting his head, said, "How can I help you, Sergeant?"

Saito asked, "Where were you on the night of the firestorm, Doctor?"

"My wife and I were on a train to Nikko, where my wife's family is. Why do you ask?"

"I am asking the questions, Doctor," Saito said arrogantly. "Why did you leave, and did you have Kempeitai's permission for this travel?"

"Why, of course, we had travel permits issued here in Tokyo. I still have them. As to why we went, my brother-in-law had taken ill. We went to check on him. I returned two days later when I felt assured of his stability."

"So, you left your Tokyo home unattended?" Saito zeroed in on Fujita.

Dr. Fujita smiled. "It was not much of a home, but it was where we chose to live – near common people, people without any means. It was a place to sleep and take meals when we were not at the hospital."

"Do you ever check your air raid trench, Doctor?"

"Rarely, Sergeant. If an air raid sounded, we would leave immediately for the hospital. Of course, we complied with the neighborhood association regulation by having a full barrel of water and some sand on hand for fire-fighting."

"And why would you not stay and ensure your home and property are protected?"

Fujita breathed deeply, showing apparent impatience; he retorted, "Because our first duty is to our patients – and potential patients!" He glared back at Saito. "Is that all, sergeant," he added with authority and indignation.

Saito stood silently for a moment. Then he dismissed Fujita, who left the room.

Dr. Yahara took up the imperious demeanor and ordered Saito to remove his upper garments. Gunji assured Saito the doctor knew best and persuaded him to remove his clothing. Reluctantly, Saito complied. Deep red sores were on his back, and Saito winced when the doctor touched them.

"Hmm, possible infection has set in." Dr. Yahara said. "You should have seen a doctor immediately."

"Hundreds of people should be seeing doctors. Why should I?"

"Because you are a soldier," Dr. Yahara said as if Saito had asked an unreasonable question.

He ordered Gunji to prepare a syringe. When Saito saw the needle, his head rolled back, his knees crumpled. The man passed out and fell to the floor.

"Oh my, the brave sergeant is allergic to needles. He hit his head; don't you agree, Lieutenant?"

"Yes, Dr. Yahara. Maybe a concussion. We should probably keep him for observation."

With that, the doctor knelt and injected the syringe's contents into Saito's arm.

"He will be out for several hours. Have an orderly get him to a bed. Then go do what you need to do."

Gunji retrieved the key from Saito's jacket pocket and left the office. He went by his room and packed a suitcase resembling one in Saito's closet, then took a taxi back to the Kempeitai field office.

A young soldier stood guard at the entrance, and Gunji knew there had been a change of guard since his earlier morning visit. As Gunji signed in on the logbook, the young private eyed his suitcase suspiciously after Gunji showed his identification.

"I'm here to see Saito. I'll be leaving after my visit here for the train station," he gestured to his case.

The soldier nodded and allowed him to pass. Once inside, Gunji checked the hallway, darted into Saito's office, and softly closed the door. The first order of business was to secure travel permit forms from Saito's desk. He used the stamp and ink pad, authenticated several forms, folded them, and placed them in his jacket pocket. He walked over to the closet, and using Saito's purloined key, Gunji opened the door.

He was stunned to see the closet empty; the suitcase was gone. Fighting his panic, he considered what could have happened since their departure only two and a half hours earlier. Had Saito given someone else permission to remove the case without him knowing? He closed and locked the door. Gunji decided to leave the key in the desk drawer. He did not want to be caught with it. He looked to see if there was a file on the Fujitas. Finding none, he checked what was Tanaka's desk. It, too, was empty of any case files.

Retrieving his, he stepped out into the hallway, preparing to exit the building; he heard his name called.

"You are wanted in here." A man in a lieutenant colonel's uniform motioned to him. Gungi walked back down the hall as innocently as he could and stepped into another room. The man looked at him severely and his suitcase. Gunji noticed his mixed ancestry.

"Why are you staring at me, Lieutenant? Do you think I look funny?"

"Uh, no, Sir; I'm umm," Gunji stuttered.

"I am a thorough Japanese," he said curtly.

"Uh, Yes, Sir, of course. Uh, you needed me, Sir?"

"Yes, Lieutenant. Your activities have brought you due credit. We have decided to transfer you to another station where your talents may be of greater use."

"Transfer, Sir?" Gunji was now greatly concerned. He did not want to be separated from Yuki.

"Yes, we are sending you to military headquarters at Hiroshima Castle. They have a clinic where you can keep your ears tuned to matters of interest."

"To whom will I report?" Gunji asked nervously.

"To me. I will give you instructions on how to contact me. Of course, you will report to the hospital commander for your medical duties."

"Elements of the Fifth Division are in Hiroshima, if I am not mistaken."

"Indeed. I have it on good authority. We will be establishing an Army headquarters there soon. You will leave tomorrow morning. Your orders, personal instructions, and travel permit are in this envelope. Don't open it here."

Gunji took the envelope, hoping his face did not show disappointment.

"I see you are already packed?"

"Uh, yes, Sir; I hoped to take a few days' leave starting today."

The officer regarded Gunji's suitcase suspiciously. "Unfortunately, it is urgent that you get moving quickly. Be on the early train tomorrow morning. Your ticket is also in that envelope."

"What about Major Tanaka? I have always reported to him."

The senior officer regarded him with disdain. "He's out of action for the time being, as I understand it. We received word a few minutes ago that he will be recuperating for several weeks, if not months. He is not your concern."

And with that, he dismissed Gunji, who left and headed straight back to the hospital.

Gunji tried to look puzzled. Saito, a cigarette hanging crookedly from his mouth, brought the case and set it on his desk. Opening it, he smiled.

"I'm surprised; that's a radio transmitter!"

"Yes, Lieutenant, a forbidden radio transmitter I found at the Fujita house the night of the raid in their air raid trench. The major felt it was evidence of treason and told me to safeguard it. He planned to arrest Dr. and Mrs. Fujita that very night."

Gunji remained calm, displaying a false curiosity. He was, after all, a lowly medical student. Yet he needed a way to seize the case and make it disappear. Then the idea came to him.

"I will let Major Tanaka know you are safeguarding it. I am sure the hospital commander will notify Kempeitai headquarters that the major survived and is recovering from the raid."

Saito looked up sharply, calculating he did not want his superiors learning of Tanaka's safety from any other source. Saito was not one to lose face or lessen his importance. He sat silently for a minute, then exhaled more smoke, "Perhaps I should go with you now and check on the major personally before reporting to our superiors. Maybe you could persuade the medical staff to let me speak with him."

"Possibly, especially if you insist. But you must not give away my cover." Gunji desperately tried to play a convincing role as a secret informant while remaining calm and assured.

"Yes, I will come with you to see the good Major Tanaka. But we will safeguard the evidence here." With that, Saito returned the suitcase to the closet. After locking it, Gunji saw him place the key in his right jacket pocket. Gunji wondered where the file on the Fujita family was.

"Shall we go, Lieutenant?"

On the ride to the hospital, Gunji remained silent. Finally, Sergeant

Saito finished his cigarette in one extended inhalation, slowly blowing out the smoke. He seemed to be thinking about his options.

"Our superiors will be delighted to know he is alive. And you are there to watch over him – and the suspects. But it is more appropriate that I should be the one to inform them, Lieutenant."

He lit another cigarette. He offered one to Gunji, who declined politely.

"Yes, you are probably right, Sergeant."

"They need to know one of their senior officers is safe but under treatment."

"You know this is so strange," Saito continued to smoke his cigarette. "We found very incriminating evidence at the Fujita house. I am surprised the major would now say someone is framing them."

Gunji blinked in a puzzled manner. "Evidence?" he asked innocently.

"Yes, Lieutenant. I have it locked up here. If Tana – if the major did not report today, I was going to his superiors with it."

Gunji wanted to tell the sergeant he should talk to Tanaka first but decided he should not push. He feared he would appear anxious. Better to let Saito figure it out.

Saito continued to smoke, thinking, oblivious that the commissioned officer Gungi was in his presence. The senior sergeant could not have been less impressed with junior officers.

Finally, he opened his desk drawer and removed a key. Then he walked over to a closet and, using the key, unlocked the door and pulled a suitcase from the interior. Gunji recognized it at once as the one he had carried for Yuki that awful night.

"This, Lieutenant, is the evidence I spoke of."

Saito broke the silence.

"Did you know I met the Fujita girl once at the Kure Naval Hospital?"

"Really? I knew she had served there and at Yokosuka."

"Yes, Tanaka was suspicious because it seemed Yuki met a strange woman on a park bench during her breaks. Then the woman disappeared. I got sloppy. I should have immediately apprehended this woman when I first saw her. The girl denied knowing her and having any meaningful conversations."

Gunji sat quietly for a moment. Then he asked, "Why would you have been curious about her sitting with this woman?"

"No obvious reason." Saito paused. "Except the girl worked on a ward where highly classified information could leak. It was just before we attacked the American base in Hawaii. There was a young navy pilot who was injured training for the mission. He had a reputation for being talkative."

"And you suspected she talked to him about this training?"

"Or that he talked in his sleep. We were covering all possibilities. We had the Imperial Navy transfer him to a hospital ship sailing to the southern fleet."

"But surely that alone is not enough to suspect the Fujita family of treason!"

"Oh no, Lieutenant, not at all. However, we also knew they had a close relationship with an American family before the war. Tanaka interrogated one of the Americans but got no useful information. Still, they stood out. In addition, the Fujitas are Christians." Gunji noticed the disdain in Saito's voice.

"I understand there are many loyal Christians in Japan."

"Maybe. It is a Western religion, you know, white man's religion."

Gunji nodded but remained silent. Saito seemed talkative on his own.

Saito lit another cigarette as they rode slowly through the streets toward the hospital. "You know, I find it interesting that a witness saw someone at the Fujita house with a bundle, as you say. We questioned one of the neighbors, they had seen no activity or were unaware of much activity at the Fujitas that evening. Only that they had gone out earlier."

Gunji saw an opening. "That's not surprising. The Fujitas were in Nikko that evening. They had received permission from your headquarters."

Saito turned to Gunji, obviously surprised by this information. "Really? I wonder why Tanaka did not know."

Gunji remained silent. Saito had posed an interesting question. Since the Kempeitai had to approve travel permits, an officer in headquarters or the field office must have signed off.

As they were approaching the hospital, Gunji let the thought drop. The next phase of his plan was imminent. He hoped his ruse would work. If not, he would be taking more decisive action.

When they arrived, Saito marched imperiously into the ward where Tanaka lay unconscious. He summoned an orderly, demanding to see a doctor. A tall man in a white lab coat strolled in, a stethoscope draped around his neck.

"I am Dr. Yahara. You wish to see me?"

"You are treating Major Tanaka? I wish to know his condition."

"And who are you?" Dr. Yahara appeared unimpressed with Saito's attitude.

"I am Kempei Master Sergeant Saito, his assistant. I need to know his condition and if he has spoken."

"His condition is quite serious, but we think he will pull through with

Twenty-one

Nikko
March 1985

Okita was still spinning a good yarn, and I wondered how much was true.

Why had he not just told me what happened to the Fujita family, especially Yuki? He seems determined to relate these long-ago events as a drama to be played out. How is it that he knows so much about them? Time and again, I was tempted to ask him to get to the bottom line or at least tell me why he related the history as he did. His interest in my past was at the back of my mind, especially concerning my college buddy and me. *Did he know something?*

"This fellow Gunji seemed to be going out of his way to protect Yuki and her family,"

"Yes, he seemed very brave, determined, and in love."

"Naturally, I'm most anxious to hear what happened to him and Yuki. Did they marry?"

Okita smiled at me knowingly. "And I am most anxious to know what happened to you and your friend, Captain Wade, who helped burn Tokyo."

I must have been staring at him because his eyes riveted on mine. He expected an answer, and for an unexplainable reason, I felt compelled to tell him.

"Well," I hesitated. "It seems we both were in trouble after that mission."

Saipan, the Marianas
Afternoon, 10 March 1945

He sat on his bunk with his head in his hands. Captain Sam Reid knew he had almost killed another crew by unloading his ordinance over Tokyo Bay. He tried to tell himself his aircraft was in danger with engine trouble, but he was too good a pilot to know that was not true.

Sam's crew knew it. His flight engineer told him they could make the bombing run and still make it home. His men had looked away when they exited the aircraft after landing. It may have been a suicide mission, but this bunch would never run from a fight. During the debriefing, he admitted he had made a hasty decision without mentioning the B-29 below his own.

Not cowardice caused him to turn away from the alarming glow ahead of the bomber. His thoughts were of a girl, an innocent, pretty Japanese girl, and he loved her. He knew he could not participate in burning that city. He loved her people.

Sam had changed uniforms earlier, anticipating the summons from his squadron commander. *I don't need to be relieved from duty looking sloppy.* He shaved and combed his dark hair.

His commander had been on the mission. He knew bombers had turned back for mechanical reasons. He also knew the scuttlebutt that Reid had turned at the eleventh hour after unloading his payload, nearly taking out another plane and crew. Yet Sam was considered a terrific pilot, probably one of the best. Their conversation had been brief. The commander's decision was merciful in a sense.

"I've got a bit of influence up the chain of command. We're transferring you to Tinian, away from everyone here. You get a fresh start. This incident won't go on your record."

Sam had merely nodded.

"But Sam," his leader continued, "don't let something like this happen again. We lost some good crews on that raid. They deserve better from the survivors. Clear?"

"Yes, Sir." He had heard the rumors that less than five percent of the B-29s failed to return. He also knew the brass considered that an "acceptable" loss rate.

"Pick up your orders in the morning. In the meantime, pack your gear and move over to the staff tent. Should be a C-47 flying over to Tinian on a mail run tomorrow or the next day."

And that had been the end of it. Sam was to be moved out of the squadron and off the island of Saipan.

Two days later, he lugged his duffle bag aboard the C-47 cargo plane bound for Tinian. Not long after landing, he bumped into an old classmate and fishing buddy.

Nikko
March 1985

Okita regarded me quizzically and with a penetrating stare. I shifted uncomfortably in my seat.

"Then you met your friend on Tinian? We all know Tinian Island was the site of the atomic bomb unit." He paused. "You were not part of that, were you?"

I knew the use of the atomic bombs against Japan remained a sensitive issue in Japanese culture.

"No," I answered. "That unit was more or less isolated from the regular bombing units. We were in a different group, though all of us were on Tinian's North Field."

He grunted. "What happened to the two of you?"

It took several minutes for me to answer, but Okita waited patiently. Pondering how much to tell him, I stalled by asking for another cup of coffee. Okita suggested we return to the garden. After refreshing my cup, we sat on the bench under a cherry tree.

Though it was now warmer outside, a chill seemed to grip me.

"You were saying," Okita prodded gently, "the two of you were reunited on Tinian."

"Yeah, ironically, the same squadron on the same day."

"A small world indeed."

Sipping my coffee, I tried to frame the next revelation. Finally, I spoke.

"It's a long, complicated series of events. We had just arrived and checked into the squadron administrative section. We were told to report back in the morning for processing. The young clerk seemed overwhelmed with his work. As we turned to leave, he told me that I was on a mission for the next evening. He handed me my orders. I was to be a co-pilot. The bottom line is my best friend took that mission in my place and never returned."

"I'm so sorry," Okita said softly. His sympathy was genuine.

"Surprisingly," he added, "that makes sense now."

I looked at him.

"In war and even in times of peace, we lose people we care about. You lost your family." His tone was empathetic, but I had no interest in empathy. I wanted answers.

"Well, what happened to Gunji after he left the Kempeitai office?"

Okita inhaled slowly and breathed out even more slowly.

"I think you may have discerned that the hospital had, shall we say, a very friendly contact within the Kempeitai."

I had not, but from how he told the story, I could easily see that it was believable. I held my peace. My desire for him to get to the end of this tale was compromised by my enthrallment with the yarn.

"Gunji himself was not privy to all the details and intrigues. For sure, Dr. Fujita had a confidant and friend in Dr. Yahara. It was Dr. Yahara who had the secret contact. He also was the one who wanted to triage Tanaka to the hopeless ward. Yahara told Gunji to follow his instructions to protect Yuki and her family."

"Were these people aware the war was winding down?"

"Yahara and Fujita knew the war was doomed." He sighed. "But they knew it was far from over. Yahara knew that as soon as Tanaka was well enough, he would be after the Fujitas. He came up with a plan."

"How long could the Fujitas stay in Tokyo?"

"They figured they could count on only a few days, a week at most. They could keep Saito under sedation during that time, but he would report the strange events to his superiors as soon as he woke up. That would negate and even jeopardize his mole in the Kempeitai. Yahara had instructed Gunji to obtain several travel permits from Saito's office if possible. Gunji's new orders came with several such permits."

"Wait a minute. Where were the Fujita family all to go? You told me Gunji's orders were to Hiroshima; what about Yuki and her family?"

Okita smiled at me. "All of them would have orders to Okinawa."

"Okinawa!" *Very few Japanese survived that battle.* "The invasion was only a couple of weeks off – around the first of April if I recall correctly!"

"Their orders were false. In reality, they went to Hiroshima, except for Yuki. She would stay behind for a while."

"You mean to tell me the Fujitas were sent to work in Hiroshima?" I was exasperated.

"Yes," he said evenly. "No one knew it would be the target of the first atomic bomb attack."

My heart sank.

"Have you ever wondered what became of your old friend Michi?"

Okita again diverted the storyline away from Yuki and her family.

I must have displayed considerable annoyance at his tact because he quickly added, "Patience, my friend. It is all interrelated: their lives and these events, these memories we revive."

"You sure seem to know a great deal about this family," I said in a deprecating tone, disregarding the social conventions expected in the home of a gracious host.

Again, he merely smiled. "You said the two of you were close as youths. Did you not expect he would be caught up in the vortex of war, just as you were?"

"Yes, Michi and I were very close, almost like brothers. I knew he flew for the Imperial Army or Navy. I feared we would face one another one day. Fortunately, I was spared that ordeal."

My host sipped his coffee thoughtfully, his face unreadable.

"Michi's engineering studies took him along a similar path as yours. He became a fighter pilot in the Imperial Army Air Force. An outstanding pilot, so I learned. He reportedly brought down a few of your B-sans, one on the Night of the Black Snow."

I grimaced at the term the Japanese gave Operation Meetinghouse. On that March night when we burned Tokyo, more than a hundred thousand people died – according to some estimates, more than in either Hiroshima or Nagasaki.

"There were few fighters reported that night." My mind swirled in the memories of an orange glow on the horizon across a darkened bay.

"Yes, we heard about it much later. Our Navy and Army air defense efforts were poorly coordinated." Okita stopped to catch his breath.

I rubbed my face.

"Although it would not have made much of a difference, I think."

"You haven't told me about Michi's fate. We corresponded a few times before the war. I remember he enjoyed my stories about my fishing expeditions in Georgia."

Okita sipped his coffee, deep in thought. "He became a kamikaze pilot."

Stunned, I stood reflexively. "What?" I stammered.

Okita's face was a mask of somberness. He motioned me to sit.

"Yes, it seems our friend Saito had some influence. Michi refused to volunteer for the Special Attack Units when the call went out. He explained to his commander that his Christian beliefs forbade suicide."

"I suppose he was ostracized for this."

"Not at first. Young pilots were not coerced early on, merely encouraged through propaganda and a call to national honor."

"You told me Saito had something to do with his volunteering."

"Yes, it goes back to when Dr. Yahara hospitalized Saito. They could not keep him down too long; that would have been suspicious. After a few days, Dr. and Mrs. Fujita were on their way to Hiroshima following Gunji. Yuki came here to Nikko to visit family. Once released from the hospital, Saito heard of Gunji's and the Fujitas' departure for Okinawa to assist in the coming battle. He did not question the story when he saw their orders. He returned to work but remained suspicious because of the radio transmitter."

"Well, what about that missing suitcase with the radio?"

Okita chuckled, "Oh, the suitcase was back in his closet. Saito did not even bother to check until Tanaka walked in one day in late July."

"You mean they held Tanaka that long in the hospital?"

"Long enough. The major went into rehabilitation."

"Rehab? But where?"

"To a sanitarium in the northern part of Honshu, well out of the way. It kept Tanaka out of action. Again, Doctor Yahara's friend in the Kempeitai was most helpful. Eventually, he came back to Tokyo determined to find the Fujitas. The first person he sought was Yuki."

"What did Saito have to do with Michi? How does this all tie together?"

"While Tanaka recuperated, Saito was busy. He became suspicious about the ruse against the Fujitas. After all, who would want to frame the good doctor and his wife? Let's be honest; it was a stretch. From Tanaka's files, Saito knew of the Fujitas' extended family in Nikko. He found that Michi was assigned to an air base near Tokyo."

"He went to Michi to find the Fujitas?"

"Yes, but Michi did not know where they were. His only information pointed to Fujita's transfer to Okinawa. Yet he had seen Yuki in Nikko while on a short leave. It seems Saito suspected as much. He also learned from Michi's more ardent flying mates that he had failed to volunteer for the Special Attack Unit. He used that as leverage."

"Meaning?"

"The short version is that he told Michi he knew Yuki's location and would arrest her if he did not join the Special Attack force. He lied and told Michi that his cousin was guilty of having a proscribed radio, and the proof was in his possession. Michi, being loyal to his family, felt he had no choice. They sent Michi to a base in southern Kyushu to help train young volunteers on flying. He worked with both Army and Navy teams. Of course, given limitations in fuel and the pressing crisis on Okinawa, the training was very abbreviated. He flew his last mission against the invasion fleet anchored off the island."

Twenty-two

Special Attack Unit Airfield, Southern Kyushu, Japan
Tuesday, 29 May 1945

The cherry blossoms came as usual that spring. Michi had enjoyed them during his brief leave with his family in Nikko in April. After their blooming peak, the gentle breezes blew like a delicate blizzard; petals covered the ground like a blanket of pink snow. As the train carried him toward Tokyo, Michi looked out the window. The spreading tree canopies on the hills reminded him of distant snow-covered mountains. His heart sobbed, knowing this probably was the last time he would enjoy their beauty.

Michi arrived at the southern Kyushu training base, where the blossoms were no more.

Japan's military leadership, however, desperate to turn the tide of continuous disastrous defeats, had another type of cherry blossom in mind. In less than a month, Michi had taught three young men to pilot a Kyushu K11W Shiragiku, a two-seat training aircraft. The plane was a Navy trainer, but to Michi, an airplane was an airplane. He quickly mastered its mechanics.

Within a few days, he flew it with a precision that impressed his superiors. He then began to teach boys in their late teens the nuts and bolts of flying. Seated in the rear seat, he gave direction and encouragement, knowing he was teaching teenagers to operate a machine whose ultimate purpose was to end their lives in a vain attempt to stop the American advance toward the home islands.

The old trainer aircraft was a slow, plodding machine; any tactics dictated a night or early dawn attack. The ponderous plane could carry a crew of five; however, for the one-way missions envisioned by the Special Attack Corps leaders, only two would make the journey – a pilot and a navigator. It would carry an extra fuel tank in the cockpit and a single five-hundred-pound bomb.

The senior officers assigned Michi as a navigator rather than the pilot in case he decided not to complete the mission. They briefed the crews on how to approach and plunge into an enemy ship. The plan was to take off at dusk and attack the American fleet anchored off Okinawa at midnight under the waning full moon.

Michi thought of his American friend, doing his duty, bombing the homeland where he had grown up. They had corresponded several times before the mail exchanges ended. He also knew enrollment in the college officer preparation courses would result in an officer's commission in the American Army upon graduation. Michi felt the irony of a savage conflict where the two were on opposing sides. Such was the way in a fallen world.

The night before his mission, he wrestled to express his feelings in poetry, then prayed earnestly for his family and friend. Though he knew it was unlikely, he also asked that he be spared from the coming suicide mission. Michi asked that the bitter cup of tomorrow's mission be removed. Michi wondered if he had done the right thing. It was to protect his cousin Yuki, but he had doubts about sacrificing his life this way. His only consolation was Saint Paul's admonition to Timothy that if a man does not care for his own family, he is worse than a heathen. Either way, he knew he would have to fly the mission in the morning or risk execution.

When the morning came, Michi rose to watch the sunrise. The rays beaming behind a dull gray cloud framed by a bright, almost blinding corona of light was stunning. Breathing the sweet, damp air, he abruptly felt a peace he could not begin to explain.

Suddenly, a large, red-crowned crane soared across the vista. Its snow-white wings, trimmed by contrasting black tips, flapped twice as it glided gracefully through the air. *Strange,* he thought, *why is it so far south?* Its natural habitat was far north on Hokkaido.

Should he take this as a good omen, Michi wondered. Maybe it was an answer to his prayers. This rare and beautiful breed was a symbol of good fortune and longevity. Legends held that it lived for a thousand years.

He watched until the graceful bird disappeared in the distance and mouthed a prayer for its species' preservation. He carried a mental image of the great bird throughout the day. Late in the afternoon, after the ceremonial supper, the crews received their final briefings. They drank sake for a final toast. Then, they boarded the trucks that took them to their planes.

Michi's young pilot, Kenji, sat stoically across from him on the ride to the parking ramps. Just past his eighteenth birthday, the young man had expressed his desire: remembrance at the temple in Tokyo for his sacrifice. Michi rated him a mediocre pilot, someone to whom he would not ordinarily entrust his life and limb.

But this was a one-way journey with no hope of return for a life of happiness and fulfillment. For Kenji, to die was to live eternally in the shrine as a god. Michi knew the lad carried Buddhist omamori amulets for good luck on his mission. While respecting that tradition, Michi had a small wooden cross, a small New Testament, and a family photograph. Otherwise, his pockets were empty.

Oddly enough, both men wore a life preserver. Michi was unsure why they had such a garment; perhaps if they had to make an emergency landing at sea, there would be hope of rescue for another try. Kenji wore a red and white hachimaki headband around his leather helmet, a symbol of courage that Michi opted to omit. He wore an airman's simple flight suit with gloves and headgear.

After a stirring exhortation by a senior staff officer, the men walked to their assigned planes and took their positions. Labor service maidens, girls of high school age, stood nearby waving plastic branches of cherry blossoms. Kenji finally let down his guard and displayed his nervousness. Michi had to instruct him on how to start the aircraft. Afterward, they taxied out to the runway, and one by one, the squadron's planes lifted into the evening sky. Each crew choose its route to the Okinawa fleet anchorage. Because of Kenji's inexperience, Michi instructed him to fly a direct course over Amami Island, north of Okinawa.

They reached their 3,000-foot cruising altitude just as the sun settled in the western Pacific; he thought this sunset was as lovely as the sunrise he'd watched that morning. Michi whispered a silent prayer of thanks.

Michi estimated it would take almost six hours to reach the target area in the slow, lumbering aircraft. At about ten o'clock, he observed the dark Pacific. He saw the phosphorescent water caused by millions of tiny marine animals. The chemical structure of the animals emitted light as oxygen dissolved in the surrounding saline waters. *Is this a result of the sea's turbulence or from a ship's wake?* After a while, the phenomenon passed, and the plane droned on in the moonlit night.

After a few hours, they had flown past Amami Island and headed for the western side of Okinawa. Kenji radioed Michi excitedly, "Look, Lieutenant! Is that lightning ahead?"

Michi stood in the rear cockpit, observing the wind stream buffeting his head. To the south, he saw flashes of light, red tracers. "No, Kenji," he answered calmly, "that's anti-aircraft fire. Some of our comrades are in action already. Time to lose a little altitude. Take it down to three hundred feet."

The young airman complied. "I hope we get a carrier." Enthusiasm exuded from Kenji's body language.

"Perhaps, but I doubt they will be in the area."

Still standing erect, his arms resting on the open canopy windshield, Michi thought he saw a dark shape ahead, moving toward them. A picket destroyer, perhaps. At this point, he was supposed to pull the toggle to activate the bomb; he did not, and Kenji was too excited to notice.

"Lieutenant! A battleship!" Kenji exclaimed. The excitable youth had not studied the silhouettes of American ships adequately. The ship ahead was too small to be a battleship or a cruiser. It was a destroyer.

"Yes, I suppose so," Michi replied as Kenji attempted to move his glide path to hit the bridge of the newly discovered, fast-approaching vessel.

The ship's forward anti-aircraft batteries opened, and tracers flew by their plodding plane. The inexperienced Kenji completely misjudged his glide path to the target, a fact Michi easily recognized and decided not to correct. Kenji overshot the vessel and splashed the old trainer into the ocean.

Michi was thrown back into his seat and wondered if the bomb would explode even though he had failed to arm it. When it did not detonate, he pulled himself back up and realized the plane was sinking. Kenji was still strapped in the forward cockpit, unmoving. Michi stepped out of the aircraft, onto the wing, and activated his life vest. He made his way along the wing next to the fuselage to Kenji and found him unconscious. He unbuckled his seatbelt and activated his life preserver; as the water flowed in, Michi lifted Kenji from the sinking aircraft. Both airmen were adrift in the Pacific.

Kenji had a deep gash on his head, a wound in his shoulder, and blood flowing freely. Michi worried that the blood would attract sharks. He also noticed a pain in his back where he had been slammed into his seat when the plane hit the water. Still, Michi felt he might be able to swim to land. He had seen the island five miles distant before Kenji began the descent. Michi would face an enormous challenge when swimming that far with the wounded man. Still, he held the young flyer close and tried to paddle his way toward the landmass visible in the moonlight.

Weary from his struggles, Michi thought he had a vision as the water glowed with the phosphorescence he had observed earlier during the flight. Now, he was floating among the creatures of the eerie light. What seemed like eons later, a dark shape passed between the two Japanese pilots and the island, and then a glaring light blinded him.

When Michi regained some of his night vision, he saw the destroyer had stopped before them, shining a searchlight on them. They drifted closer to the vessel. Exhausted from the exertions, Michi slipped into unconsciousness. When he opened his eyes, he had been hauled onto the destroyer's deck. He felt someone searching him, and he passed out again.

When he awoke, he'd been strapped to a bed, his wet clothes removed, and covered with a blanket. Turning his head, he saw no sign of Kenji. How long he lay there, he did not know. After a while, the door opened. A tall man in an American Navy uniform came and stood over him. He placed what Michi knew to be a stole around his shoulders. He wore the rank of an American Navy lieutenant on his collar, and Michi saw a cross on his pocket lapel. The officer placed his thumb on Michi's forehead and muttered words in Latin.

Michi spoke in broken English, "Thank you, Father, you need to know I am a Protestant Christian."

The American Chaplain rocked back, stunned by Michi's pronouncement in decent English.

"You aren't dead, nor do you seem to be dying."

"I hope not sincerely!" Michi gave a weak smile, grateful to be alive.

"I was told one of you was dying. A cross and a pocket New Testament Bible were found during the search. We believed one of you is a Christian."

"Kenji, dying?" Michi asked.

"Well, one of the lads who pulled you two out of the water thought so."

"Please ask a doctor to see him, Father."

"Yes, of course, my son." He turned to leave. "We don't have a Protestant chaplain on board, I'm afraid."

Michi turned his head to follow him. "Your good prayers are appreciated anyway, Father."

Off the Coast of Okinawa
2 June, 1945

Two days later, the destroyer pulled alongside a brilliant white hospital ship bearing a large red cross. They transferred Michi and Kenji by breeches-buoy. They offered to let Michi go unbound, but Kenji was belligerent and had to be restrained. Michi asked to be bound also. Once on board, an intelligence officer, a lieutenant commander named Orser, had a long chat with Michi. They got nowhere with Kenji.

Michi talked freely about his family in Nikko, his American friend, and his parents who had lived in prewar Japan, and finally, he could freely admit his reluctance to join the Special Attack forces. Dubious at first, Commander Orser began to trust Michi's words.

"You know, Sir, I'm required only to give name, rank, service number."

Both men smiled. Michi had given much more. The sessions were painfully slow and protracted due to Michi's attempt to communicate in English, which he hadn't spoken in the six years since his American friend left.

They discussed the special attack units, and Michi's description of the buildup of suicide men and material bothered Commander Orser.

"Why did Kenji join the Special Attack unit?" Orser asked, trying to understand the psyche of young Japanese men.

"Kenji very … how you say, rash? Believe he wants to be a god. Believe dying this way make him a god to be worshipped at our shrine." Michi shook his head sadly, "Men not make very good gods."

"No, that's true," Orser agreed.

"Military believe we kill enough of you, your leaders ask for peace; Japan no surrender."

Orser reflected on this for a moment and nodded his head in understanding.

"May I ask favor?" Michi asked.

"You've earned it, Lieutenant."

"As a Christian, I need Holy Supper."

Orser regarded Michi for a moment. "I'll speak with the ship's chaplain."

The following day was a Sunday, and Orser and a Marine guard led a handcuffed Michi into the room set up for worship. They sat on the front row, passing through a phalanx of staring patients and medical staff.

Someone muttered, "Dirty Jap" and the room hummed. Orser and the chaplain had anticipated a hostile reception for good reason. A month earlier, a kamikaze pilot had deliberately targeted another hospital ship, killing thirty people, including six nurses, four surgeons, and seven patients.

The service began with a hymn. The entire congregation was genuinely shocked when Michi joined in and sang Amazing Grace.

The chaplain deliberately changed his sermon when he learned Michi would attend the service. He began by recounting Jesus' prayer in the Gospel of John for all his disciples to be one. Then, he recounted the tragedy of religious wars in Europe between various Christian factions. He summed up by admonishing the attendees that despite all the hatred boiling out of the Pacific war, Christians are admonished to love their enemies.

His sermon flopped.

The battle ranging on Okinawa was proving deadly, and the kamikaze attack on the American hospital ship weighed heavily on everyone's minds.

As he began the service of Holy Communion, the chaplain knew this, too, would be controversial.

"On the night he was betrayed," he began, "our Lord took bread and broke it …"

After reciting the rite, he picked up the plate with the bread and motioned to his assistant to secure the wine goblet. Then, in a calculated move, he walked straight to Michi and offered him the sacrament.

There was an audible stir in the room.

"The body of Jesus, broken for you," the chaplain served Michi.

Michi took the bread with his bound hands. He indicated he would dip the bread. The assistant holding the chalice looked quizzically at the chaplain and received a stern glare. The young man then offered the cup to Michi, who dipped his bread lightly in the fluid and swallowed the element.

The chaplain returned to the front and invited the worshippers to line up to receive the sacrament. Only a few did.

After the benediction, Orser and the Marine guard led Michi up the aisle. As they went by, one wounded soldier stuck out his hand and sneered, "Hey Jap, are you really a Christian?"

Michi smiled and answered, "Yes, Sir. You Christian too?"

The man seemed stunned by the question, but he merely nodded.

"Good," Michi said gently, "Then you love God and neighbor. You are brother in Christ."

Commander Orser led Michi away, leaving those in the room stupefied.

A few days later, the ship's captain administered a letter of reprimand to the chaplain.

Nikko
March 1985

I grinned. *Religion, again.* I remembered Michi had been quite devout.

"What happened afterward?"

"Because of Michi's cooperation and knowledge of the Special Attack Corps, he and Kenji were sent to America and held in a camp in California until the end of the war. Michi gave them a great deal of information about the kamikaze campaign planned against the invasion of the home islands. I think it had a sobering effect on the strategic planners in your military."

"And after the war?"

"They returned to Japan in early 1946. Administrators at the camp arranged for them to stay with a Nisei family until they could be repatriated. Because of your Supreme Court rulings, the Nisei were released in early 1945 to return to their homes or resettle elsewhere."

"How did Kenji take the surrender?"

"Devastated. He wanted to die. But Michi worked on him. At first, he considered Michi a traitor and threatened to kill him. When Kenji realized he would go home to his family, his attitude changed. Michi slowly shared the Gospel with him."

"I bet he loved that."

"No. Not in the beginning. However, his attitude toward that also softened. Michi gave him his water-damaged New Testament."

"Did Michi ever hear from him after they returned to Japan?"

"Quite so," Okita smiled again. "Kenji went back to school and later became a very successful businessman. He made a lot of money!"

"And Michi, what happened to him? I tried to no end to learn about all my Nikko family after the war. I could not travel to Japan in the immediate aftermath of the war. When I hoped to find them through other intermediaries, I got nowhere. I assumed all of them perished."

"Michi came home and became a Christian minister."

"What happened to Tanaka?" I asked, wanting to get off the subject of religion.

"Oh, he returned to duty in late July, quite healthy and determined to find the Fujitas. That quest had become an obsession for him."

"The Fujitas went to Hiroshima. Did they stay there for the duration?" *Surely, the duration ended the day of the atomic bombing.*

I continued my query. "And why did Yuki not go to Hiroshima when her parents did?"

"She planned to join her parents in their work there in August. August the sixth."

I must have looked startled.

"And that is when – and where Tanaka found them."

SCATTERED BLOSSOMS

194

Twenty-three

Kempeitai Field Office, Tokyo
Sunday Morning, 5 August 1945

Tanaka sat at his desk, eyeing his paperwork. Saito sat across the room. Summer sun heated the office, and humidity permeated the shattered city. Both men had chained-smoked three cigarettes since commencing their work. Tanaka had little evidence to go on to corroborate his finding the radio at the Fujita shanty in March.

"Major," Saito interrupted both of their studies. "Do you remember much about your time in the hospital, particularly the first days?"

Tanaka looked up and stared impassively across the room. "Not really. I was under sedation most of the time. Why?"

"Our old comrade Lieutenant Gunji told me you mumbled a few words about the Fujitas. You thought they had been set up."

Tanaka leaned back in his chair, took a drag from his cigarette, and exhaled the smoke.

"I recall no such thing. And I am sure I never said that. Why would I?"

"Well, one of the doctors also confirmed that story. They denied knowing what you meant – if you said it, that is. They also suggested a Fujita neighbor told you a stranger had come by the Fujita house with a package."

"I'm sure that is not true either, Sergeant. I spoke only to the neighbor across the way; I heard nothing like that. She only denied knowing the Fujitas' whereabouts. I recall that vividly."

"Strange." Silence hung in the air as each man regarded the other. Then he added, "Isn't it also strange that Lieutenant Gunji and the Fujitas were suddenly assigned to Okinawa?"

Tanaka thought for a moment. He never believed the Fujitas had gone to Okinawa. Gunji's whereabouts had not concerned him. He was a mere informant.

"Do we have their orders?" Tanaka asked.

Saito opened a desk drawer and rummaged around. He found a folder and withdrew it.

"I found Gunji's orders. He left Tokyo on March 15. They disclosed this information to me after I was released days later from the hospital. If he went to Okinawa, he no doubt perished with most of the other troops and civilians on the island."

Tanaka thought for a moment, "If indeed he went to Okinawa."

"I do not have the Fujita orders. I found it odd that civilian medical people would be ordered to Okinawa and odder still that they would volunteer to go to an island about to be invaded."

"You think these orders are falsified, Sergeant?"

Saito studied the paper he identified as Gunji's orders. "It looks legitimate. Shall I call Army headquarters to verify their authenticity?"

"That might be worthwhile, Sergeant," Tanaka answered. "By the way, is the radio safe?"

"Yes, it's locked in the closet. Shall I retrieve it?"

Tanaka nodded. Saito rose, took the key from his desk, and stared at it.

"Something wrong, Sergeant?"

"You know, Sir. My memory is pretty good. I recall showing the radio to Gunji after locking it away; we left for the hospital. I know I put this key in my pocket. I have never thought about it until now."

"And you say you went to the hospital immediately afterward?"

"Yes, and I had to remove my jacket and shirt when they treated my burn wounds."

"We'd better check the closet," Tanaka replied apprehensively.

Saito crossed the room, opened the closet, removed the suitcase, and set it on his desk. He opened the case, and to Saito's horror, the radio was missing, replaced by heavy books stuffed inside. He slapped his hand on the desk and swore.

"What?" Tanaka asked tersely.

Saito stared in disbelief. "It's ... it's gone!"

Tanaka was on his feet in a flash and across the room to Saito's desk. He gaped at the books. He looked accusingly at Saito. "Are you sure this is the case?"

"Yes, I recognize the scuffs. Someone has been in here."

"Careless fool! Why did you take that key with you?"

"But Major, who and how could anyone remove it from this building without being seen?"

Frantic, Tanaka tried to think clearly. He marched back to his desk, sat down, and lit another cigarette.

"Who else knew about this suitcase?" he asked. He now reverted to his police training. Ask the right questions, and sift and sort information.

"Just Gunji, unless he told someone else."

"And Gunji disappears the next day – to Okinawa presumedly."

"But he could not have taken it from this office without being checked."

"Unless," Tanaka said analytically, "unless he had help inside or possessed an identical case, he brought it with him and switched them."

"It would have to be the latter," Saito reasoned. "How could we possibly have a mole here?"

"Yes, you're probably right, but we cannot be too careful. Check the duty rosters for the guards on the day you had Gunji in here."

Saito left the room and returned in fifteen minutes. "I checked through the records," he held the logbook. "Gunji signed in twice that day; he came the second time after I was hospitalized. I have summoned the guard who was on duty at the door."

"Ah," Tanaka nodded.

In a few minutes, a young private knocked and bade to enter. He saluted Tanaka and stood at rigid attention. Tanaka nodded for Saito to proceed. Saito strolled over to face the unfortunate, intimidated soldier.

"Private, you remember the day Lieutenant Gunji came here." He pointed to the entry in the log.

"Why yes, Sergeant," the man's voice quivered. "He came to see you. He had a suitcase and planned to depart as soon as he left here. He said he was going to the train station."

"Did he leave with the same suitcase?" Saito asked. Tanaka silently observed the interrogation. He did not like questioning private soldiers. That was a sergeant's responsibility, and Saito was good at it.

"Yes, Sergeant."

"Did you inspect it?"

"No, Sergeant." The youngster was distressed now.

"Was it like this one?" Saito gestured to his desk. The soldier looked over, gulped, and nodded. Sweat poured off his brow.

"Thank you, Private. You may go."

The soldier turned, saluted Tanaka, and left the room hurriedly.

"Assign him to the beach defenses."

"I will see to it. The idiot let Gunji leave without a cursory look in his suitcase."

"You'd better check Imperial Army headquarters on Gunji's orders."

Saito nodded and went to the phone. Tanaka got up and walked down the hall to the latrine. He passed a lieutenant colonel who was heading toward the exits. The officer did not look familiar, nor did he look pureblooded Japanese.

When Tanaka returned, Saito sat at his desk smiling.

"What?" Tanaka demanded.

"Guess where Lieutenant Gunji is right now?"

"I'm not in the habit of guessing, Sergeant. Tell me what you found." Tanaka answered sharply.

"Yes, Sir," Saito responded to the rebuke as humbly as he could pretend. "He's in Hiroshima at Sixth Army Headquarters."

"Call and verify," Tanaka ordered.

After a few frustrating minutes, as connections were made, lost, and remade, Saito finally reached the offices of the Sixth Army at Hiroshima Castle.

"Verified," Saito hung up the telephone.

"And that isn't all I discovered. Gunji is with the Fujitas!"

Tanaka's eyes widened perceptively. Though he tried to look severe, he could not help but smirk.

"The Fujitas are working at the military medical facilities?"

"No. They help but mostly remain at the Shima Clinic in the city."

"Arrange a flight to Hiroshima tomorrow morning. Get one as early as possible. We will round up this nest of spies all at once!"

"I am already on it, Major," Saito answered. Then he paused and said, "But who arranged their orders?"

Tanaka thought a moment. Then he looked over at Saito.

"Do you know a lieutenant colonel who is working here? One who does not look full Japanese?"

Saito thought for a moment, then shook his head.

"Strange," Tanaka said.

He left the room without further comment and turned toward the exit door. The guard snapped to attention, and Tanaka grabbed the logbook. He looked at the names.

"Which is the lieutenant colonel who left a few minutes ago, soldier?"

The soldier, a different guard than the one they had interviewed earlier, glanced at the book.

"I don't know, Sir. Here is his sign-in name."

The soldier pointed at the Kanji letters. Tanaka wrote the name down and went back to the administration offices.

When he asked about the officer, a clerk told him he was from Imperial Headquarters, often visiting to get intelligence for planning.

"Does anyone know him?" The clerk shrugged, he did not know of any relationships with the staff.

When Tanaka returned to his office, Saito hung up the phone. "We depart at 0400 tomorrow. We will be on a Hakajima transport. Exclusively yours." Laughing, Saito looked at Tanaka for approval.

"Very good," Tanaka said dismissively. His mind was on the lieutenant colonel. *Who was he, and what was his real business here?* Tanaka decided to check on the man with his sources at Imperial Army headquarters upon their return from Hiroshima.

Before taking his seat, Tanaka cast his sights toward the open suitcase on Saito's desk. "You'd better lock up your books, Sergeant."

Hiroshima, Honshu, Japan
Monday Morning, 6 August 1945

After a three-hour flight, Major Tanaka's plane landed at Hiroshima Army Airfield south of the city at 0715. An Army sedan and driver were waiting for him and Sergeant Saito. Tanaka and Saito wore their standard Kempei uniforms. Each man had one small valise. A few people were emerging from various shelters. Their driver explained that a B-san had just passed over the city, triggering an air raid alert. Tanaka told him curtly, "Take us to the Shima Surgical Clinic."

At that moment, a specially modified B-29 that history would remember, named *Enola Gay*, was approaching Shikoku, one of the main home islands directly south of Honshu. The bomber, carrying the first atomic bomb to be used in warfare, sped along at 230 miles per hour toward its initial point about eleven miles east of Hiroshima. Two other B-29s accompanied the fateful bomber, dropping instruments to measure the weapon's effect and photographing the event.

The Kempei major was blissfully unaware of the impending catastrophe about to befall the city. As they rode to the clinic, Tanaka reveled in his plan. *Today is the day I will finally arrest Dr. and Mrs. Fujita before the hospital staff.* They would then travel to Hiroshima Castle, apprehend Lieutenant Gunji and begin interrogations. Due to the morning traffic congestion, reaching their destination took more than thirty minutes.

As they neared the clinic, Saito asked Tanaka what he had learned of the mysterious lieutenant colonel at their field office. Tanaka had spent the afternoon tracking the man's activities through a friend at Imperial Headquarters.

"Do you remember the Richard Sorge spy ring back in 1941?" Tanaka asked.

"Yes," Saito answered. "Sorge was a Communist agent of German-Russian descent, as I recall. He worked as a correspondent for a German newspaper. While secretly working for the Soviet Union, he tried to warn Stalin of the pending Nazi attack on the Soviet Union in June 1941. Our government sentenced him to death last year. I believe. No one in Moscow believed him."

"Correct. According to my sources, Lieutenant Colonel Nakamura – was one of the key players behind the scenes in breaking the case and Sorge's arrest. He is a virulent anti-Communist."

"Then he is a good man. And Sorge was a good spy."

"Yes, and Sorge protected his clandestine radio for a long time."

Saito realized this was another slap at his carelessness with the now missing evidence. But not to worry, they had methods of making people talk.

Tanaka surveyed the morning traffic.

"I must get to know this Colonel Nakamura when we return to Tokyo."

Saito was silent, then spoke lowly, "I hear rumors of a peace proposal to the Americans."

"Yes," Tanaka answered, "Nothing will come of it. The Cabinet has a solid veto of any proposal that yields in any way to this Potsdam Declaration the Americans and her allies came up with. Of course, the unconditional surrender clause will kill any negotiated settlement. We have nothing to fear. When the Americans hit our beaches, it will be a bloodbath their people will never tolerate."

"But I hear the Soviet Union annulled the neutrality pact with our government. That seems ominous." Saito worried.

"It was expected. Russia has much to gain if she recovers territory, not to mention the loss of face for her defeat by our forces in 1905. But I think we have adequate forces in Manchukuo to handle the Red Army."

"You are sure of the cabinet holding firm?" Saito countered.

"Indeed. General Anami will refuse any terms unfavorable to the Empire. All he has to do is resign, and the government will fall. Then the Emperor has to find a new Prime Minister."

Tanaka was speaking of the War Minister and his role in the Cabinet.

"No, Sergeant," Tanaka continued, "You need not worry about our Empire cowering before the Americans. We will fight to the last man, woman, and child. Nothing will cause us to accept their terms."

"Sadly, we have defeatists in high places."

"And that is why our mission today is so important, Saito. When we bring in a nest of spies, the peace movement will tremble. That is why we, the Kempeitai, exist – to keep defeatists in their place. Better yet, to root them out."

Saito said nothing more.

They passed over the T-shaped Aioi bridge, turned right, and then left into the parking area of the Shima Clinic. The two Kempei men dismounted from the vehicle and strolled straight into the building. The time was 0755. At that moment, the Enola Gay approached its initial point, and the pilot prepared to bank to the west, directly toward the city.

Met by an orderly who did not know about their visit, Tanaka demanded to see the clinic director. The orderly told Tanaka in a stammering voice that his director was away from the city. Tanaka then demanded to know where Dr. Fujita was at the moment.

"I am sorry," the orderly bowed deferentially, "He and Mrs. Fujita just left for Hiroshima Main Station to meet their daughter, Yuki; she will arrive today from Tokyo."

Tanaka smirked. He would arrest the entire family at the station.

"Let's go," he told Saito, then paused. "No, Sergeant, you stay here if his information is wrong. Detain them until I return."

With that instruction, he proceeded to the waiting car and directed the driver to proceed to Hiroshima station. It was now 0800. The drive to the station took more than ten minutes to cover the one-and-a-half-mile.

The *Enola Gay*, soaring at 31,600 feet, was approaching its release point almost three miles east of the city. At the same time, the train bearing Yuki was slowly approaching the station where her parents waited patiently on the platform by the tracks.

Dismounting from the vehicle at the station, Tanaka observed an approaching trolley off to the side as passengers queued up for boarding. Tanaka glimpsed up at the massive concrete facade as he entered the station. The three-story structure's interior provided some semblance of coolness in the warm summer morning. Strutting out to the arrival platforms, he saw a train engine three hundred yards down the tracks, slowly chugging in, its steam obscuring its shape. It appeared almost motionless.

Then, he saw the Fujitas waiting on the platform beside a large concrete pillar. The doctor wore the brown national uniform required of civilian men and carried the medical bag always required of physicians. His wife sported a long-sleeve gray blouse with her monpei trousers.

Checking a clock on the far wall, he saw it was just past 0815. As he started to move toward his quarry, the clock and the wall disappeared in a blinding flash of blue-white light.

The *Enola Gay's* bombardier had set his instruments so that when the crosshairs of his bomb site aligned over the T-shaped Aioi Bridge, the bomb named Little Boy would be released from its pinions. It fell, increasing to the speed of sound, covering more than two and a half miles to its designated target in forty-five seconds.

The B-29 immediately veered to its right, diving hard, accelerating to escape the coming shock wave. In that forty-five-second interval, the bomb traveled its trajectory, detonating just five hundred feet from the Aioi Bridge, 1,900 feet above the Shima Clinic with a force of 15,000 tons of TNT. Sergeant Saito, along with everyone in the clinic, died instantly.

At Hiroshima Station, before Tanaka could even think of raising his hands to protect himself, there came a loud clap followed by a force of the super-hot wind that sent him flying toward the tracks right where the Fujitas had been standing.

There was an eerie silence in the station for a moment, then bedlam erupted. People screamed or cried in pain. The roof had collapsed. The Fujitas, shielded by the massive concrete pillar out on the platform, had been knocked over by the shockwave. As they helped each other stand up, they carefully checked each other for injuries. Then, they noticed a man lying on the tracks beneath their feet. Instinctively, Dr. Makato Fujita leaped down to examine him.

"He's unconscious; his head is bleeding. Hand me my bag." As Tanaka surmised, Dr. Fujita usually carried his medical bag with him. Quickly applying a bandage against the wound on the man's forehead, Fujita noticed the burn scar on his face. He knelt, scrutinizing the man as if in a trance.

"What's wrong?" Sumiko asked.

For a moment, Dr. Fujita did not answer. Then, looking up to his wife, he said, "I have treated him before. In Tokyo, after the March fire raid. He's the Kempei officer who is looking for us."

Then he lifted Tanaka to his feet and sat him on the platform. They carefully laid him on his back.

"Yuki! Her train is here!" Sumiko shouted as she rushed down the platform, joining other people waiting for their family members. People stumbled out of the carriages. Folks were bleeding, obviously from broken debris. Searching through the crowd of injured passengers, and despite the dust that coated the young woman's face, Sumiko immediately recognized her daughter squatting near one of the cars. Yuki's head was bleeding, and held her left arm with her right hand. Heart pounding in fear and relief, Sumiko knelt in front of her daughter; she gasped, "Oh my Baby, you are injured." Momentarily, Sumiko was unsure what to do – embrace or lead her away.

Yuki looked up, obviously suffering from shock, looking vacantly past her mother.

"What happened, Mama?"

Sumiko whispered. "The city was bombed."

She called for Makato, who was already rushing toward them.

The doctor had been thinking of others a moment before but had now turned his full attention to his daughter. His facial expression could not hide his fatherly concern. He checked the wound on her head,

"Superficial cut from glass, I think," his voice betrayed his concern. "Please get my antiseptic and cotton from my bag." Sumiko did so and held Yuki while he cleaned the wound. "Yuki will need stitches, for sure."

"Her arm," Sumiko said. "She is holding her left arm."

Dr. Fujita carefully ran his finger over the sleeve. A bone protruded through the torn, blood-soaked garment. Without looking up at his wife, he said, "Yuki has a complex fracture; we must immobilize it."

"Yuki, did you travel alone?"

Still dazed, Yuki could only mutter, "Yes," and fainted.

"Lay her down. I'll make a sling, but first, let's bandage it." Dr. Fujita turned to his wife. Mama looked around the platform and saw several small cases scattered along the ground. She grabbed a bag and opened it. Finding a few blouses, she took one and tore it into strips. Dr. Fujita opened his medical bag and withdrew a syringe and a bottle. "This may help for a while. I need more supplies." He injected Yuki's arm. "Thank God you are alive," he whispered. Seeing that Mama had Yuki's arm immobilized and bandaged, he rose.

"I will check outside. Maybe we can get her to the clinic."

Dr. Fujita carefully stepped around the injured and the dead. His instinct again was to stop and treat people, but he knew he did not have the medical supplies he would need.

When he reached the station's front doors, he stood stunned at the scene before him. The city had disappeared. It happened in seconds. To Dr. Fujita's left, a curtain of dark, purple smoke boiled upward into a mushroom-shaped cloud hundreds of feet into the morning sky. Through raging fires out beyond the station parking area, beyond the flattened buildings, he saw that the bomb had practically leveled everything. He looked where Shima clinic should be and saw nothing but a wasteland. Not far from the station entrance, a trolley burned, and he saw the smoldering bodies of people who minutes earlier had been waiting to board the transportation to the city's interior. There were many more dead and dying people laying out before him. Others stumbled about as if looking for something or someone. Several were half-naked and seemed to have skin dangling from their arms. He shook his head and went back to his wife and daughter.

"Can we get Yuki and any of these people to the clinic?" Sumiko asked.

"There is no clinic; I did not see anything resembling an intact building," he answered numbly.

Mama Sumiko started to the front, but he held her arm. "You may not want to see this."

"I've seen Tokyo. There is very little that can shock me now. You stay with our daughter – and Mr. Tanaka."

She returned a few minutes later, her face ashen.

"The city is gone; nothing is there."

Makato Fujita looked about. The doctor knew he must treat people with whatever means he had. Looking back down the tracks, the train Yuki arrived on seemed intact; another lay on its side on an adjacent railbed. The engineer of Yuki's train was standing by his locomotive as if trying to determine if it was workable. Fujita walked down the platform and spoke to him.

"Did you see anything?"

The railman shook his head.

"Only a glaring flash; I applied the brakes, and the jolt knocked me down instantly. When I could stand, I found my assistant engineer … unconscious. I saw a big dark purple cloud rising in the air."

"Is your train workable? Will you be returning on your route today?"

"I don't know."

"I am a doctor. Take your time; you are in shock; sit and rest a while. I see no hospitals from here. Shortly, we must find a way to evacuate people up the line to medical facilities."

"Yes, that is probably the thing to do." The engineer seemed to be coming to his senses.

When Makato returned to the women, Tanaka was staring at them. He mumbled something about arresting them. Makato smiled and thought, "You are in no shape or position to arrest anyone, my friend."

Yuki was slowly recovering from her earlier state of shock. She held her hand out to her father. "Gunji-san is at the castle. Do you think it is okay there?"

He looked at her sadly and shook his head. "I could see nothing in that direction but fires."

Yuki bowed her head, a tear trickling down her face. At that moment, Sumiko realized the small house they rented no longer existed. What they now owned here in Hiroshima was on their person. All their other possessions remained in Nikko.

The rest of the morning, Dr. Fujita and Mama helped survivors as much as possible. He met another doctor who tried to help people until he ran out of supplies. Dr. Fujita then decided to conserve the limited supplies in his bag. He would use what he had left to care for Yuki.

"We cannot possibly help all the people who were injured. Several died as I attended to them," the other doctor told Fujita.

Dr. Fujita nodded. He had limited capabilities under the circumstances. Both men knew their limitations as well as their obligations. Sumiko used her nursing skills as best she could to make people comfortable. Survivors wandered into the ruined building, seeking help because there was nowhere to go. Now, Sumiko looked around for assistance, but the other doctor had disappeared. Without warning, black rain fell —large marble-sized drops, cold to the touch. Several blotted Makato's jacket before he found shelter with Sumiko and Yuki.

Around noon, the engineer of the intact train told them he would take injured refugees up the line. Fujita told him they had travel permits. The engineer, joined by the conductor, told him travel permits were not needed; this was a disaster. The assistant engineer, now recovered, blew the engine's whistle.

"We must get to Tokyo, then Nikko. My guess is a Tokyo train will be up the line. I will stop where there is more medical help and offload passengers. Then I will come back and take more."

As they started toward the train, Sumiko put her hand on her husband's arm.

"What about him?" Gesturing toward Tanaka, who sat propped against a stone pillar in stunned confusion. "We cannot leave him here."

"But he is trying to arrest us!"

"For whatever reason, he has been delivered into our hands again. We cannot abandon him. I sense we are to care for him. Our Master said to love our enemies. We cannot leave him here to die."

Yuki also looked at her father and nodded her assent. Makato Fujita knew it was fruitless to argue with his wife and daughter. He handed his medical bag to Sumiko, lifted the injured Kenpeitai officer to his feet, and walked him to the train. They found a car with room for the four of them.

Shortly after the hour, the train backed out of the partially destroyed structure. Along the way, it stopped where there were medical facilities to drop off the wounded. Makado replenished some of his supplies and found time to reset Yuki's arm. In smaller villages, people offered the passengers water and some rice balls. They changed trains once.

It took two days for them to reach Tokyo. They decided to push on to Nikko. Their long-held travel permits allowed them to make the last leg unmolested. Tanaka slept most of the time, concussed. Yuki's arm remained in the sling, and she rarely complained about pain. Yuki stared out of the window of the train, grieving the loss of countless lives and the beautiful Hiroshima.

Before the train departed for Nikko, the Fujitas had heard rumors that a super bomb had hit Hiroshima. Three days after arriving home in Nikko, the Fujitas heard about the devastation in Nagasaki. Now, more than ever, they felt confident the war was over.

212

Twenty-four

A sense of relief settled over me. Knowing my Japanese family had missed annihilation by the Hiroshima bomb brought a sense of peace to a decades-old anxiety.

Just as I was about to ask about the rest of the story, Okita asked me about the rest of my life. My host controlled the pace of our interrelated stories; my life after the war piqued his interest. *There's not much to tell.*

"In late September 1945, my crew and I flew a bomber back to the States. I was assigned to Robins Field in central Georgia. My discharge from the service came a few months later. Eventually, Robins became a mothball site for B-29s. I went into business for myself. I wanted to be part of the Occupation Force, but there was little need for B-29 pilots in the Army Air Force.

"Since I could not return to Japan, I tried to find out about the Fujita family through military and diplomatic sources. Word came back that there was no record of them. I gave up. I was … bitter. Eventually, I married and had a child. Regretfully, my wife and I separated, but that was after my daughter had grown up and graduated from college."

Okita held his words. We were quiet for a few minutes.

"Friends are coming by in a while to meet you. I trust you do not mind?"

"Not at all, but then I must travel back to Tokyo."

"I am curious: did you ever run into any of your wartime friends or colleagues?"

I laughed. "It's funny, you should ask. Ironically, a few months after the war, I met up with my old nemesis, Major Max Adams. I was working in the military personnel office at the base in the States when his service record crossed my desk."

**Military Personnel Office, Robins Field, Georgia,
Thursday, 24 January 1946**

"Captain Reid," the senior non-commissioned officer said, "look at this guy's record. He's a genuine war hero!" He passed the personnel file over to the officer's desk.

"Hmmm, this guy sounds familiar. What did he do to be a hero?"

His record denoted a Silver Star, a Distinguished Flying Cross for valor, and three Air Medals. Perusing the assignment record, Sam noted that Major Maxwell Adams had spent his entire time in the Pacific in the Photo Reconnaissance Squadron. He then checked the flight mission record. None of the officer's very limited flying had been over Japan. Instead, he had flown over a few of the outlying islands of the Marianas on a few training missions. Such activities were unlikely to result in combat situations, leading to daring acts beyond the call of duty.

He then checked the citations and was shocked to learn that Major Adams had flown on the 10 March fire raid on Tokyo with a unit on Saipan. That was utterly impossible since he had been on Guam on the morning of March 10. It was on this mission that he supposedly was awarded the Silver Star. Few Silver Stars were handed out in the XX Bomber Command. The criteria were strict, restraining awards of the Distinguished Flying Cross and the Air Medal. He noted Major Adams also received the Distinguished Flying Cross and Air Medals for bombing missions over Japan when he was the assistant operations officer of the recon squadron. In other words, his record of unit assignments and his flight record did not match the citations for the awards.

"Why are you smiling, Captain?" the old Master Sergeant asked.

"Want to help me hang an officer who falsified government documents?"

Puzzled, the sergeant looked at him quizzically, then grinned and nodded.

Piece by piece, they figured out that Max was assigned to the Supply Squadron. Captain Reid found a number and called him. He introduced himself as an acquaintance from a previous assignment at the Boeing plant in Wichita in 1944. He invited him to drink at the Officers Club Friday evening at 1900. Then, he opened the Yellow Pages of the phone book and found a costume store in Macon, eighteen miles up the highway.

Friday evening, arriving fifteen minutes late, Reid strutted into the Officers Club bar wearing a dark civilian suit and sporting a graying mustache, hair-piece, and a pair of tinted glass spectacles. He sighted Max standing at the bar in his service uniform, displaying all the fraudulent ribbons. He walked over and introduced himself.

Max looked at him closely, "You look sort of familiar. Where did you say we met?"

"Wichita, 1944," Sam answered as he ordered Max a drink, a double Scotch. "I was working with Boeing there. We were producing B-29s there like hotcakes. You were there to pick up a new B-29." He ordered a club soda for himself, feigning a stomach ulcer.

Max continued to stare at him. "You remind me of someone."

Sam laughed, "You know, a lot of people say that about me. Anyway, I heard you were assigned here and thought I'd look you up for ole times' sake. I know so few people here."

"You have a Southern accent. What do you do here at Robins?"

"I'm from southern Georgia. I'm a contractor here, unlike my work in Wichita. You remember I was with Boeing there."

Max looked a little confused. He gulped his scotch and muttered, "Oh yeah, I think I remember." All to say, he did not but decided to be polite to someone paying for the drinks.

"So, Max, what did you do in the war?" Sam asked. "Looks like you saw a lot of action."

Max swallowed another gulp. "Yeah, it was pretty rough out there. Flew out of the Marianas."

"Oh, which island?"

"Mainly out of Saipan and Tinian. Spent time on Guam at first, Tinian was the last place."

Sam twirled his mustache, knowing he had just heard a fairy tale.

"Any missions over Japan?" he asked.

"Oh yeah, I got all thirty-five required ones in as an aircraft commander. I can't talk about the ones at Tinian."

"Nah," Sam faked his disbelief, "Don't tell me you were the 509th Composite Group!" The 509th was the unit responsible for the atomic missions against Hiroshima and Nagasaki.

Max poked out his chest and took another drink. "I really can't talk about it. Let's just say I helped end the war."

"Well, I'll be!" Sam shook his head. "You aren't radioactive, I hope?" Sam held out his hands, then stepped back mockingly.

Max finally showed some humor. "I only glow in the dark when there's no full moon."

"So, what do you do here?"

Max took another sip, emptying his glass, saying, "I can't talk about it too much. I have a cover over at the Supply Squadron."

Sam ordered another round of drinks, ensuring Max was getting doubles. They continued to chat for some time. By and by, Sam asked Max to join him for dinner in the dining room.

"On me," he added, "The least I can do for a guy who put his life on the line with thirty-five missions over Japan."

"Sure," Max assented, and they headed to the dining room.

Over dinner, Sam deliberately kept Max's wine glass full and ordered another double Scotch for him as they discussed the war and the rebuilding of Japan and Germany.

"I tell you, we ought to let the Japs rot. Don't help 'em at all. Kill 'em all, the slant-eyed monsters."

He went on interminably with this manner of insults and degrading commentary to Sam's ire, But Sam kept a straight face.

"Did you ever meet any Japanese?" Sam asked.

"Hell, no, and I don't want to. The only good Jap is a dead Jap. We should have A-bombed the entire country."

"Tell me about your Tinian adventures – I mean, what you can talk about."

Max drained his wine glass. "Can't say much," he started slurring his words.

"It was pretty unnerving hauling those bombs, though."

This guy is so full of himself. The lies he's making up will catch up with him. After dinner, Sam bought him one more drink, then suggested they drive up to

Macon, pick up some women, and see what the night brings. Max agreed. In the Club parking lot, Sam insisted he drive Max's car as he knew a good place to go.

Max tossed him the car keys without argument and crawled into the passenger side. He was already half asleep. Sam drove around on base for a few minutes. When he heard Max snoring, he headed into the officer family housing area, straight to the base commander's house. He made sure the lights were out in the home.

The commander's wife had a reputation for her beautiful camellia bushes adorning the front yard of the expansive senior officer quarters. Sam used his handkerchief to wipe his prints off the steering wheel and then aimed the car across the lawn into the camellia flora. The vehicle drifted slowly over the curb across the winter grass and smack into the bushes.

He quickly exited the vehicle. With the motor still running in neutral, Sam hastily pulled Max's inert body across the cloth-covered seat so that the man was lying near the steering wheel.

Then Sam walked away. It was just a short distance back to the Officer's Club, where he had parked his vehicle.

Monday would be an exciting day.

Nikko
March 1985

Okita's expression remained bland. Oh, but reading the disapproval in his eyes wasn't hard.

"You left him for your military police?"

I laughed. "Indeed I did! Yes, he was in trouble enough with the base commander's wife for the destruction of her precious camellias, not to mention driving while intoxicated. That was nothing compared to the report my personnel sergeant sent up the chain late Friday afternoon. Major Max Adams suddenly was under investigation for falsifying government records by Monday afternoon. Even more reprehensible were his false claims in those records of being something he wasn't. A lot of people died doing what he claimed he did."

"What happened to him?"

"Eventually, he resigned his commission in lieu of court-martial. That's the last I ever heard of him. Max tried telling the investigators about a civilian contractor who drove his car. It's a shame he couldn't be more convincing or have any evidence, but the investigators held the falsified records. I hear he turned pale when they showed him the contradictions."

"Hmmm."

"If you think I regret what I did, I have never lost a moment of sleep over it."

"Yes, I see," Okita tugged at his earlobe.

"And did you ever hear from any of your old crew-mates?"

"No, not the ones on Tinian. I did run into a couple of Dallas' old crew in Georgia. They were transferred to a new unit on Guam late in the war."

"Ah?" Okita said with interest, "Why were they transferred?"

"Well, a new bomber wing arrived at Guam in April. The primary targets became Japan's oil and coal industry."

"I recall my country was recoiling from such attacks,"

"Yes, Pop, Dixie, and the others flew the unit's last two missions. As a matter of fact, I heard they flew the last bombing missions of the war."

I continued, "As I understand the situation, those final bombing missions occurred while your government was struggling to surrender."

Northwest Field, Guam, The Marianas
Mid-Afternoon, 14 August 1945

Sweltering inside their bomber, Pop, Al, Dixie, and the other crewmembers waited impatiently for the order to start engines for their second mission with the 315th Bombardment Wing.

The members of the *Lake Blackshear* crew were ordered across the island to replace a crew quarantined with a tropical rash. The new modified B-29B was a step above their beloved *Lake Blackshear*; equipped with Eagle radar, the bomber was capable of all-weather precision targeting. The plane's bottom was painted black, affording it protection against searchlights on night missions. The aircraft's first crew had stenciled the name *Pitch Black* on her nose. Unlike *Lake Blackshear*, which had retained the capability to have its four gun turrets operational, the newer bomber lacked those defenses and had only its tail gun.

They had flown with the regular aircraft commander on a mission the night of 9 August against an oil refinery at Amagasaki. Al Rocco, who earned his pilot status in his former unit, flew as the co-pilot. A new bombardier took Al's old position. At Northwest Field, their newest member, a new radar operator, joined the crew and sat beside Bill Meeks at the navigator's desk. Amagasaki had been a rough mission with severe anti-aircraft flak. The team returned safely, but the aircraft commander came down with the same symptoms as his sick crew members the following day. Squadron headquarters assigned a pilot who happened to be senior to Al Rocco by two weeks.

First Lieutenant Richard Thomas was a real martinet who immediately alienated the crew with his arrogant military bearing. He called the men together and dressed them down, telling them he would not tolerate sloppy uniforms and familiarity between the officers and enlisted men.

"You will not speak to me or each other by first names," he ordered, strutting back and forth as the men stood at attention in the tropical heat.

"You will always observe strict radio procedures; I will not put up any informal chit-chat." The crew inwardly boiled. The one thing they knew about him was he had never flown a combat mission. They had ten under their belts.

"Dismissed," he flung out, and waited for their salutes. As the pompous officer turned to walk away, Pop Warner decided something needed to be said.

"Lieutenant Thomas, I need to speak with you," Pop raced to catch up to his rapid pace.

"What do you want, Sergeant?" His reply was curt as he continued walking.

"I want to give you some good advice, Sir, before you foul up a very great crew."

"That's pretty insubordinate of you, Sergeant Warner, isn't it?"

"That's my name, Lieutenant, and you haven't seen insubordination yet. But keep that attitude around this crew, and you will. Now listen to me carefully, sonny."

Thomas' face turned purple with rage, but Pop, who stood several inches higher, closed the gap between them and glowered down into the man's face before he could speak.

"We know about you, Lieutenant. You've never flown a mission against the Empire or against any other Japanese fortification except the milk runs out to Truk Atoll. But this, this will be your first real combat mission. This crew has survived ten, and it wasn't because they were sloppy in their duties. They're experienced professional airmen who know their jobs.

"They survived close calls and never failed to deliver the mail to the enemy. I'm telling you what they expect of you, whether you want to hear it or not. You had better know how to fly that damned bomber through heavy flak and thermals. Because if you don't, you and the rest of us won't be coming back."

Pop paused, caught his breath, and continued, "Am I clear, Lieutenant?"

The young officer stood motionless, shocked; he scowled toward the ground. His anger, still visible, was turning to embarrassment.

"Okay, Sergeant Warner," he swallowed hard, "what do you suggest?"

"Lighten up. Your co-pilot is a rated officer who can fly the plane when you need him; treat him as a professional. He's got a helluva lot more combat hours than you. Get to know your crew as fast as you can. All this peace talk we're hearing may come to nothing. No telling how many more missions we have ahead of us."

Pop saluted smartly and turned to walk away, then stopped and looked over his shoulder, "Don't worry, we'll bring you through; we always do. We expect the same of you."

That evening, Thomas caught up with Al Rocco coming out of the mess tent. They walked together until Thomas broke the silence. "Say, Al, can we talk about these missions?"

"Yes, Sir, Lieutenant. What would you like to know?"

"Uh, just call me Dick," Thomas tried to sound friendly.

Al stopped and turned to face Thomas.

"What's the catch?"

"No catch, I'd like for you to tell me about the flak and the thermals."

"Okay, then, Dick. Flak speaks for itself. Nothing you can really do about it. If they have your number, they hit the plane. So far, we've been lucky.

What you want to do is dodge the searchlights. Once they lock onto you, the enemy gunners have a target. We'll be dumping lots of the aluminum foil strips to confuse their radar. So, be ready to dance and weave that monster of an airplane to get out of the light beams."

"You've been through that experience?"

"Several times. It's hairy, but you get the hang of it. We've been lucky – or maybe blessed."

Thomas nodded "What about these thermals?"

"On my first mission – I was the bombardier then – we got caught in severe thermals. It was on Operation Meetinghouse."

Lieutenant Thomas gaped noticeably, astonished. "You were on Meetinghouse?"

"Yep. Thermals hit us just after bombs away. Flipped us on our back. Now that was hairy!"

"You were inverted over the target?" Thomas asked, clearly in awe.

"Yeah, you looked 'up,' and all you saw was an inferno. Of course, we were being pushed several hundred feet higher in altitude."

"How did you get through it?"

Al looked directly at Thomas. "The best pilot in the Army Air Force," he answered proudly, almost reverently.

"Our pilot remembered his small plane training; he dropped the nose and let the air currents continue the flip until we were right side up. We were still diving toward the flames below, but he leveled us off, and we got the hell out of there. No, our pilot did it all, including an all-or-nothing landing as we ran out of fuel. I think a few other planes experienced this phenomenon."

"Did his co-pilot help him?"

Al scoffed. "His co-pilot was a junior flight officer fresh from the States. The man froze; went into shock. I believe they shipped him home once the mission ended. I became the co-pilot on the way back from that mission and helped to get us back to Guam."

"Where is that pilot now?"

"Oh, he got transferred out to Tinian the next day. Word is he cold-cocked a senior officer, a real prima donna major that no one liked. The squadron commander did not want the hassle of a court-martial even though several of us would testify it was self-defense."

Al stopped talking and looked down at the ground.

Thomas saw something like sadness flicker across Al's face. "So, is he still flying out of Tinian?"

Al shook his head. "Nope, His plane went down over Osaka; he didn't come back. A friend wrote me about it."

"Who was this guy?"

Al looked up and respectfully said, "Wade, Captain Dallas Wade."

The two lieutenants were silent as they continued to walk toward their officer quarters.

"Have you piloted through thermals?" Thomas asked.

"Oh, yeah, Nothing like Meetinghouse, though. Never been flipped. You learn to anticipate it and fly through it. You will have to be alert over those oil refineries. It's going to be hot and windy. Don't worry; I'll be there beside you. We'll make it through."

Thomas nodded. "Okay."

"Look, Dick, you have a good, seasoned crew. The bombardier who replaced me hits his targets when you turn the plane over to him. The other guys are experts; for instance, Dixie stays alert on the radio, and Bill Meeks is a great navigator; he'll work well with the new radar operator. Our tail gunner has bagged a couple of fighters who got too close to our rear. Larry Wynns saved our rear ends on the Meetinghouse mission by spotting another bomber about to unload his bomb directly above us. Pop Warner? He's the best flight engineer in the command; he'll keep those darn unpredictable engines humming."

Al paused as Thomas looked over at him.

"You'll see, we're a pretty good team."

"I've never taken a fully loaded bomber off before," Thomas admitted. "You hear stories about those that don't get into the air and …"

"Don't fret over it. I'll be by your side calling off the ground speed. At the right moment, we gently bring the yoke back, and we'll let it fly itself off the end of the runway."

"Okay, thanks for the advice." Thomas nodded. "Here's my hooch. See you tomorrow."

At noon, 14 August, the crew received their briefing on the night's mission. They were startled to learn they would fly the longest mission of the war – 3,800 miles to an oil refinery at Akita in northern Honshu. They were hoping for confirmation of the surrender rumors. Five days had passed since the second atomic bomb had detonated over Nagasaki.

Before boarding *Pitch Black* at mid-afternoon, Dick Thomas pulled Al aside.

"Al, disregard the date of rank stuff. How about you fly as aircraft commander tonight and let me be co-pilot?"

Al questioned his suggestion but said, "Okay, let's go." They climbed up the ladder in the nose wheel to the cockpit. Before taking his seat, Thomas stopped at the flight engineer station.

"Have we enough fuel to make it, Pop?"

The older man looked up from his gauges and smiled at the young officer. "I'll save us a gallon or two in case you want to take a victory spin around the island."

Both men chuckled.

The crew waited several minutes before they received the "go" signal, and Al radioed to Pop to start the engines.

As the four engines reverberated in the tropical heat, Al glanced at Thomas, carefully studying his gauges while gripping his yoke.

"Maybe this will be the last mission, Dick."

"Let's hope so."

"Yeah, my first — and last," Thomas replied.

Near 1600 hours, the island's radio station received an "urgent" bulletin from Japan's Domei News Agency that stated an Imperial message accepting the Potsdam Declaration would be forthcoming. Shortly thereafter, the B-29s began to shut down their engines. Hopes soared that the mission was a scrub. But half an hour later, the start engines signal came. The mission was on.

Twenty-five

I discontinued telling my story. I remembered I wanted to know about the man with the suitcase. *Is this a good time to switch the subject from me to someone else?* I took a whiff of fresh, crisp air to clear my lungs and change the conversation.

"What happened to the man – Mr. Nakamura, who came to the Fujita family before I left for college? He had a connection with the Kempeitai from what you have told me."

My host nodded. "Mr. Nakamura was a Kempei officer. He knew of Major Tanaka's interest in the Fujita family."

"So why was a Kempei officer acting against Japan's interests – or her foreign policies?"

Okita spoke, almost as if he were speaking to someone else, somewhere else.

"Nakamura was a loyal, patriotic Japanese citizen. Yet he had a more pressing interest. You see, Reid-San, my friend, Nakamura deeply respected the Emperor, as did his wife. Yet he despised the militarists who were running our country."

"Wait a minute! Did not your Emperor play his role in leading Japan into war?" Without waiting for his response, I kept the questions going. "And prosecuting it?"

Memories of my youth flooded back. Growing up in Japan under the so-called Imperial Way, I had seen its aggression in Manchuria and China. While I had not seen the photographs of Nanking that Mr. Nakamura had shown the adults in 1939, my father told me about them.

How could the Emperor not know these things?

Okita, discerning my strident accusative tone, stroked his chin, thoughtfully. "Yes, in a manner of speaking. But you see, someone, especially from a Western democracy, can't understand just how dysfunctional our government was."

He paused as if gathering his thoughts. Then he continued, "You probably realize the so-called Manchuria Incident was contrived and executed by the Imperial Army on the Asian mainland without cabinet consent."

"Yes, the Kwantung Army Group," I muttered knowingly.

"So, you also know that this aggression was executed without sanction from Tokyo?"

I nodded, confirming my awareness of that step toward World War II.

"Yes," he continued, "you can say the Emperor acquiesced to this incident. But you also must appreciate his overall role in the government."

I nodded for Okita to continue.

"As a young man, the future Emperor was trained to be a father figure to his people. While he would assume his role as head of state, he would do so without ever directing any specific policy. When he spoke at all, he usually did so in the vaguest of terms."

I had heard this before from other sources when I debated how Japan and the West stumbled into a disastrous war. But it did not make much sense to me. Okita was right; I didn't clearly understand it. I started to say so when Okita turned back to look at me and continued.

"Tradition was – and is – very important in Japanese life. The Emperor would not withhold his consent once the Cabinet and the military leaders agreed on a policy or a course of action."

"But was not your Emperor the commander in chief of the military, with the same authority as our president?"

"Yes, of course," he answered. "Under the Meiji Constitution established during his grandfather's reign, he held that authority and, by default, the responsibility. But please understand the way people thought back then. The Emperor was revered as a god to the people, including the military. Not like the Christian God but a man-god descended from the gods. He commanded great affection as well as obligation."

"It still doesn't make much sense that the military could just lead Japan into war."

"From your perspective, it is true. But, events took on a life of their own. Well, let us say the military just took responsibility for national policy unto themselves."

"But still seeking his approval."

"True, but often in retrospect." He looked directly at me and continued, "For that reason, your perspective is correct, but from a westerner's point of view. Yet he did assert his authority to end the war. Even then, it was a near-run thing. And that is where our friend, Mr. Nakamura, comes in."

"A near-run thing?" I asked, obviously puzzled. I thought I knew the sequence of the war's end. President Truman and British Prime Minister Churchill demanded unconditional surrender, and the Japanese government refused. The United States dropped two atomic bombs, and six days later, they quickly accepted the Allies' terms.

"You're telling me the surrender was more complicated than most of us assume?"

Cherry blossoms drifted down around us. I noticed a chill in the spring air. I tapped one foot, then the other, to keep circulation going.

Okita again looked beyond me into another time and place. Describing the defeat of Napoleon at Waterloo in June 1815 as a "the nearest run thing you ever saw …", the Duke of Wellington's victory pronouncement could well have applied to the end of the Second World War.

The Fujita family's confidence that World War II was nearly over was premature by almost a week. The B-29 crews in the Marianas anxiously awaited good news on August 14. They waited in the hope this mission was truly the last. More likely, most hoped they would not have to fly that night. They could not know the excruciatingly slow pace of the Japanese government's decision to surrender.

Okita continued, "The way to war's end was complicated and contentious among Japanese leaders. Even after the second atomic bomb attack, die-hard militarists in the Japanese cabinet insisted on fighting the decisive battle on the home islands."

"Ketsu-go," I spoke knowingly. Our intelligence people learned later this strategy involved elaborate plans for inflicting massive casualties on allied invaders – both at sea and on the beaches – using not only military personnel and massive suicide teams, but civilians as well.

"Yes, indeed," Okita added. "They hoped to bring about a termination of the war on terms favorable to Japan. You see, following the March firebombing of Tokyo, the Emperor toured the devastated area. He knew Japan was defeated but needed a way to bring about an early conclusion. The defeat of Germany and Italy left Japan alone against the world. That fact served to bolster his convictions. Then came the loss of Okinawa."

"So why not just end it and spare all the misery?" I asked accusingly.

"That is where it got complicated. Within our cabinet, there was a sub-cabinet – The Supreme Council for the Direction of the War. Known as the Big Six, it consisted of our Prime Minister, Foreign Minister, War Minister, and Navy Minister, as well as the Chiefs of Staff of the Army and Navy. Any war termination decision required unanimity, not consensus, within the Big Six and the full cabinet. Furthermore, the resignation of any cabinet member would cause the government to collapse. A governmental collapse would ensure the continuation of the war."

"It's a wonder any action could be taken." I could only shake my head.

"True enough. When the allied leaders demanded unconditional surrender at the Potsdam Conference in May of that year, it only hardened the militarists' resolve. Even the Soviet Union's entry into the Pacific war did not shake them from their determination."

"How did Japan get to the surrender decision?"

Okita's head dropped toward his chest as if he were praying. He remained silent, collecting his thoughts. I felt no urge to rush him. I sensed he must be remembering his painful times. Finally, he went on.

"The Emperor spoke." After another few moments of silence, he continued, "He had to say it twice, once on August 9 after the Nagasaki atomic bomb and again on August 14. He stated his loss of confidence in the military and asked his subordinates to 'bear the unbearable.' It was very difficult."

"Why did he have to say it twice?"

"Because of the demands for preserving the Imperial system, our Kokutai. Some felt the allies' response to the Emperor's status was vague. Yet, during the final conference, the Emperor assured he had confidence in the allies' goodwill. And so, we got full cabinet approval to accept the allies' Potsdam Declaration. It was then just a matter of the Emperor recording a rescript announcing this to the nation on August 15."

I remember my bombing missions before the surrender. "We continued our bombing right up through the night of August 14 and the following day."

"Unfortunately, yes."

"But then, perhaps not so unfortunately, because that is where our friend Nakamura plays his part."

Twenty-six

Ana Oshima peeked down at her breakfast of miso soup and half of sweet potato, whispered a prayer of thanksgiving and crossed herself. Ana looked up at her husband, Lieutenant Colonel Fujihara Nakamura, who returned her look with a loving and sympathetic face.

"I am sorry there is not more. It is sparse in the markets."

"We're better off than many of our neighbors," he answered to encourage her and lift her spirits. "You have done a marvelous job caring for our home and preparing a feast with so little. I will see what I can bring home this evening."

As a Kempei officer, he had sources of food that ordinary citizens lacked. Many people tried to go to the countryside and bargain with farmers, bartering for food, but that activity became challenging. Farmers now were hoarding their products as shortages increased, or they demanded exorbitant prices. It was no secret that many Japanese people were on near-starvation diets.

Nakamura and his wife Ana were anxious about food, but they had heard nothing of their parents and other family members in Nagasaki, which added to their anxiety. Nakamura had asked a colleague in that city to see what he could learn. So far, all they knew was the Roman Catholic cathedral had been destroyed. Both parental families, as well as siblings, lived near the church. It was hard not knowing. Ana's parents' European features caused them to stand out among the more ethnically pure Japanese, and they became subjects of suspicion among their neighbors. Nakamura had requested his colleague to try to protect them. Ana's features had helped her play a role in the pre-war years as she had contacts in the Portuguese Consulate. That time seemed far away, surreal.

The young nurse at Kure Naval Hospital had learned too late of the plans for the Pearl Harbor attack. Ana had to make a hasty but fortuitous departure from the meeting place at the park bench before Tanaka could detain her.

"I will try to learn what happened in Nagasaki."

He watched her for a reaction and saw only sadness in her face.

"I understand they are dropping leaflets telling us to evacuate cities,"

"Yes," Nakamura stood up, took his cup of tea, and walked to the sink.

"They plan to firebomb all our cities. The Americans are humane in one respect by warning civilians to get away."

"Did they warn Hiroshima and Nagasaki?"

He shook his head. "Not that I have heard. I am not sure it would have made a difference."

"Will they continue to use this weapon?"

"I hear our leaders do not believe they have any more such weapons. They are difficult to manufacture." He swallowed, "Yet if they have such weapons, they have demonstrated a resolve to use them to achieve their purpose."

Nakamura did not tell Ana how his Kempeitai colleagues had interrogated an American fighter pilot shot down near Tokyo. After torturing the man, he confessed to them Tokyo was the next target of the atomic bomb. *Those young officers are determined to fight the Ketzu-go final battle. The interrogators were fools. How would a fighter pilot flying out of Iwo Jima know about a top-secret program?*

Still, it was plausible; there was not much to bomb in the devastated city. That was another reason to ensure the war ended sooner rather than later.

"I may be late tonight," Nakamura continued. "There is talk of a coup."

Ana looked up, startled. "A coup? Against the Emperor?"

"Not so much against the Emperor directly, against the peace faction in the cabinet. We need to identify them."

"Surely, their senior commanders would not allow such a thing, not if the Emperor forbade it!"

Nakamura sipped his tea and thought walked back to his seat. "No, I fear there may be an undercover plot of which the senior officers are unaware. Lieutenant Ida is helping me."

"I think he is a competent young man," Ana said. The couple had hosted the junior officer for dinner a few nights before. Nakamura nodded. "I do not like that he also has a sense of ruthlessness."

"Then why do you stay in the Kempeitai?" Ana asked.

Nakamura hesitated even though he fully trusted his wife. "Because it is where I perhaps can control events."

"You play a dangerous game, dear husband. We both have."

"I am in good standing ever since the Sorge case. I have tried to watch over certain people. I have used my means. And no one suspects you, be at ease about that."

"Please be careful, my love," she admonished. "Your clandestine activities may be your downfall."

Nakamura rose from his seat and reached for Ana, pulling her to her feet, and kissed her tenderly.

"Please try not to worry. But pray to your God that all will go well today."

"First, I must pray for your safety, my love," she whispered in his ear.

He smiled, and as he turned to leave, he saw Ana looking forlornly at the scraps of breakfast. He noticed, not for the first time, how thin Ana had become. His uniforms were looser.

Laying his sword across the handlebars, Nakamura rode his bicycle the six miles to the headquarters close to the Palace grounds. The August heat and humidity hung like an oppressive, hazy drapery over the city. He had become so accustomed to surveying the sights of destruction and ruins of Tokyo on his route to work that he feared becoming too callous toward the plight of his fellow Japanese. He turned his attention from the shanties and lean-tos that served as make-shift housing for people left homeless and hungry by the fire raids. Dodging bomb craters, debris, and dead animals, he pedaled swiftly to his office. Nakamura arrived at 1015, his uniform damp with sweat.

Lieutenant Ida followed behind as he entered his small office, holding a leaflet.

"Did you see these, Colonel?" Ida asked, handing the paper to Nakamura.

Nakamura took the document, and as he read the message, his heart was stricken, but he remained stoic. At that moment, a non-commissioned officer knocked at his door and bowed.

"The Commandant wishes to see you immediately, Colonel."

Nakamura walked out without replying to Ida, clutching the leaflet. As Nakamura entered the office, the Commandant stood behind his desk facing the window. He spoke without turning to acknowledge Nakamura's presence.

"It's going to be a long day, Nakamura," he sighed, "and a long night."

"More rumors, Sir?"

The commandant nodded and turned to face Nakamura. "We have reports from the field units demanding a fight to the end. I told the Chief Cabinet Secretary yesterday morning that an insurrection was possible. I also firmly suggested that we fight the final battle." The general seemed to expect a response. However, Nakamura remained mute. "And I have heard other disturbing rumors."

Nakamura waited for the senior officer to reveal the rest of the news troubling him.

"We may have a secret cell within our ranks, bent on their own will."

Nakamura inhaled audibly. The news unmasked his calmness. The Kempeitai was a ruthless organization known for its brutality with prisoners and suspected traitors and defeatists. Nakamura knew rumors of a special Kempei unit, known as the Kamo detachment in Manchukuo, that conducted gruesome medical experiments on Chinese civilians and prisoners of war. To have such people on the loose with their agenda was more than troubling. Nakamura waited for his superior to continue.

"We must keep a close watch on events, Nakamura. Check your records and see if you can detect any behavior pattern that warrants our attention."

"Yes, Sir," Nakamura replied. The commandant waved a hand, a sign for Nakamura to leave.

Since the Sorge case, Nakamura had moved to administration, keeping tabs on personnel assignments and promotions. Nakamura's reputation as an investigator was legendary within the Kempeitai. Most of his fellow officers knew he abhorred torture. The commandant refrained from pressing him into those roles. But his efficiency as an administrator and an investigator was beyond reproach. If there were potential rebellious members of the Kempeitai, Nakamura was the best man to find them.

Returning to his office, Nakamura found Lieutenant Ida still waiting and realized he still had the leaflet in his hand. Printed in Kanji characters, the paper informed the Japanese people their government was about to accept the Potsdam Declaration. Nakamura knew if it got into the hands of fanatics, the peace process could be derailed.

"So, Colonel," Ida persisted, "is it true?" He pointed to the paper in Nakamura's hand.

Nakamura's forehead furrowed. "That's not for us to debate, Lieutenant. We follow the will of the Emperor. Is that clear?"

The young man frowned and nodded.

"Now, I need a few personnel files."

Nakamura spent the rest of the morning and early afternoon checking the files of twenty officers in grades lieutenant to major. He found nothing out of the ordinary.

Unknown to Nakamura, during his morning work, the Emperor of Japan had called an Imperial Conference of the Cabinet and supreme counselors in the Palace air raid shelter. After hearing the militarist's positions favoring the decisive battle and the peace faction, the Emperor spoke. In a strained voice, he told the assembly that he wished to accept the Potsdam Declaration and end the war. He left the room as members of the gathering broke down in tears.

At noon, the Cabinet met in the Prime Minister's official residence bunker to ratify the decision. Under the Meiji Constitution, an Imperial decision still required ratification by the Cabinet. They began to debate the wording of an Imperial Rescript to announce the decision to the people of Japan.

At 1400, Nakamura rose from his desk and gave Ida another list of files he needed.

"I will be out for an hour or so, have these on my desk when I return." He departed the building and rode his bicycle to a familiar location. An old bearded man stepped out of a shanty and handed him a bag.

"Salted fish and a quarter kilo of rice," he said and stated the price. Nakamura paid an exorbitant fee for the black-market items. Then he pedaled back to his home. Entering, Nakamura called for Ana. When she did not answer, he looked around the small house and discovered a note taped to the crucifix on the wall. It read:

My Dearest Husband,

I hear of plentiful rations near Kumagaya. I am taking the train there. I will stay with my cousin and return tomorrow.

Your loving wife, Ana

A sinking feeling of despair fell over Nakamura. Today was not the time for Ana to be on a train. People continued to flee the city. Even with a Kempeitai pass, she may not find a vacant seat. Her despair concerning the food shortages pushed her to drastic measures, but that was the state of things now. He left his bag on the kitchen counter. He surveyed his dwelling, which suddenly seemed enormous and empty. Nakamura looked back at the crucifix and dared to ask Ana's God to protect her. Only a short time after, Nakamura departed for Kenpeitai Headquarters.

When he arrived at 1530, several more files had been stacked on his desk. Nakamura began to review them carefully, making copious notes. He wanted Lieutenant Ida to assist him, but the young officer was nowhere to be found.

While Nakamura had been out, the Imperial Cabinet began work on the Rescript and, also unknown to him, the Domei News Agency had sent out a FLASH message in English, signaling that the government was accepting the Potsdam Declaration.

Lieutenant Ida stepped into his office and bowed. "Sir, I looked over most of those files. I know these officers. None would fail in their loyalty to the Emperor."

Nakamura nodded and thanked Ida. "I still must check them, but thank you for your initiative. That is very helpful."

The young man seemed pleased and bowed out of the office.

As the day wore on, Nakamura continued scrutinizing the files, making notes, and cross-checking items that recurred in each man's record. By 1700, Nakamura was tired, and he stood and stretched. Looking down, something in his notes suddenly caught his attention. Several of the officers were graduates of Tokyo Imperial University. That was no great surprise, but he suddenly noted most had studied National History under Professor Kiyoshi Hiraizumi. Again, that would not seem surprising since Hiraizumi was a leading faculty member of the history department.

Nakamura looked out his window, rubbing his aching forehead. The mist had not lifted, obscuring his vision of the Palace southwest of Kempeitai headquarters. He thought of the small, shy, bespectacled man who symbolized Japan, a living god to most of his seventy million subjects, but not to Ana with her Christian beliefs, not to Nakamura himself with his secular views of the world. Yet to both, the Emperor was their appointed ruler. Even so, Nakamura knew that the Army controlled the government and Japan's decisions for the war.

As he stepped away from the window, he turned back to see the mist clear, granting him a clearer view of the Palace grounds. The mist that clouded his mind seemed to clear also. Then it hit him.

Of course, he thought, Hiraizumi taught the mythology of Japan's origins as if it were a fact of natural history. He practically brainwashed his students in the belief of emperors who, according to legend, had existed from the beginning of history. The professor asserted that Emperor Jimmu was a real person who descended from the sun goddess Amaterasu and had ascended to the throne around eighteen hundred years ago. These theories, taught as fact, would cause adherents to feel boundless gratitude and devotion to the Emperor. Was that gratitude enough to cause a coup to prevent the Emperor from the humiliation of surrendering his permanent status with the Empire?

Nakamura began to recheck the files, but was summoned to the commandant's office. Several senior officers gathered as their leader relayed an order from the War Minister. The Kempeitai would obey the Imperial command. After dismissing most of the officers, the commandant held Nakamura and two others back. Closing the door, he snorted, "Of course, you realize we will all be considered war criminals when the Allies arrive?"

No one answered, and he waved them out.

As Nakamura walked back to his office, one of the other officers confessed to him, "I have concerns about a friend of mine."

Nakamura looked at him curiously.

"He's in the War Ministry, very close to the Minister himself."

"I'm checking files now to see if we may have problems within our own nest," Nakamura shared.

"It's going to be a long night," the officer moaned as he walked away.

Unknown to Nakamura, at that time, *Pitch Black* and other bombers of the XXI Bomb Command were heading for Japan. By 2030, the Emperor of Japan had signed the Rescript announcing the acceptance of the Potsdam Declaration.

Continuing his work, Nakamura identified nine officers who were students of Professor Hiraizumi. He called Lieutenant Ida and asked him to determine their location and status. Then Nakamura sat back to worry about the pending announcement, mainly about Ana. He tried not to imagine her on the crowded train to Kumagaya.

Simultaneously, coup leaders were deploying rebel Imperial Guard troops on the Palace grounds.

At 2300, Nakamura stepped out of the building for a breath of fresh air. It continued to be stifling hot and humid, even outdoors. Then he heard the wail of air raid sirens, and the city was suddenly cast into darkness.

About that time, the Emperor had completed recording the Imperial Rescript in the Household Ministry on the Palace grounds. Imperial chamberlains secured the two copies of the recording and hid them in a safe behind a stack of papers.

At 2310, the Foreign Ministry transmitted the official acceptance of the Potsdam Declaration to the Allies through Swiss diplomatic channels.

Nakamura returned to his even more humid office, and by candlelight, he stared at the list of potential rebellious officers. He called for Lieutenant Ida, who did not respond. Nakamura rose from his desk and went in search of him. A guard at the door advised him the Lieutenant had departed the building just before Nakamura had gone outside for his break.

"Did he mention where he'd be?"

The guard told him no. Nakamura returned to his office again, sat, and thought about Ana. She should have told him about contemplating the trip to Kumagaya. Then he realized Ana knew he would forbid it and that she desperately wanted to find more provisions.

Lieutenant Ida irritated him. The young officer should have informed him of his intentions. Yet he had shown initiative in the past, so Nakamura put the thought aside and returned to his tedious work. He heard a wailful sound permeate the room as he studied the files. The lights went out.

Twenty-seven

One minute after midnight, another air raid sounded. Tokyo remained dark from the blackout.

Reports began coming into Kempeitai Headquarters about unusual activity at the Palace. Shortly after 0130, the Commandant summoned Nakamura to his office. The room was stifling hot, especially with the curtains covering the windows. Dim lighting produced by the unit's generators made seeing difficult but kept the building less detectable to enemy aircraft.

"I am concerned. One of our sergeants reported something about the murder of the commander of the Imperial Guards and a fake order being issued in his name to secure the Palace."

"Shall I go over?" Nakamura asked, clearly concerned about events.

His commander deliberated. "No, send one of the junior officers to investigate. I may need you here."

Nakamura finally saw Lieutenant Ida in the building.

"Where have you been?" Nakamura demanded.

"I went to check on the men you asked me about. All seem to be at their post or off-duty."

"Good. I have another mission for you. Go over to Imperial Guards Headquarters at the Palace, check on any unusual activity, and call me from there."

Ida bowed and departed. The Guards' headquarters was just a short walk across the road and moat.

Twenty minutes later, Nakamura's phone rang. Lieutenant Ida reported nothing unusual as far he could tell. Nakamura told Ida to return to headquarters. He reported Ida's finding to the commandant.

Aboard B-29B **Pitch Black**
0135 Hours, 15 August 1945

"Landfall," Bill Meeks radioed Al Rocco as *Pitch Black* flew over the Boso Peninsula east of Tokyo Bay, shortly after midnight.

"Roger, Bill," Al responded. "Tokyo is west of us, but it's completely dark over there."

They had hoped to receive a recall message signaling that the war was over, but Dixie assured Al that no such report had come through.

Five minutes later, they headed northwest toward their IP, an island in the Sea of Japan, west of Honshu. The bombardier entered the bomb bay to arm each of the 100-pound bombs. Half an hour later, Al turned the bomber on its final heading to Akita. Ahead, they could see the glow of the burning refinery, fires started by the fifteen or more bombers ahead of them.

"It'll be quite bumpy, Dick," Al radioed his co-pilot. "Just follow my lead. We'll turn the controls over to the bombardier in a few minutes."

"Roger," Thomas replied.

Remembering that harrowing night above Tokyo Bay in March, Al radioed Dixie and Larry Wynns, seated in their observation domes.

"Make sure we don't have a bomber above us!"

"Roger, Skipper," Dixie replied.

"All I see are the stars," Larry reported.

It was indeed a turbulent ride through the target area, but they held her steady, and as soon as he heard bombs away, they awaited the reports of cleared bomb bays. Then Thomas sealed the airplane, and they flew into the darkness northeast of Akita. On the way home, they could see the stream of B-29s still heading for Akita.

"A milk run," Dixie radioed dryly from his observation dome.

"It isn't over yet, Dixie," Al responded. "Keep your eyes open for fighters."

Tokyo
Early Morning, 15 August 1945

By 0330, the Commandant, Nakamura, and the rest of Kempeitai headquarters knew a full-scale coup was in progress at the Palace. The rebel officers had murdered the commanding general of the Imperial Guards and forged a fake order.

More disturbing reports filtered into the Kempei command center. Members of a super-secret Kempeitai gang, known as the "Thought Police," had attacked the residence of the Lord Keeper of the Privy Seal. The gang knew this Cabinet official controlled access to the Emperor. They were determined to neutralize his influence. However, loyal troops had repulsed them. Then came the report that another dissident group had attacked the Prime Minister's official residence. Fortunately, the Premier was staying elsewhere. Finally, a city policeman came in to report that a regiment of the Imperial Guards had surrounded the Japan Broadcasting facilities.

By 0615, the East District Army commanding general responsible for the Tokyo area defense had taken control of the situation and ordered the rebel troops out of the Palace grounds. The Emperor's recordings remained hidden.

Earlier, the commandant went to the War Minister's official residence, but was denied entry. When he returned just after dawn, he reported that the War Minister had committed seppuku.

At 0720, Radio Tokyo came on the air to make a special announcement alerting the country of a pending Imperial Rescript at noon.

Events appeared to be reaching a climax, and Nakamura believed they would make it through the day without further incident. Nevertheless, he continued to check the personnel files on his desk. The names of the "Thought Police" came in, and when he checked, he found they were on his list of suspicious officers.

By 1100, the recordings of the Imperial Rescript were delivered to the Radio Tokyo building and locked in a safe. The commandant ordered several officers to go over to protect the studios. Nakamura sent Lieutenant Ida with them.

At 1130, Nakamura still perused the files before him. He could not put his finger on it, but something bothered him. Then Nakamura remembered. He had not looked at Lieutenant Ida's personnel file. He withdrew it from a file cabinet, quickly scanning the education section. The hairs stood up on his neck. There it was. Ida had been a student in Professor Hiraizumi's class. Several of his classmates were in the secret "Thought Police."

Nakamura charged out of the building, leaving his sword and pistol behind. He grabbed his bike and pedaled toward the radio station about a mile away. It was now 1135. He should make it in less than four minutes. The front tire burst without warning, and he tumbled to the ground, striking his head on a stone in the road. Slowly, he picked himself up and stood. The bike was useless, and he stepped off with a limp. Ignoring pain in his leg and head, he tried to run, it felt like he trying to move in knee-deep water. It was 1140 when he looked at his watch.

Lieutenant Ida stood with other policemen in the hall outside Studio 8 at the broadcast station with his hand on the hilt of his sword. He noticed a distinguished-looking man carry a wooden box through the crowd, bow, and hand it to someone Ida knew to be the head of the news department. Ida edged closer to the door as the recipient turned, bowed, and passed the box to another man inside the control room. It was 1150, ten minutes until the broadcast announcing the end of the war was scheduled to be made. Ida looked up as if saying a prayer.

A senior officer noticed Ida gazing at the ceiling and rebuked him for not staying alert for the Emperor's broadcast. Ida leaped forward toward the studio door as if awakening from a deep trance. Drawing his sword, he screamed, "There will be no broadcast! Traitors! I will kill you all!"

As Ida finished screaming, Nakamura charged into the corridor, rushed forward, and tackled Ida. As they fell to the floor, Ida slashed at Nakamura with his sword, cutting a gash on his cheek. Despite his injuries from the bike tumble and the wound Ida inflicted, Nakamura pinned the younger man to the floor. Other military policemen quickly assisted by helping lead the screaming young lieutenant away.

An officer handed Nakamura a clean cloth to apply to his facial wound. He was advised to see a doctor, but he refused. "I will remain for His Majesty's rescript."

At noon, the announcer bade everyone to rise. Across the Empire of Japan, millions of listeners stood to their feet in respect.

Then, the mournful strains of Kimigayo, the Japanese national anthem, filled the studio, flowed out of the building down the rubble-filled street of Tokyo and across the airwaves to a defeated and ruined nation, to people in devastated cities and those around a solitary radio in small villages.

Nakamura, tears streaming down his face, found himself softly singing to the tune,

> *"May your reign continue for a thousand*
> *generations,*
> *Eight thousand generations.*
> *Until the tiny pebbles*
> *Grow into massive boulders*
> *Lush with moss."*

For the first time, many of the people of Japan heard the voice of the Crane:

> *"To Our good and loyal subjects…"*

Pitch Black encountered no fighters, and thanks to Pop's efficient fuel management, the big bomber landed at Northwest Field with a few gallons to spare just after the lunch hour, sixteen hours after takeoff. On the way home, they heard the broadcast that the war was over. On the last night of the Pacific War, 14 August 1945, the XXI Bombardment Command struck several cities.

One of them was Kumagaya.

Nikko
March 1985

Okita's story was intriguing, but I wanted to know what happened to Yuki and her family. "Now, will you tell me what happened to Yuki and her family and that Tanaka?"

Okita's face was enigmatic. "Let us go inside for a moment and refresh our coffees."

Okita was quiet as he refilled our cups. Taking a sip of his own, he continued his exasperatingly slow story. "The war ended a few days later. By the time of the broadcast of the Emperor's acceptance of the Potsdam Declaration on August 15, Tanaka's concussion had healed enough for him to comprehend that Japan had surrendered to the Allies."

"Who told him?" I assumed he was in Nikko.

"He listened to the broadcast with the Fujitas. Here in this house."

I must have swayed on my feet, a little off balance at this revelation. "You mean Tanaka was staying here with my family, in this very house, this house I lived in? How do you know this?" I asked.

"As I told you, I knew this family quite well. It was no secret. He stayed in your old room."

The idea that such a monster had slept in my room and home galled me, but I wanted to get to the bottom of this saga.

"How did he take it – the surrender, I mean?"

"Utterly distraught, he broke down and wept like a child."

Okita wasn't looking at me. He looked straight through me as if conjuring up a memory.

"Did he kill himself?" I asked hopefully. Okita massaged the back of his neck. I placed my coffee cup on the table.

"He planned to kill himself – after he killed the Fujitas."

My muscles tensed.

"What … what happened?" I stuttered.

Twenty-eight

Nikko, Japan
Sunday Morning, 2 September 1945

Japan formally surrendered to the Allied powers on the morning of 2 September. The formalities occurred aboard the battleship USS *Missouri* in Tokyo Bay. The Fujita family and Tanaka listened to the worldwide broadcast. The solemn occasion concluded at 0925, with all signatories affixing their names to the document. A few moments later, a massive air armada of B-29s and US Naval aircraft flew over the vast American fleet anchored in the bay as if to solidify the event and conclude it with a roaring show of military capabilities and performance. The ceremony lasted about twenty-three minutes and was broadcast around the world.

Although the Fujitas shed tears, the family breathed a sigh of relief. The war had ended. The killing would stop; soldiers in far-away places – isolated Pacific islands, mainland Asia, and allied prisoners of war camps – would be repatriated. The disarming of the Japanese military became a reality. American troops would occupy the home islands.

Japan's surrender loomed over Tanaka's life like an ominous storm; the impact was nothing short of catastrophic; his heart raged. He plotted his revenge.

Late that afternoon, he furtively entered Dr. Fujita's home clinic and retrieved an instrument to enact his plot. He checked the house. Doctor Fujita and Yuki were in the backyard pruning the cherry trees, and Mama Sumiko was in the kitchen preparing dinner. He decided he would kill her first.

Despite his work in the Kempeitai, Tanaka never killed anyone. He had witnessed the beheadings of dozens of Chinese civilians in Nanking and the execution of captured Allied airmen. He was personally responsible for the arrest and prosecution of dissidents in the government, the military, news media, and industry. The major had interrogated and roughed up others.

However, Tanaka had never taken another human's life; now, shattered, he was ready to kill three.

Sumiko turned from her work in the kitchen to see Tanaka standing three feet away with a surgical scalpel pointed at her. She could see the evil in the man's eyes, the utter hopelessness.

"What do you think you are doing?" *He will not know my fear.*

"I am going to kill you, all of you. You're traitors!" He spat out his words, each syllable laden with a seething disdain to emphasize his determination and hatred.

"And then what? What will that gain you?"

"I will commit seppuku to atone for my failures to defend my country!" Then he dropped his head, raising the scalpel high above his head. "It will be my apology to the Emperor."

"You will not kill anyone!" Mama Sumiko countered, her voice rising, speaking with an authority that a Japanese soldier would understand, even from a woman.

"How dare you come in here holding a weapon on me and threatening me and my family! My family saved your life, not just once but twice! My beloved Yuki, a nurse, cleaned your filthy body and begged for your life when they wanted to consign you to the ward of the hopeless. My husband restored your burned face and body and then rescued you from death in Hiroshima even as people died around him. This family has cared for, fed, clothed, and treated you more kindly than you can understand.

"And now you stand here threatening to kill us! Do you not know life is a precious gift from a merciful and loving God? Suicide is nothing more than self-murder. I forbid you to think like that under my roof! Did you not listen to our Emperor's words? Are you too weak to bear the unbearable? You are no better than Ronin! You dishonor the Emperor!"

"The Americans will come and enslave us," Tanaka began.

"They will not! You have listened to the lies of the militarists' propaganda for so long that you believe them. You have to believe what you want. Now, in the name of Jesus Christ, I command you to put that scalpel back where it belongs. You get out in the garden and help Makato and Yuki prune the trees. You, Matome Tanaka, will act like a decent man while you stay under my roof!"

Mama Sumiko's scolding declaration had been short, assertive, and decisive. Tanaka lowered the scalpel. "Soon, they will come for me and put me on trial."

"Not if I can help it."

"What can you do?" he choked. The man was broken.

"We will think of something; now go to work!"

Tanaka left the room.

Sumiko bowed her head in prayer, "Lord, help me think."

***Dai Ichi Building, Supreme Commander Allied Powers
Headquarters, Tokyo
4 October 1945***

The young American lieutenant looked up from his reading to see the diminutive Japanese woman standing before him. She wore a plain black western-style dress that cut below her calves, and he would have guessed her age to be mid-sixties. His quizzical look evoked a response.

"Good day, young man. I have an appointment with the Supreme Commander."

"Oh yeah," the man answered condescendingly.

"Yes, Mrs. Sumiko Fujita. I am expected at two o'clock sharp. It is about one forty-five, so I am a bit early." She spoke in clear English.

The lieutenant looked at her with contempt and then at his appointment book. He picked up the phone.

"Have a seat, The General is very busy. It may be a while before he sees you, if at all."

Sumiko smiled and turned to take a chair.

The man dialed three digits, "A Jap woman is here; says she has an appointment. A Sumiko Fujita."

The lieutenant's face underwent an abrupt alteration in expression; his demeanor suddenly changed from sarcastic to stark.

"Yes, Sir! Right away. No, Sir."

Looking at her with a chagrinned expression, he said,

"Uh, Mrs. Sumiko, you may go up. Sergeant, escort Mrs. Sumiko up to SCAP's office."

A Staff Sergeant in khakis appeared behind her and gestured to an elevator.

The noncommissioned officer escorted her to an office where a secretary and an American colonel were seated. The officer rose as she entered, walked over, and shook her hand.

"Mrs. Fujita? Welcome. Just a moment." He walked to a closed double door, knocked, and entered. She heard him announce her name, open the door, and gesture for her to enter.

Sumiko walked through the portal with a gracefulness befitting royalty, but bowed to the man standing before his desk. He was dressed in the American Army winter uniform that, except for his five-star rank insignia, was bereft of any medals or ribbons. He stood erect, self-assured, his manner gracious, as he smiled and walked toward her to offer his hand.

"Mrs. Fujita, it is a pleasure to meet you. How is your husband, Dr. Fujita?"

Taking his hand lightly in hers, she held it for a moment. "Thank you, General; he is well and sends his kindest regards and his prayers for your good health."

The General of the Army smiled and beckoned her to sit in one of the comfortable chairs. He took one next to her.

"Now, how may I help you?" he asked. Sumiko noticed the colonel and another person sitting a short distance away; obviously, one was to take notes.

She looked straight at the Supreme Allied Commander and began her well-rehearsed message.

"General, I will not waste your valuable time. You are a very busy man doing so much to rehabilitate our country, yet I know no one else to come to."

He nodded, obviously pleased with her flattery.

"You received my letter explaining our relationship with the American medical missionaries," she continued. "They both died in Japan. They had a son who became like a son to us. He left in 1939 to return to the United States to complete his schooling. He entered an engineering school in Atlanta, Georgia. We believe he served in your Army Air Force and was perhaps a B-29 crewman. We want to know his fate. We fear he died during the war, but we desperately want to be sure."

Sumiko felt exhausted, an unmistakable sadness in her tone.

The General nodded. "I will do all in my power to learn his fate. Can you give my people his full name and any other information that may help them learn what became of him? I do hope he survived the war."

Sumiko nodded.

"In your letter, you had two requests," the Supreme Allied Commander said.

"Yes, dear General. I know you will be conducting tribunals soon for suspected war criminals."

He stared without any discernible expression. Sumika stared back and finally spoke in a firm voice.

"We believe we are hosting someone in our home who may be on your list. We have medically rescued this man twice. I sincerely believe his heart is good, and he can be rehabilitated."

"War crimes are serious, Mrs. Fujita," the General said gravely. "Perhaps it is best for a court to decide."

"We appreciate your sense of justice, dear General, but we also know you're bent toward mercy, just as our Lord Jesus showed us. Please consider my plea."

Her face bowed respectfully, Sumiko noticed the slight change of expression in the great man's face. Then he patted Sumiko's hand.

"I assure you, Mrs. Fujita, I will do all in my power to help you."

The Fujita Home, Nikko, Japan
Saturday, 10 November 1945

Yuki thought the man at the door looked vaguely familiar, though he wore the uniform of an American Army officer. His uniform bore no ribbons or adornments other than the insignia of rank and his cap tucked beneath his arm. She believed him to be a Lieutenant Colonel. He appeared to be Japanese. Yuki noticed a scar on his cheek. He spoke, and she recognized a voice from the past.

"You have grown into a lovely woman, Yuki-san," he said in Japanese.

She gasped. It was the man who had brought the suitcase to the house that day so long ago.

"Mr. Nakamura," she whispered and bowed.

"May I come in?" he asked politely.

Yuki bowed and stepped back for him to enter.

Nakamura removed his shoes and slid his feet into the guest slippers. Yuki went to summon her parents. The four of them met in the dining area. Sumiko and Dr. Fujita seemed startled initially but graciously offered the visitor tea. He accepted, and Yuki left to prepare the service. They sat at a table and exchanged pleasantries.

Yuki served the tea to their visitor, who thanked her sincerely. Dr. Fujita boldly asked Nakamura why he wore an American uniform. "Mr. Nakamura, tell us; were you an American spy when you came here in 1939?"

Nakamura shook his head. "My wife and I wanted to avert a disastrous war we knew we could not win. I tried to use every advantage I could to prevent the tragedy. I am of Japanese-Portuguese ancestry. In the sixteenth century, Portugal sent explorers to Japan. My ancestor married a Japanese woman whose descendants lived near Nagasaki."

"But, were you a spy for the Americans?" Mama Sumiko insisted.

Nakamura smiled and answered, "No. I was Kempeitai then. I used my contacts in the Embassy of Portugal to pass on information to the American Embassy."

Yuki remembered her time in Kure. "There was a woman I met in a park, Kure, and passed information to."

"Yes, someone from my network," Nakamura admitted. "She was my wife, Ana. She befriended a Portuguese diplomat with whom we shared anti-militarist sentiments. I told you there was no active spy network in Japan for the Americans. I decided I would be a surrogate for them. I also had an important position in the Imperial government that aided my efforts. I honestly wanted to avoid war. After the surrender, the Supreme Commander Allied Powers offered me a position with his staff."

"What is your work with the occupation forces all about?" Dr. Fujita asked.

Nakamura smiled. "Let's just say I try to prevent any unnecessary uprisings – and trouble among dissident groups."

Mama Sumiko followed Nakamura's eyes as he looked at the simple wooden cross hanging on a solid wall above a picture of the Emperor.

"My dear wife kept one similar to that."

"The cross?" Yuki asked.

He nodded, "Hers had a man on it."

"Ah, was she of the Roman Catholic faith?"

He nodded again.

"And where is your wife today?" Mama Sumiko probed.

"She died in a raid the night the war ended." Still staring at the wall, he looked pensive.

The room was silent as his words sank into their minds and hearts.

"We are so sorry, Mr. Nakamura," Mama Sumiko said warmly. "But if she trusted the man on that cross, her soul is safe. Of that, I am convinced."

They were all silent for several moments. Then, Nakamura sipped his tea and looked at the Fujita family.

"Mrs. Fujita, I believe you wanted to know what became of an American pilot who lived here as a child?"

"Yes, Sir," she answered cautiously.

"I regret to inform you he was lost in action over Osaka in March 1945. I'm very sorry to bring you this news."

Although visibly shaken, Sumiko also seemed resigned to the terrible news. He noticed tears streaming down Yuki's cheeks.

"Thank you, Colonel; we now have closure."

"I believe," he continued, "you asked the Supreme Commander about a pardon for a Major Tanaka?"

"Yes, Sir. That is our request."

"I'm sorry, but our records indicate Major Tanaka and a noncommissioned officer named Saito died at Hiroshima in August when the atomic bomb exploded. Neither man was ever heard from again. We assumed they perished. Therefore, SCAP cannot pardon a dead man."

Sumiko and Dr. Fujita regarded each other, wondering what to say and what not to say.

Their visitor quickly continued, "However, I believe you have a guest staying with you. He may be of interest to us for other reasons. May I speak with him privately?"

There was no reason to argue. Dr. Fujita led Nakamura to the garden where Tanaka sat, trying to read a Bible. The doctor bowed and left them alone.

Tanaka looked up and regarded the officer with trepidation, then stood and bowed.

"Please sit," Tanaka sat beside him on the bench, and looked skeptically at the man, *I am sure I have seen him before.* Nakamura opened the briefcase he carried and took out a few papers.

"This is a full pardon for a man named Tanaka. It comes with a price."

Twenty-nine

My host finished the story. Tanaka went to work for the United States occupation forces. His skills proved useful in combating Communists and other dissenting parties in the war-ravaged country.

"You mean they pardoned him on the condition he works for the American counter-intelligence and anti-Communist efforts in post-war Japan?" I asked, chagrined at this news.

Okita told me Tanaka received a new identity and was a tool of the Office of Strategic Services, which was the precursor of the Central Intelligence Agency.

At that moment, Okita's story was interrupted by a commotion inside the house. His daughter Riko entered with a bag of groceries and two children. One was a boy of about six and the other a girl of perhaps four years.

Okita's face suddenly brightened. The children ran to him, and he embraced them with grandfatherly affection. Riko set the groceries on a counter and smiled as her father delighted in his grandchildren.

"Permit me to introduce the rest of my family, this is Nitobe Inazo," nodding to the lad, "and this pretty little blossom is Yuki Sakura." The little girl smiled shyly and hid her face in Okita's trouser leg.

I could not help smiling. I turned to Riko and said, "Your children are beautiful."

Riko returned my smile. "Yes, and they are a handful, but they love to come to their grandfather to be spoiled." We all laughed except the children.

Asaka Okita turned to his daughter. "We will be in the garden; when our guests arrive, please send them out."

Okita explained, "There are a couple of people I want you to meet in a while."

We sat on the bench and took a moment to watch the cherry blossoms drift from their tenuous perches on the tree limbs. It was not lost on me that the little girl's second name was Japanese for cherry blossom. I was curious about the boy's name and said so.

"Nitobe Inazo was one of our early twentieth-century statesmen, an idealist. He converted to Christianity and then studied at your John Hopkins University in the U.S., He married an American woman. His vision was to shape a more peaceful and even democratic world order. Inazo served as an under-secretary of the League of Nations."

"I see."

"My grandson also has an American name, after the boy who lived in this house. His American name is Dallas."

For a moment, I sat silently. My coffee cup had grown cold as I gripped it tight enough to rewarm it.

"How did you know?" I asked finally.

"Ah, my friend," he laughed gently, "I told you I knew a lot about the Fujita family. I have lived in their house for many years. After the war, I told you Tanaka was recruited into the CIA, where he could be helpful and find out many things."

I turned sharply and did a double take.

"You are Tanaka!"

He bowed his head to conceal an apologetic smile.

My head was spinning. I had begun to suspect that Okita could be Nakamura. *I've been fooled the entire time by his tale.* I was sitting with the man who held responsibility for my father's death, a man who had persecuted his fellow countrymen, who had pursued the family I had loved, the girl I had loved. Loathsome! I despised this person in the last few hours, hoping he had met a terrible fate. Now, I learned my government had employed him. He lived here in my old home. I felt cold, angry, confused, lost.

"You tell me what happened to my family."

The compassion in his voice matched what I saw in his eyes. "Sumiko and Makato passed away in 1952, both had leukemia. We believe it came from radiation exposure in Hiroshima from the black rain. Yuki survived until 1970 and passed after a short illness. Pneumonia."

"So, my entire family is gone?"

"Are they?" he asked. "Don't you have a daughter?"

The bitterness welled up in me. "Yes, but we are estranged."

"Hmmm, she is half Japanese?"

I looked at him coldly, "You know a lot about me, too much."

"Please continue your story."

I looked down at the ground and wiped my hands on my pants. "I mentioned after my discharge in 1946, I went into business for myself and made a good bit of money. I wrote to Sam's girlfriend, Mary Kurahara, using my real name from a post office box. In 1947, I traveled to California to meet her. Mary and her family had moved back to the home they had before their internment. The morning of Sam's mission, I learned his plane had exploded in midair. There were no survivors. I had a dilemma. Sam took the mission for me, as Dallas Wade. Therefore, the casualty records would show that Dallas was KIA – you know, killed in action. I told her I had taken Sam's identity and it was best to keep it that way.

"I still had our personnel files, switched our photographs, and became Sam. Each of us had the government's servicemen's life insurance policies. Sam died as Dallas Wade, so I changed Dallas' insurance form to list Mary as the beneficiary. By the time I turned the records in to the personnel sergeant, he nor anyone else ever knew the difference. Mary received the death benefit. As you know, Nisei lost millions in seized and abandoned property in the hysteria after Pearl Harbor. Anyway, the money helped Mary and her family get back on their feet after their release from the concentration camp in early 1945. One thing led to another. We married and had a daughter."

"Your daughter was born in 1952, I believe."

"Yes, Mary named her Yuki. She knew where my heart was. We tried to make a go of it, but Mary and I separated in 1971. I saw Yuki on weekends and holidays. Everything was going great. Yuki got into medical school – at Emory, just like my Dad. My daughter finished with honors. She had it made for life."

"Then she disappointed you." Again, he used a statement of fact, not a question.

"Yes," I admitted. "Yuki and her husband, also a physician, decided to become medical missionaries, just like dear ole Dad. Yes, as far as I was concerned, it was such a waste."

"Where is she now?"

"Somewhere in Africa, treating pygmies, I guess."

"Just how did you manage to pull off your charade of the identity switch?" Okita asked curiously. However, I had a feeling he already knew.

"The day Sam and I went to our new squadron's administration hut, we eagerly presented ourselves for check-in. The scene was chaotic. The overwhelmed clerk struggled to manage the workload; he was inundated with tasks, leaving him unable to process our entry into the squadron. The clerk directed us to return the following afternoon or whenever we could. It was evident the guy ran a sloppy shop. We still had our personnel files. Sam wanted to take the mission assigned to me to make up for the one he aborted, the Night of the Black Snow. He flew using my name. When Sam did not return the next evening and was listed as missing, presumed dead – as Dallas Wade – I decided to become Sam. That way, there would be no repercussions for my missing the mission.

"No family was waiting for me. We shared similar appearances down to our height and weight, so I switched our photographs in the personnel files, and two days later, I was processed as Sam Reid. I had changed the insurance form to make Mary the beneficiary of Dallas' policy. No one knew; no one cared. Neither of us had living relatives."

"Yet you both had fingerprints. I verified you were still alive with those. The rest was easy to track. But Yuki had passed away by then."

"How did she die? Did she marry?"

"Yuki passed peacefully in her sleep. I was by her side."

"You?"

He bowed his head and scratched the back of his neck. Okita watched my face.

"Yes, I am Yuki's widower. Riko is our daughter, and of course, had Yuki lived; she would have those two wonderful grandchildren."

We sat in silence for a while. I was speechless. The unexpected end to his story nearly knocked the wind out of me; I sat my cup down and rubbed my face with both hands. "I don't know what to say."

Minutes passed before I could speak.

"What became of Colonel Nakamura?"

"He was my control. We uncovered a few Communist nests in the Soviet Union planted here. He became a bitter man, as you well may understand. His dear wife died needlessly as the war ended."

"I must confess. I flew that mission to Kumagaya on the last night of the war."

Okita nodded, "Ah so."

He paused, then continued, "For a while, Nakamura despaired of the surrender and wished Japan had fought the decisive battle. He would have been on the beach defenses had it come down to that. But, after turning himself into the Americans, he became one of their prime agents. After retirement from the CIA, he finally went home to Nagasaki. He is a deacon in the Cathedral there."

Another Japanese Christian, I thought to myself.

Finally, I said, "Do you know where my parents are buried?"

Okita stood and bade me to rise. He led me to a corner of the garden.

He brushed away the snow and withering blossoms to reveal six blue stone markers with etchings in Japanese and English and a simple cross on each. Two of them bore my parents' names; the others marked for Yuki, Sumiko, and Makato, and one for Masao Gunji.

"How?" was all I could utter; a tightness in my throat almost prevented my breathing. The remains of the people I had loved were below my feet.

"They had your parents' cremains removed from the church cemetery in 1948. They believed it best that the whole family be together."

"Gunji?"

"A survivor at the Hiroshima Castle military grounds remembered he had left for the Nagarekawa Methodist Church downtown about ten minutes before the explosion. The church itself, less than a third of a mile from ground zero, was destroyed, with only a shell remaining. Of course, his remains were never recovered, yet the Fujitas wanted him remembered."

"He became a Christian?" I asked, still noting the cross on his stone marker.

"Yes, Mama Sumiko continued where Yuki left off. He accepted the faith a few weeks before the bomb fell."

"And you, she converted you too?" I pondered the irony.

"Oh no. Sumiko converted no one. She shared the story, the good news, as they say, and left it to her God to change hearts."

Still, my head was swirling. I did not know what to say.

"You need to know something else, Dallas-san; Yuki was a devoted wife to me. Yet Yuki always had a room in her heart for you. You were part of her family. She never forgot you. But this change of identity. Well, she had the report that Dallas Wade had perished in a raid."

I felt like cursing the day I switched identities.

There was a noise from the house, and Okita turned to look. Then he nudged me gently.

"Come and sit; my friends are here."

Turning toward the house, I saw the two men I had seen the day before at the church. Both wore clerical collars, black shirts, tan slacks, and very nice ecclesiastical uniforms. They walked toward me. I could not help but gawk at one of them, the one who looked oddly familiar.

"Don't you remember me?" he asked, grinning from ear to ear.

My expressions of disbelief and incredulity were such that I laughed and gasped at the same time. The aging process had not changed certain distinct features. Now, my memory had awakened.

"Michi?" I muttered hesitantly.

He smiled and held out his arms. I walked forward until we were a mere foot apart. Then I reached out and embraced him, a gesture he returned.

"Old friend."

"You … you're alive! Thank goodness you are alive!" I sniffled.

"Oh yes," he laughed as he pulled back, so we could look each other in the face. "I am quite alive and healthy."

I laughed also and patted him on the arms. "Okita-san said you had survived the war. I was much relieved."

"And you survived as well. Okita-san told me a few years ago when he tracked you down. I wanted to write to you, but we then decided to let you come to us. We believed you would eventually. And you did, much to our joy."

Okita came up and beckoned us to sit. Michi and I sat together while Okita and the other man sat across from us.

"Tell him," Okita faced Michi.

"Do you remember writing me about fishing at a place called Lake Blackshear in Georgia?" Michi asked, watching me with his dark, penetrating eyes.

"Yes, of course. You would have loved the place."

"And do you remember the Night of the Black Snow, the night you encountered two fighters over Tokyo Bay?"

Now, it was my turn to give a penetrating stare. "You?"

"Yes, I saw the name on the nose of the B-29. Even in the dim moonlight, it was visible. I flew by twice to make sure. Intuitively, I knew that you were flying that bomber."

"Another plane dived on us. A headshot. Our guns jammed. Yet it exploded in front of us."

Michi held his hand toward me, palms up.

"My young wingman, Akio, would make the ultimate sacrifice. I could not let him kill my old chum who saved me from drowning."

"You! You shot him down?"

Michi merely nodded.

I rested my chin on my hand as I remembered that act of – what, treason, compassion, friendship, grace?

"Well, it would be foolish to say I'm not grateful. I'm sorry you had to turn on your countryman."

Okita spoke up, "I believe you sent a radio message a few days before the fire raid."

I nodded. "Yes, I made an excuse to get my radio operator away from his station as we approached Tokyo Bay. I quickly typed out a warning to Mama Sumiko. I used the code she gave me years before and urged them to flee the city before the March 10th raid. I had only a moment, and there was no real hope she would receive it; I mean, what were the chances? A million to one? Ten million to one?"

The other man sitting across from me said, "The doctor and Mama Sumiko were already on the way to Nikko to see Sumiko's sick brother, Michi's father. Yuki did receive the message and believed the raid would be on March 9 during the day. So, in the early hours of March 10, Yuki was caught in the midst of it. She survived. As did I, thanks to her."

I regarded the clergyman closely. Yamaguchi was his name, as I recalled.

"You were the child Yuki rescued?"

He nodded, smiled, and bowed his head. "Then she brought me to Nikko to live with Michi's parents."

An impossible series of events unfolded before me. Had I traveled all this far – in space and time, as Okita had suggested in our first conversation? Back to discover a saga of improbable human interactions. Had I come back sooner, would it have been different? A deep sense of loss and regret overwhelmed me. I looked over at the man who had been Tanaka, the beast. His name change should be of no consequence; he was still the same man. Or was he? He spoke across the path to me now as my gracious host, Okita.

"You were a good pilot and leader," he said. "I saw your military records. Except for your encounter with this Major Adams, you had an almost spotless record."

"He deserved it."

"Hmmm, perhaps. Who is without sin? Did you not alter government records when you assumed Sam Reid's identity? Would you like to know what happened to this Major Adams you hated so much?"

I looked up, obviously surprised. "You know about his later life?"

Okita smiled again. "I learned much about you, Dallas-san. And when it became obvious you had something to do with Max Adams' arrest and subsequent resignation, I used my resources to track him down – and help him."

"What? Help him? How?" I exclaimed.

"I found him in California. As you Americans say, in bad shape, down and out. I arranged for a Nisei family to hire him in their seafood restaurant. He did quite well, working his way up in the business. He has worked with Kenji on several ventures."

"Kenji?"

My curiosity was aroused.

Michi interrupted, "He is the Japanese businessman you have been dealing with in Tokyo the past two weeks."

I could not contain my amazement. "That Kenji was the pilot of your Kamikaze mission?"

They all laughed at once.

"Well, I'll be," I laughed too. "Kenji's a shrewd fellow but ethical." Then I again thought about the Max. "But Adams was such a racist, especially toward Japanese."

"But Dallas," Michi asked, "were not most Americans anti-Japanese during the war? Both sides based much of their official and unofficial propaganda on the racial distinctions of their enemy. Think of the way your own country, with its Jim Crow laws, treated your black citizens, many of whom fought bravely for their country."

Remembering my time in Marianas and Georgia, I had to agree. I nodded.

Michi tapped my knee, "You once shared a deep faith with our family. Why did you abandon it?"

It was an easy answer for me, but perhaps a shallow one. "Everything I cared about was taken from me – my parents, my adoptive family, the girl I loved. Then, I return to kill the very people I lived among during my formative years. What kind of callous deity sanctions that?"

Okita spoke gently but firmly, "Dallas-san, your heart has been torn asunder for decades since that day you boarded the ship to go back to America. The war only exacerbated the rift in your soul. It may have played a part in the failure of your marriage. Now consider a man like me. I lived in darkness for years, following a blind obedience to a code that wrought havoc on my people as well as people of other lands. Yet, a strange, alien grace was bestowed on me.

My heart was changed."

The clergyman in Michi spoke to me with the kindest tone, "Dallas-san, the Asia-Pacific war was a horrible and brutal event. It tore families apart, killed millions, and it nearly destroyed my nation. All of us, you included, were like these blossoms, scattered by a malevolent tempest to the ends of the earth, if not literally, then spiritually. You lost people you loved. You think you are still lost in a whirlwind. Yet my nation is restored. This family is restored. We have found redemption. And you can also."

"It's too late," I responded.

"No!" Michi spoke forcefully, "It is not too late. The Scriptures record the loving and forgiving heart of God. He offers you a way back; he stands at the door of your heart and knocks. Will you not invite him back in? God gave you a heart of flesh, not of stone. Don't you remember what the prophet Malachi wrote: 'Return to me, and I will return to you'?"

The three of them suddenly stood in unison. Okita said, "You will always be welcome here, Dallas-san. My home will be a second home to you. But it would be best if you considered the other family you left. I do not know the dynamics of your marriage, but I sense Mary Kurahara is a wonderful, decent woman. Your daughter followed a different calling than this world offers. I beg you not to forsake her for that. We now leave you to your thoughts."

They walked back to the house, and I stared at the ground, unaware of the time. Sensing my aloneness, I stared at the blue stones marking the resting place of my family. The blossoms drifted around me, settling in my hair and shoulders.

A gentle wind blew through the garden, and my heart raced. Suddenly, I felt my heart being pulled, as it were.

I uttered audibly, "Leave me alone."

I heard a voice in my head.

"No."

It was as if someone had spoken aloud.

I arose, went into the house of my childhood, retrieved my things, and walked quickly to the train station.

Epilogue

I will restore to you the years that the locusts have eaten…
Joel 2:25a

A Medical Clinic, Uganda, Africa
Late Afternoon, a Sweltering Day in June 1985

Seated at a small desk near the clinic entrance, a young nurse studied her paperwork as the hot, late afternoon sunlight filtered through the doorway. Her neat white uniform contrasted sharply with her beautiful, deep ebony complexion.

As a shadow fell across her work, she saw a tall white man, his silver-gray hair framing a tanned, taut face. He wore a sweat-stained khaki shirt and wrinkled, matching trousers and carried a small valise. He removed his aviator sunglasses and looked at her sadly.

"May I help you, sir?"

"Yes, please," he answered. "I'm looking for Dr. Cox."

Then he added, "Dr. Yuki Cox."

"I am sorry, sir, but she and her husband left for the day. They will not be back today unless there is an emergency. I expect them at six tomorrow morning."

"I need to see her before then. It is important."

The woman smiled again.

"Are you a friend of the Doctor?"

"Yes," he paused as if unsure what to say further; "she is … she is my daughter."

The nurse sensed it had been difficult for him to confess this. Her smile deepened with gentle and sympathetic understanding.

"Then, obviously, you have come a long way."

The nurse laid her papers aside and pushed back from her desk.

"Come, I will lead you to their home. It's a short walk."

"Thank you; I hate to interrupt your work."

"It will be here when I return; come."

She rose and walked out and pointed the way up a rust-colored double-rutted road wide enough for one vehicle. True to her word, the walk lasted only a few minutes, and they stood before a small cottage. He nodded, mumbled a thank you, and approached the small, covered porch. Setting his valise down, he made a fist to knock at the door with his hand. Hesitating only a moment, he lowered his hand. Securing his valise, he turned and walked back to the road.

"Is there a problem?" the nurse asked.

"This is probably a bad idea, Ma'am." His voice cracked as he tried to speak further. There was a throbbing in his throat, and his eyes seemed suddenly misty.

"You have been estranged far too long, Sir. It is time to end this separation."

"But what if she won't see me?"

The sound of children laughing caught his attention. He saw a young lad run around the corner of the cottage to pick up a stray soccer ball. The boy, perhaps five or six years old, turned and looked at the two people on the road. Then, after a curious moment, the youngster ran back behind the house.

"At least you will know." The nurse said. "But I think she will see you; it is time for you to find out."

The woman nodded her head in the direction of the backyard. She gently patted his arm. The man nodded and walked toward the corner of the house.

The young woman watched as he stopped and looked at the joyful commotion hidden from her view. The noise ended suddenly. A quietness as deafening as thunder held the moment. She watched him step around the corner and disappear.

Then she whispered a prayer and walked back down the road back to the clinic.

The End

Author's Afterword

The idea for *Scattered Blossoms* leaped into my head during a visit to Quebec City in 2017. I was thinking about the day my wife Randi and I had spent in Nikko, Japan, during Hanami in March 2001. The memory of snow and cherry blossoms dancing together in a gentle breeze became vivid in my reflections. Then, searching the internet, I found the poem quoted at the beginning of my story. Suddenly, the idea for a story germinated. I recalled a book I had read – *Downfall*, by Richard B. Frank – in which he relates the firebombing mission on Tokyo on the night of 9-10 March 1945. The story began writing itself in my mind. I trust the reader sees the connection between the scattered cherry blossoms and the scattered lives of the people in the story.

When we were youngsters, growing up in Crisp County, Georgia, my brother and I used to crawl around inside a World War II B-29 bomber (I later learned it was an F-13 reconnaissance bomber) in the Georgia Veterans State Park at Lake Blackshear, about nine miles from our hometown. That airplane has since been removed to a fenced-in enclosure to prevent vandalism. I learned from Park officials that the plane had flown out of Guam, and the crew received the Distinguished Flying Cross after flying through a typhoon on just two engines. This airplane is named *The City of Lansford*, after the small town in Carbon County, Pennsylvania. In my research, I learned that a citizen of Lansford, Alfred "Fredo" Baldwin, the tail gunner on that bomber, was responsible for getting the airplane named for his hometown. I also remember seeing the mothballed B-29s sitting next to the highway whenever we passed by Robins Air Force Base in the early 1950s.

I have loved B-29s from the days of my youth. In researching material for this story, I read several books on the bombers and their missions in World War II. Many of the action described in *Scattered Blossoms* is based on accounts of the missions flown out of the Mariana Islands. I also gleaned ideas about the Kamikaze mission from stories in several history books on the war in the Pacific. Other books that shaped my thinking for this story include *Mission to Tokyo* by Robert Dorr, *I Saw Tokyo Burning* by Robert Guillain, *Bringing the Thunder* by Gordon Bennett Robinson, Jr, *Japan's Longest Day* by The Pacific War Research Society, *Behind Japan's Surrender* by Lester Brooks, *The Last*

Mission by Jim Smith and Malcolm McConnell, *Inferno* by Edwin P. Hoyt, *Whirlwind* by Barrett Tillman and *Blankets of Fire* by Kenneth P. Werrell.

The sub-theme of racial hatred by both the Japanese and Americans in the war era is particularly relevant today. How we see the "other" shapes our perspectives when they become enemies or neighbors. It is even worse when we dehumanize them. In the Asia-Pacific war, that racial animus went both ways.

I also learned that there is an Anglican Church in Nikko, Japan. Known as *The True Light Church*, it was originally built of wood in 1899, rebuilt in stone in 1914.

I owe a special debt of gratitude to Professor Joshua S. Mostow, University of British Columbia Department of Asian Studies, for his permission to use his beautiful translation of *Ki no Tomonori's Poem 33*.

I also am deeply grateful to:

My friend Colonel (Retired) Gary Gresh, former Army colleague and published author who advised me on writing and publishing.

Colonel (Retired) Don Boose, an Asia expert and former faculty-mate at the United States Army War College, who gave me valuable insights into Japanese culture.

My good friend Skip Orser, who read the first lines and encouraged me to continue.

My brother, Dr. Sam E. Wood, for his medical advice.

My dear friend Mari Fitz-Wynn, editor, coach, and friend who pushed me to finish.

Becky Bock, who was a beta-reader.

Jennifer Parser, who suggested a title change.

And my wife, Randi Leigh, who is a loving nitpicker and encourager.

John I. Wood and *The City of Lansford*, Lake Blackshear, Georgia

SCATTERED BLOSSOMS

About the Author

John I. Wood is a retired career Army officer who served four years in Asia. He commanded at company, battalion, and brigade level. A graduate of the U. S. Army War College, he also served on the school's faculty before retirement. He and his wife Randi served together as missionaries in The Anglican Diocese of Egypt. They live in North Carolina. John is working on a second novel.

284